THE ART OF CORRECTION

When Judith returned, things were looking even better.
There was a neat pile of clothes on the floor and the young
pair sat side by side on the sofa, naked save for the skimpy
items she had handed out. Keeping hold of the trimmed
sole of an old gym shoe, she laid down the cane and sat on
the table with one leg stretched out along its edge.

'We'll take you first, girl. Out here and bend over.'
Judith indicated the expanse of bare thigh then pushed
Sandra face down across it. She felt the body heat through
the thin shorts and ran a hand over the buttocks. 'Hmm,
quite warm already. Soon you're going to be a whole lot
warmer.'

'Yes, Miss Judith. But please don't spank me too hard.'

'Whatever it takes, my child.'

By the same author:

DRAWN TO DISCIPLINE
RITUAL STRIPES
BENCH-MARKS

THE ART OF CORRECTION

Tara Black

This book is a work of fiction.
In real life, make sure you practise safe, sane and
consensual sex.

First published in 2004 by
Nexus
Thames Wharf Studios
Rainville Road
London W6 9HA

www.nexus-books.co.uk

Typeset by TW Typesetting, Plymouth, Devon

Printed and bound by
Clays Ltd, St Ives PLC

ISBN 0 352 33895 4

*All characters in this publication are fictitious and any
resemblance to real persons, living or dead, is purely
coincidental.*

Contents

You'll notice that we have introduced a set of symbols onto our book jackets, so that you can tell at a glance what fetishes each of our brand new novels contains. Here's the key – enjoy!

cp (traditional)

cp (modern)

spanking

restraint/bondage

rope bondage/hojojutsu

latex/rubber/leather/enclosure

fem dom

willing captivity

medical

period setting

uniforms

sex rituals

On File

RATING: 7.8

Name: Judith Wilson

Date of Birth: 15/02/1981

Employment: Joined the Nemesis Archive
                               2000, promoted to assistant
                               Director 2002. The institution
                               was established in the heart of
                               the old university town by a
                               funding initiative from Oceanus
                               Inc of Chicago (other clients on
                               file at #151 and #167-2). In effect
                               Ms Wilson is sole curator of its
                               unparalleled collection of
                               materials concerning sexual
                               submission and domination
                               amongst women.

Publications: 'Sadistic Women of the 20th
                               Century: A Reading List', *The
                               Flagellant 2: 12–14 (2002)
                               Bulletins from The S/M Divide*:
                               'The Case of Jana and Frau K',
                               NemArch (in press).

Physical Parameters:	Height 1.67m; close-cropped dark hair, brown eyes; straight nose, full lips. A build well suited to traditional discipline is emphasised by the habitual costume of tight black trousers.
Sexual Parameters:	Ongoing development of an idiosyncratic brand of assertive masochism. Giving the lie to any vulgar notion of 'the submissive', she is known to court subjection to rigorous corporal punishment and take her satisfaction therein.
Sexual Status:	Live-in relationship with Archive employee. Volatile; indications are it will not be long-lived, although the same-sex preference is expected to be maintained.
Prognosis:	Candidature very strong. Exposed to the right conditions she has potential well beyond the numerical assessment above. However, despite the qualities noted, it is unlikely to be fulfilled through exposure to situations for which she might ordinarily volunteer.

The summary was followed by a detailed psychological assessment and a batch of surveillance material but the woman peered at the date-stamp on the top and pushed it all aside with a grunt of irritation. The target had been primed last September, so six full months had passed without any response. She swept the hair back from her face and scanned the page again: it was hard to believe that someone with these credentials would not rise to the bait. Perhaps there had been a simple failure to connect that had no special significance. The case should not have been left for so long. It was time to arrange for a prompt. Her fingers moved rapidly over the keyboard while she checked the words that came up on the screen.

From: constance@ac.co.uk
To: sm@theprogram.cz
Subject: #175-3

No reaction as yet. Can I recommend a cryptic reminder of last summer's trip?

Always, C.

She clicked on SEND and watched the message vanish with a little smile. Give it a couple of weeks and something might happen. With a stroke of luck. And *then* they would be able to start things moving.

PART I

1

Walkout

'Right, that's it. That's fucking *it*. Get those pants down and get over that chair. This time I'm going to welt your arse for you.'

'Shit, no. No way, not when you've lost the rag like this. Gracie, all I did was *look*, like the whole bloody street was doing. One wiggle too far and the back seam would have been away. And then we'd have really had something to gawp at.' The attempt at levity was a mistake, for the eyes narrowed and the lips set in a tight line.

'Last time was going to be *the* last time, remember? And if you ever did that again it was going to be a proper beating. No messing. A *punishment* beating. So I'm waiting.' She bent the rattan rod into an arc then swished it through the air. 'We'll start with a dozen and see how we go, OK? If you mark up nicely –'

'Jesus fucking Christ, Gracie.' Judith felt a surge of annoyance at the hectoring voice. 'It was a bum in tight threadbare jeans, the tightest I've seen in an age. I was just looking, for God's sake. You're coming on like I ripped them off her and had my tongue up her juicy cunt in front of all the punters. Get a grip, girl.'

'Judith. You *promised*.'

'I'm not taking a thrashing for a peek at a tasty bum. Not for a small thing like that. I'd sooner walk away.'

7

The thought hadn't been in her mind, but somehow the words were out hanging in the air between them.

'Oh yeah? Do it then, boss, do it. Walk away.' For a short space she took in the high colour and the twisted mouth then Judith felt her fists clench in a rising tide of anger.

'If that's what you want, I will.' There was a brief attempt to wrestle down the emotion but it was too little too late. She had come close to it before, but this time a boundary had been crossed. 'Should you decide to have a change of heart you will find me at the usual place at work.' Of course it was *her*, not the secretary who had taken the step away but Judith was in no frame of mind for analysis. The exit line had been delivered and resisting the temptation to underscore it she closed the door of the flat with a quiet firmness and made her way down the stairs.

The route to work lay across the park where the water of the pond sparkled in the cool breeze of a bright spring afternoon. As the flow of adrenaline abated she felt a little shaky and sat down on the nearby bench. There had been a finality to the angry exchange – the gauntlet of a break thrown down and picked up at once – that left her with the feeling of being *outside*. It had been a stormy affair of half a year since the honeymoon period of the early autumn but she had always been fully engaged, even when the flirting and punishment games that had served as a cover for her promiscuous tendencies became more and more extreme. Until now.

Her eyes followed the raucous wheel of a flock of starlings that took them into the topmost branches of the trees coming into bud opposite. It was time to face facts. However much she pined for the romantic idea of devotion to beauty – and Grace had that to the max – Judith knew in her heart of hearts that she found the excitement of the new too much to resist. She glanced in the direction of a couple wending their way entwined across her view and shook her head slowly. It wasn't for her and that was that. Hell, it probably wasn't for them either once the novelty had worn off. Lots of people felt like her, she was just a bit, well, more so than most. Judith stood up and smoothed out the creases in the snug fit of her trousers: there was a job to do and after that she was going to the pub for a beer or six. Her friend Marsha was always juggling at least three girls half her age with a shamelessness that was guaranteed to make her feel better.

Two minutes took her out of the far gate and in another five she was turning off the High Street into the stone-walled hush of a quadrangle. The old Porter's Lodge, now unmanned, had been turned into student bedsits, while the main building of the former University Library had been lavishly decked out as new premises for the Psychology Department. These financial benefits had eased the transformation of the book stacks into a repository for their present disreputable collection, the existence of which no longer attracted much attention except among first years given to sniggering knowingly about what they called 'S&M'. Ignoring the looks and whispers of just such a group who had spotted her destination, she crunched her way along the short gravel path and entered a security code to open the heavy outer door. In the small lobby there was a brass-plated declaration, THE NEMESIS ARCHIVE, and beside this Judith pressed the button that would deliver her directly to the third floor. She was not due to report to her boss until the following week and she wanted to keep well clear of the office and Grace's return from lunch, to say nothing of the gossipy assistant Penny.

Emerging from the lift, Judith crossed the cast-iron structure of shelves and aisles layered vertically above and below to a spiral stairway that gave access to the topmost level. There, recessed into a corner, was her

9

computer station with its batch of manuscripts awaiting attention. She sank into the padded desk chair that reclined and swivelled at a touch and reached for the blind. It was not a day for contemplation of rooftops and spires or the newly greening grass below, nor was it one for burying the head in a piece of autobiography, however spicy. What she needed was the distraction of pure pornography, blatant visual porn made with only one purpose in mind, and what she had right to hand should fit the bill exactly. A flick of the wall switch powered up the large flat screen in front of her and she reached for the small pile of DVDs that had recently arrived.

While the Director herself made notes and comments on a few incoming items, she was of an age and disposition to savour the erudite turn of phrase and the finely executed line-drawing of a scene of chastisement. Not for Miss Samantha James the stilted dialogue and action typical of the burgeoning market for 'CP' shoots, so when it was decided that the best of such materials should be archived in their collection it had fallen to Judith to do the necessary evaluation and selection. But who gave a fuck about hammy performances? In her present mood the sights and sounds of a cane's repeated impact on helpless buttocks would make the perfect diversion from the real-life troubles she was afflicted with. The title in front of her was hardly original, but the girl in the picture looked pretty enough, so she inserted the disc of *The Academy of Discipline* into the player on her desk and settled back in anticipation.

In the event, it was at first a somewhat dispiriting experience. The four she took from the top of the pile each had the agent of retribution cast as a 'dominant male' who upbraided his female victims in a sneering tone that made Judith cringe inwardly. To her mind it was one symptom among many – like the violence of her first good lover or the devious betrayal by her one-time associate in London – of a typically masculine disregard for the feelings of others. But despite her distaste for the macho style, the scenes being played out were beginning to have a cumulative effect. Acting ability was hardly the point when you were getting real cries of pain from real strokes that left real marks and there was an unmistakable seepage from Judith's crotch to show for it. Then at last she found the gem: a schoolmistress scene with a long-legged beauty of a pupil who was plainly in for a protracted and intimate corrective experience. As the stern-faced teacher waited, ruler in hand, for the white knickers to come off, Judith unzipped and slipped a hand down inside her own. Then the girl was bending, ankles clasped, the red bands multiplying across her firm high cheeks while Judith's fingers found her slippery folds and her nose caught the scent of her own arousal. She rocked gently back and forth, savouring the interplay of the two figures as the girl was drawn eventually across her mistress's knee. Now the older woman leaned forward, breasts spilling out of a shirt unbuttoned through her exertions and spread the coltish legs to expose a vulva as wet as Judith's own while a short, thick paddle smacked low into the crease between buttocks and thighs. Ouch, ouch and oo-oo-ooh! It was all too delicious to bear and the juices overflowed. Spasms rippled exquisitely through Judith's body and, as they slowly subsided, the onscreen errant schoolgirl was led into an adjoining room leaving the camera to a brief glimpse of a sumptuous bed before the fade-out on a tightly closed door.

Judith lolled back for a few moments, letting the images play through her mind and relishing the salacious implication of the final frames. Then she realised that the blind she had drawn against the outside was quite dark: the daylight had gone and it was definitely time for a drink. And, on the way down, a quick clean-up in the bathroom. She reached over to pluck out a clean pair of briefs from the stock kept for exactly the present purpose and for the first time took in the cover of a box she had laid aside. The paraphernalia of 'BDSM' was not really her scene, but there was something about the rear view of that black domina with the whip. It was a real peach of an arse and it struck a chord in the memory.

Judith snapped open the case and flicked the disc into the drawer of her player. Fingers drumming, she let the titles pass down while the shot panned from the bound male figure to the lady's PVC thong and on up the body to her face. Judith gasped. The expression was set in an unfamiliar and theatrical sneer but there was no doubt about it. Those were the features of an old playmate and sometime lover who had dropped out of her life at least three years ago.

'Right, Marsha, you will never guess who I've just seen.'

'Not being gifted with special powers, honey, I don't suppose I will. Though now you mention it one or two old faces have appeared again in the Easter break.'

'Not in *town*. On my screen. Starring in a vid.'

'That would be one of those sophisticated pieces of erotica you force yourself to watch for a living?'

Judith laughed and put down her bottle of Pils. 'If you rate a slave being made to drink the contents of his owner's bladder as classy. Mind you she did a stylish bit of work with the lash first.'

Now the bar manager was looking openly curious, her birdlike head with its iron-grey stubble cocked at an angle. Originally from the Pacific Northwest of the US, Marsha had over the years graduated from being a student to running a bar frequented by students. The actual amount of time this had taken had never been divulged and Judith had long before given up trying to deduce her precise age. It was sufficient for her to be

12

established as resident feminist of the 'sex-positive' persuasion and as such invariably at loggerheads with many of her university sisters. That she was a campaigner for sexual perversity in its many guises (and always in the latest jargon) was crime enough, but what really stuck in their gullets was the small but vocal entourage of young women who vied for Marsha's attention. Out of term, however, there were fewer rowdy confrontations and The Phoenix was often quiet enough – as it was that night – for Judith to occupy a corner stool at the bar while the American tended the few desultory drinkers.

'OK, I'll play. But you gotta give me a clue. I mean, Jude, given my extensive contacts in the industry –'

'Knock it off, Marsha. I haven't forgotten it was only last year you got into your first porn shoot. And anyway that's not how you would know this one.'

'Well, how do I know her then?'

'Let's say as someone I fancied the pants off that you – how shall I put this delicately? – *borrowed* for the night.'

'Shit. Was this, like, three or four years ago?'

'Uh-huh. Though it hurts as if it were yesterday.'

'And was she by any chance a lady of colour? With a butt that cried out for an all-American wooden paddle to be applied hard? And called – called – fuck, I can't remember.'

'Marsha, if you didn't bed *quite* so many gorgeous young things their names might stick a little better. It was Gwen.'

'Yeah, that's it, Gwen. She was some babe. But it doesn't still rankle, does it, Jude? Here, accept a peace offering.' Marsha looked concerned and busied herself removing the caps of two more beers. Judith chuckled and took a long pull at the ice-cold neck.

'Nah. We did a few wild things anyway and she wasn't really looking to hook up with anyone. And then she just took off without a word to a soul.'

'And became a porn star, evidently. Well she's certainly got the figure.' There was a pause while the bartender poured three pints from the tap at the end of the counter and when she came back she looked at Judith carefully. 'From the way you brought the subject up, do I detect more than a passing nod to old times? Can I guess that it's at least crossed your mind to contact the production company?'

'Damn you, Marsha.' Judith felt the hot colour flooding up her neck and she gulped more of the lager. How she hated being so easy to read. 'But you're right, of course. I sent an email saying I used to know the actress and would they forward it. And they replied in ten minutes saying it was done.'

'Jesus, Jude. Now far be it from me to say this, but aren't you a little tied up with another? I seem to recall the word *commitment* getting some exercise back in the fall.' The tone was light but the grey eyes on hers were steady and Judith looked down.

'I, well, we – er – oh, Marsha I think that might be it. End of line. I kind of walked out this morning. Though I suppose I could go back and grovel – at a price.' She thought with a grimace of the strokes of the cane that would be required before absolution was granted and they could kiss and make up.

'Honey, you know my feelings on the subject: take your pleasure and move on, life's too short, et cetera and so forth. You see beauty (I'll grant Grace that much) and want to grab it, I see a millstone. Look Jude, why don't you sleep on it? It's an old piece of advice, but none the worse for that. When I get off in a half hour I was planning to take a short walk along to the Basement. My pal Megs is gonna show with a couple of mates and I know for a fact she'll have tales to tell from the world of dirty movies. So why don't you come join us? In view of your new interest I'd say it's an invitation you can't refuse.'

* * *

Judith came to and groaned out loud. Waking up to throbbing temples, a parched throat and a severe crick in the neck was a less than happy experience and she groaned again. She struggled into a sitting position on a couch in what was plainly the small anteroom behind the bar of The Phoenix, but as for the rest . . . With a small flutter of panic she faced blank incomprehension, then the memory of the night's events began, piece by piece, to click back into place. Not that she wanted to dwell on much of it. At closing time Marsha had insisted on hosting an after-hours party at The Phoenix and Judith shuddered to recall how, tongue loosened by a mixture of beer and vodka, she had launched into a highly coloured account of her own brief hardcore excursion. The later stages remained hazy, but it looked as though she had been unable to make her way home at the end of it all. Or unwilling. Oh God, Grace. It had totally slipped her addled mind that yesterday she had walked out on her lover. Fuck! And now she had to go to work. In fact, according to the hands of the wall clock that was *right* now.

Judith pushed out through the deserted bar and the bathroom at the back where she splashed water on her face and forced herself to drink a whole glass of the stuff. Outside, lowering clouds were threatening rain and her level of apprehension notched up as she reached the Archive's lobby and pressed the button for the lift. At the second floor she crossed the small landing and took a deep breath. There was no way out of it: she had to stop by the office to check her mail. However, the room was unattended and Judith's spirits lifted as she grabbed for the small pile in her tray. But before she could make a quick getaway the door opposite opened and a figure came scurrying out.

'Oh, hi, Penny, I'm just going take these straight up. Have you, er, seen Grace?' Shit, she had to ask, however ill-advised it might be.

'No, she's gone away. Taken her three weeks' holiday that was due. But, Miss Judith, you mean you didn't *know*?'

'No, Penny, I didn't.' The puzzlement on the girl's face might have been amusing had the message not been so serious. 'We had a bit of a, er, disagreement. So what happened?'

'Well, she came in yesterday afternoon in a fine mood, saying she had to catch the evening train. Real cheeky, I thought, but the Director decided there was nothing for it and gave her the time off. And there's problems because we can't get anyone from the College for a week anyway, and even after that we – but, here, I'm forgetting myself. Miss James wanted you in her study the moment you came in. And I don't think she's very pleased.' The slow rural delivery came to a stop while the ex-maid grew visibly pink. 'I'd better warn you, Miss Judith, when I left her she was at the top shelf of the cupboard. You know, where she keeps those reformatory specials. It looks like you might be in hot water.'

2

Desktop

The slightly tentative knock elicited a forthright 'Come in!' and Judith opened the door to the wood-panelled room. It was never an entrance made casually, but that day's was accompanied by a distinct sense of trepidation. Samantha James rose to her feet and faced her visitor with a grave expression. She was a handsome woman in perhaps the later forties, dressed in black breeches and a dazzling white shirt closed at the throat by a silver brooch. While not obtrusively muscled, the body gave an impression of coiled tensile strength at the service of its owner's will. It was no doubt shortly to find expression with the aid of the cane propped against the tall punishment desk that stood conspicuously centre-stage. Judith swallowed and tried to concentrate on what the Director was saying.

'When you were first appointed, Judith, it was on the understanding that lapses in conduct would be subject to corporal correction to the degree I saw fit. I take it that you still accept that condition as binding.'

Not so much a question as a statement, it seemed nonetheless to require assent and Judith squeezed a 'Yes, Miss James' out of her dry throat.

'Good. Now before the exercise of my duty this morning I want to emphasise that in every other regard your work here is to be highly commended. The most

17

recent example, for instance, is right before me.' She snapped shut the copy of Judith's case study in *The S/M Divide* that was lying gratifyingly open amongst her papers and took it up in her hand. 'The publication of this inaugural title last month has drawn praise from some of my most exacting colleagues. I echo their approval, and I believe that the analysis between these covers sets a standard for the NemArch imprint that subsequent authors will be hard-pressed to match.'

A little embarrassed by the fulsome praise Judith waited in silence, wishing it were possible to undo the excesses of the night before. There was an agenda here she could not quite fathom and she was going to need her wits about her.

'That said, your recent behaviour has seriously inconvenienced me in the running of this establishment. In Grace's absence Penelope will have to hold the fort for a week, and even then it appears there will be no experienced staff available to step in. So I should like to know what you have to say about this situation.'

'Well, Miss James, I'm sorry for causing this trouble. Really sorry.'

'Hm. I daresay that will do for a start. Please place yourself in readiness for punishment.' For a start? What else was she supposed to say? Uneasily, Judith did as she was bid, lowering herself across the desktop and gripping its far legs low down. She felt the selected length of rattan tap against her stretched trouser seat and waited for the sentence to be pronounced. None, however, came and after a brief pause there was a perceptible grunt of effort at her back and the *crack!* of impact that drove her hips into the wood. Oh Jesus. That hurt. That fucking *hurt*. Caning always did to an extent, of course, when it was at the hands of someone who knew what they were doing. And if you wanted some sexy bottom warming as an appetiser for straight penetration then you wouldn't use the decidedly senior weapon that had been chosen.

The second stroke and then the third had Judith fighting to keep her grip on the wood as the burning smart peaked and subsided only to be forcibly renewed. In well over two years at the Archive she had not known the Director strike with quite such gusto. She clamped her jaws together, trying to quell the fear that was rising at the lack of a defined end to the ordeal. Four, five and then six left her with the whole body clenched round the frame as if it were the one thing that would save her from the storm of a shipwreck. As the worst of the smart slowly receded there was a pause into which Miss James inserted her measured voice.

'Stand up, Judith, and listen to me. You must be aware that I do not encourage sexual liaisons among my staff, for reasons that are well illustrated by recent events. So I ask you now: do you acknowledge your fault?'

'I was hasty, I didn't think she would walk out. Miss James, I didn't consider the consequences, and I'm very sorry.'

'That is not good enough, I'm afraid. You will resume the position.'

It was an order that brooked no disagreement and Judith repeated the movements made two minutes earlier to present her tautly covered behind for castigation. With, of course, one difference: the first dose had left it throbbing to an extent that the prospect of a second was filling her with dread. At the third of them she gave up the attempt to keep her mouth shut and by the time they reached the fourth she let out a sharp bark of pain. Two more appalling stripes and she was once more on her feet battling with the urge to clutch the injured parts. And once more too came the question.

'Now you know my feelings: do you admit your fault?'

God damn it, this just wasn't fair. The Director used to have decidedly close dealings with a knickerless Grace and the first secretary Helen had actually shared her bed before moving into Judith's. If there were rules they should apply to the maker of them as well as her minions. It was hard to escape the inference that this was less to do with rule-breaking than plain jealousy. Bridling with resentment Judith looked down, unable to trust herself to speak.

'Very well. If you will not answer me I am left no choice. I require you to resume the position.'

The thirteenth stroke cut low and the next caught her at the very top of the thighs. A mite less will-power and she would have bounded up; as it was she stayed put and let out a howl of anguish. This could not go on: she *had* to find a form of words that would bring the punishment to a stop. Fifteen, sixteen, seventeen took their toll in steady procession and she became aware of the sweat trickling down her face. At eighteen she jerked convulsively half-upright and grabbed at the edge of the desk while she tried to still the trembling in her legs. Then she straightened and panted out the words as best she could.

'I had an affair – that you – don't approve of – and I apologise for that. And of course I regret it went badly wrong.' The last bit came out in a rush and she waited, heart in mouth, for the Director to respond.

'I dare say that will suffice, Judith. I shall underline the statement with a final half dozen. You will please take your position to receive them.'

Another six? On top of what she'd had already? Judith told herself bitterly it was the act of a tyrant, but the spark of rebellion faded and she bowed to her fate. There was at least now a terminus and she steeled herself to suffer the closing stages with as much dignity as she could muster. At the end she flew up and stood, hands pressed to her sides, breathing hard until the atrocious hurt had begun to abate. For the duration she was all and only buttock: a bruised inflamed rump-on-legs that radiated heat and pain.

'We are done. I am going to ask you to return the equipment to its place and then we can declare this episode closed.' Judith lifted the old teacher's desk and carried it slowly and stiffly to its corner. Only once, and in another place, had she been caned hard enough to make walking difficult afterwards. That, however, would pass: she would recover. What rankled was that she had been coerced into saying something she didn't mean. Not a lie exactly, but a misrepresentation of the facts that was going to fester in her mind. Despite her condition, she could not – would not – let it go.

'Miss James, before we can move on, I have to say this. Obviously I'm upset that it went wrong with Grace – who wouldn't be? But it isn't true that I regret starting it and I shouldn't have implied that. Actually, I'm pretty sure I would do the same thing all over again. Rule or no rule.' Once the words were uttered she realised that another step had been taken. In the knowledge that she would accept no further punishment Judith drew herself up to face the woman who had beaten her so thoroughly. Miss James was still holding the cane she had used for that purpose and the grim expression she bore froze as their eyes locked in the tense silence. Then she drew back a fraction and turned half away to cast the instrument with a clatter on the oak surface at her side.

'Replace it in the cabinet, if you would, Judith, then on your way out send Penelope in to me. That is all.'

She locked the bathroom door behind her and ran the tap until the water was coming through ice-cold. Then she put in the plug and filled the washbasin to the overflow level. It was built into a solid countertop and with the aid of a low stool she was able to peel down her clothes and lower the swollen cheeks of her bottom into the porcelain in such a way that her weight was supported by the mostly unscathed flesh around the hips. It was deliciously soothing and Judith felt suddenly drained after the fraught experience. Oh God, what had she been playing at? Walking away was simply not an option: there was far too much at stake in a job that provided such unique fulfilment. But then she had surprised herself: never before had she confronted Miss James with what amounted to a refusal to fall in line. Though if the lady had not backed down what could she have done? The thought made her go cold inside. Brinkmanship was what its name implied: something that posturing males engaged in and she had no intention of making it a regular practice. She was just reaching back to run some more water when there came a knock at the door.

'Miss Judith, it is you in there, isn't it? Let me in, will you?'

'Penny, what do you want? I'm a bit preoccupied at the moment.'

'Of course you are, I couldn't help hearing. But if you let me in I can help. Don't worry, her nibs has gone off for the rest of the day.' With somewhat mixed feelings, Judith gave in and eased herself off her perch. She could imagine all too well the inquisitive young woman with her ear pressed to the door, relishing every moment. Grabbing a towel to wrap round her waist she hobbled over with trousers and pants round her ankles to release the latch.

'Oh, see the state of you, Miss Judith. Just stand still while I take these boots off, and then we can get you properly undressed. Right now, you bend forward over the bath so that I can get a look at the damage.'

Penny was a small pretty girl with greenish eyes whose thick brown curls had been done into a pageboy since she was lured from her previous incarnation as chambermaid in a country hotel to serve the Director in bed and across her knee. Considering that she had dreamed from her earliest years of being taken in hand by a dominant woman it was a match made in (a perverse) heaven.

'Goodness me, this is a sight! Some of these marks are nearly black and as thick as a finger. Now you just keep still while I give you a spray from this can. Right cunning it is, the way it works without touching you at all till the worst of the sting's been taken out of your poor bum. And then I've got this jar of cream . . .' The Private Assistant (as she had been named in a twist on the usual PA) tended the welts in silence for a minute or two and soon a glow was spreading from the punished area into the surrounding parts. Then Penny was off on another topic.

'I don't know if I should say this, Miss Judith, but have you ever seen that thing of hers? The boss's, I mean. Well today it was standing out like one of my fingers, and the juice . . .'

'Er, yes. I did once, Penny, but that was a one-off. Before you were ever here. I think that's your privilege now, yeah?'

'I suppose, though it's no skin off my nose if you, well – But, anyway, I was going to say she's never so wet down there as when she's had you over that desk. Not that that's very often, like.' Judith made a face to herself: it seemed the vindictive pleasure from thrashing the arse off her was also a big turn on. But she wasn't really complaining any more as the hands continued their gentle massage of the hot cheeks.

'Oh, Penny, don't stop. That is so good.'

'I had no intention of stopping, Miss Judith. And talking about being wet, I have to say herself isn't the only one, if you get my meaning.' Fingers curled into the vulva and Judith gasped at the intensity of the sensation.

'Penny, you don't need to –'

'Shush, Miss Judith, you just let it all go while I get down right close. I reckon you deserve this a lot more than her ladyship did and, if I remember right, you taste a lot sweeter than she does . . .'

* * *

Back at her station, Judith pulled out a stuffed leather pouffe and knelt at her keyboard. The desk chair might be well cushioned, but there was no way she was going to sit on anything for the rest of that day. But thanks to Penny's unexpected intervention – she had been off-limits since Miss James had snapped her up many months ago – Judith was cocooned in a post-orgasmic languor. It would soon be essential to get her head down for an hour or two, but first she had to see if there was a reply to the message forwarded the day before. And indeed there was, though at first sight it seemed to consist of nothing but a telephone number. However the subject box said: 'Hear me, sister!' and there was an audio file attached which Judith opened as soon as she saw it, heedless of the security warnings that tried to put her off. It took perhaps two seconds for the software to load and then the voice spoke as if Gwen herself were sitting at her elbow.

'Hey Jude, how's it going? What a fucking surprise you gave me. It's cool you rated the vid. I never was much cop with writing stuff so I got a mate to set this up for me. Give you a blast from the past. Tell you, girl, it ain't no joke what you done, taking me round with ya delivering those imp-le-ments. Remember? And now here I am in the fucking business and it's all your fault. Ha, ha! Only kidding, sister, I love it, and now I mostly dish it out. Though I still think about that time I'd been a real bitch and you whaled my arse – *intense*. Look, Jude, I'm gonna cut the cackle and get to the point. I hear you done good at that Archive place and I got a proposition for you. I ain't gonna spell it out right now, let's just say I always thought you was a bit of an exhibitionist when you got in the mood and this could be your big chance. I'm talking lights, camera, action, girl. Heh, heh. I'll be up your way next week or the week after so why

don't you give me a call and we'll have a beer. OK?
See ya round.'

All the way home Judith's mind was filled with images
from the summer of her first encounter with the Archive
when she was struggling to come to terms with her
impulses. She recalled with a smile the black girl's frank
curiosity about the tawse they were taking to a school
for models and how she ended up baring her luscious
bum for the owner to conduct a trial. It didn't get to be
a full-blown affair, but they'd certainly had their
moments. In off the street, the climb up the stairs to the
door of her flat reminded Judith just how well caned she
had been. She paused, key in lock, to put a testing hand
to the afflicted region. It was withdrawn in short order
with a grunt. Fuck it, she was going to hurt for days.

The entrance hall of the small flat was a shock. Of
course she knew Grace had gone away but this place
looked empty. As in *uninhabited*. Judith leaned weakly
against the wall that normally bulged with jackets and
coats to a degree that required her to squeeze past while
taking care not to trip over the heap of boots and shoes
that aspired to block the narrow passage at her feet. She
didn't understand how all the things had fitted into
Grace's single room for once she had moved in it
seemed to require all the space in the flat and more.
While spare of wardrobe herself and moderately tidy,
Judith hadn't minded being taken over in the least. Far
from it: the effusion of stuff was like the girl, all
unpredictable and unstable emotion. To say she was
going to miss it had to be a candidate for understate-
ment of the year. She must have worked like crazy to
get it all packed up and make the office for the
afternoon and that could mean only one thing. Judith
had not allowed herself to put the conclusion into words
but now it seemed inescapable: Grace wasn't coming
back. Ever.

She went through to her bedroom to gather up the few items of outdoor wear that hung in the wardrobe. The place would look less bare if they were back on the hooks they had once occupied. It had remained essentially *her* room, for while the bed was large enough to accommodate quite energetic couplings it was on the small side to provide two with comfortable sleeping space. Thus Grace had more often than not occupied the one next to it whose now open door and empty shelves showed that it too had been stripped of her possessions. Judith thought with a pang of those nights she had come half-awake to find a body inserting itself under the covers at her back, maybe to put the finishing touches to a process of making up. Their rituals of falling out and getting back together again had become almost a way of life. Sighing, she turned her back on the room and hung up the clothes she had brought through. It was no good pining: she was sore, hungover and short of sleep. After a nap it would all look better and she could indulge in some scheming and fantasising about the voluptuous Gwen with a blessedly clear conscience.

3

Mail

'So it's true then that this place is all about *that* stuff. Oo-er, I'd better watch out!' Tittering behind one hand the girl was pointing the other at the second edition of *The Female Disciplinary Manual* that had arrived hot off the press. In jeans and trainers, with a denim baseball cap sprouting a ponytail at the back, Sandra looked barely fifteen. Marjorie at the Business College had, however, assured them that she had good references from three years of office work, the last of which had been spent with a small 'alternative' publishing firm. But it was not a promising start, and Judith felt irritated by the schoolgirlish response to the Archive's core subject matter.

'You don't have to deal with the books and manuscripts, that's my department. All we need you to do is answer the phone and handle the correspondence, OK? And if anyone asks about real discipline, like the bench or the facilities, well that's to do with the basement. You don't need to know anything about what's down there, just put them straight through to me. Right?' The eyes watching her from under the peaked headgear had gone wider and Judith softened. The girl was obviously a bit out of her depth. Given that the reactions of bulk of the population to s/m fell somewhere between uncomfortable and downright hostile it was not surprising she felt rather nervous. Since it now looked as if they were stuck with her for a few weeks at least, it would be better to make the best of it.

'Don't worry, Sandra. If you need any help you'll get me on the intercom in the stacks or if I'm at my desk down here then just come on through. Penny will be around a fair bit as well to hold your hand, because she's been released from some of her duties as Director's Assistant. And if I were you, I wouldn't ask what *they* are. She might just tell you.' Judith grinned and the temp smiled back, wrinkling her snub nose.

'Oh, there is one more thing. The rep from Choice Instruments is coming later in the week; Julia I think her name is. You should buzz Miss James at once and send her in with Penny. Then make sure the three of them are not disturbed in spite of whatever strange noises you might hear. Important trials will be taking place, if you get what I mean.' The innuendo had caused a perceptible flush and she could not resist piling it on. 'But at other times I'd watch your step with the Director. Keep a respectful distance if you don't want to experience at first hand the weight of the leather Julia peddles.' The now salmon-pink Sandra was a study in embarrassed confusion and Judith let out a chuckle before pulling herself up. The poor girl deserved better than this and she gave her shoulder a squeeze.

'Only joking, kiddo. Pay no attention. Now why don't you make a start on the mail while I go next door and shuffle some papers about.'

By noon Judith had had enough of the formal office and fled through the connecting door into the central vault whose documentation of sadomasochistic testimony and fantasy was the Archive's raison d'être. It was her domain, and the iron clang of the steps on the climb to her top corner seemed to confirm its separation from the workaday world below. After the intervening weekend, she occupied her chair with only the smallest twinge to show for Friday's testing encounter although the morning's mirror had registered an array of purples and yellows that was not going to disappear in a hurry. For a couple of weeks at least a casual bed-partner would need to be in the know if they were not to get a shock. As if she should be so lucky. Judith swivelled her seat round and stared moodily at the dark clouds that appeared to weigh down on the rooftops: despite the constant bickering about her roving eye, for months there had not been a *hint* of anyone coming on to her.

Except of course Gwen. What else was she doing sending not merely a message but one wrapped in her voice? And what a voice it was. Rich and fruity with a husky laugh that got you in the groin every time. Like her body, it was a dark voluptuous treat that could lend some racial stereotypes a dangerous plausibility. Judith leaned back and tried to get a handle on her conflicting emotions. Grace's departure had left a void that cried out to be filled, but Gwen's track record didn't inspire confidence. When it came to the crunch she had shown herself callously indifferent to Judith's feelings. OK, it was three years ago and there had been water under both bridges. Whatever the danger, there was no letting this chance go. That was it: instead of phoning she would send a reply to the vocal email. It had come from the lady herself and if she phrased it right there might be an answer that reassured her. Or the opposite. Either way, it should help make her mind up whether to make a move.

However, the task was more easily started than completed and the afternoon light was beginning to fade when Judith gave up the remedial editing of the paragraphs of text and scrubbed the whole message. The only way was to keep it simple. She made a fresh start and after half a minute's work read what was on the screen.

Hey, Gwen, thanks for the 'voicemail'. Tell me more.
I could do stuff but then I think about some of last
time. I'm free as a bird now, how about you, girl?
   Jude

That would do just fine. She clicked to dispatch the
message, smiling at the address that had the recipient
styled 'gwendom'. It sounded like a foreign territory
over which the lady ruled, these days apparently with a
rod of iron if the video was anything to go by. Judith
gave a shiver at the thought of that whip curling about
her own naked body, teasing with little cuts at first and
then ... She shook herself out of the reverie with a
snort. One message from the tough black girl and she
was away on a full-blown fantasy. For God's sake, she
didn't even go for dungeons. It was time to check up on
the new secretary before she disappeared at five-thirty,
then the route home would take her right past The
Phoenix.

By Wednesday Sandra seemed to have the measure of
the daily business in the office and Judith was able to
leave her executive desk to examine the detailed sche-
matic of a series of television programmes about
domestic discipline. The proposal was, it seemed, likely
to receive the thumbs-up from a new cable channel
aiming to put out material that was both stimulating
and historically accurate. Where she came in was to
provide expert advice on matters of dress and instruments for a fee 'to be arranged'. It sounded promising
– and possibly lucrative – so Judith picked up the
preview tape enclosed with the package and slotted it
into the player that stood on a low side table. The
promo sheet billed the scene as one of the firm yet
affectionate correction of two chambermaids by their
mistress and the short clip opened with one holding up
her long skirts to reveal a red bottom while the other

30

squirmed over her employer's knee. The suffocating drapes and ornaments of a late-Victorian parlour looked entirely appropriate and the spanking of the already rosy cheeks was full-blooded as billed. Six more hearty slaps made the plumpish moons quiver and then she was on her feet beside the other. After that both begged the pardon of 'ma'am' humbly and thanked her for the lesson before they were told to restore their clothing and go about their duties.

In all it was a joy that made Judith impatient to see the whole thing. If the rest of the planned series was of the same ilk then it would surely be a winner. There was just one thing that niggled: the underwear. Would servant girls still be wearing those drawers that divided at the back right up to the waist in the turn-of-the-century setting the piece was aiming to reconstruct? Well, she knew just how to find out for there was in the Archive's collection a set of papers that had lodged themselves in her mind. They were from the lady of an English country house of the period and contained her quite extensive observations on the preparation of young women for chastisement. At the time of cataloguing she had only skimmed it, but it should have enough of the information needed to show the TV people how much her services would be worth.

It had become a habit of late to kick off her boots when settling into some absorbing task, so that it was in her stockinged feet that Judith padded silently through the aisles of books to the far side. What she wanted was one floor down so she swung round the squeaky rail to tread on the first stair – and froze. Surely that was another noise from below, one that sounded very like the rustle of paper. For an age she stood straining her ears for anything above the sound of her own pulse until finally she caught a faint but indisputable click, as of a door that had been ever-so-gently closed. She waited a while but there was nothing that could not be put down to overheated imaginings, so Judith made herself clomp down the steps in the half-light as loudly as socks would permit. At the bottom she pulled on the cord at the set of shelves she was seeking and took a steadying breath in the bright illumination. The folder containing the papers was easily found but as she retraced her steps something else caught her eye. There was a box file askew that a closer look showed to have been inserted upside down and when she took it off the shelf papers bulged from the lid. While no stickler for neatness, she thought it improbable she had put the thing there herself in that state. Or that Miss James had.

She squatted down and examined the contents that appeared to have been returned in haste. Under the heading 'First Times 1900–1950' there was a bundle of reminiscences, variously typed and handwritten, that ranged from a single sheet to a stapled document. Could it be that the temp was indulging – or developing – a surreptitious interest in the topic of discipline? Nah, not a chance. She was reading a lot into what was basically nothing at all. Judith tidied the papers and put the box back in its place. More than likely Penny had been sent for something and ended up rummaging about. It was time to get back to work and Judith headed up the staircase with her own material. Thus armed, she would be able to impress the producers by her knowledge of how many layers of exactly what you would need to peel away before you could give a servant girl of *c.* 1900 a spanking on her bare behind.

At last on Friday morning there was word from Gwen. It had arrived in fact in the closing minutes of the day before under the heading 'Message received' and it pulled no punches.

Gotcha, girl, but if you don't risk nothing you don't get nothing, right? You get that train when you finish work and haul your arse along to the Green Man on Greek Street. *Then* we'll see about 'doing stuff'. OK, sister?

Well, that was her told. Dithering would be fatal so she buzzed Sandra and asked her to reserve a seat on the five-thirty to St Pancras before she could think better of it. In ten minutes the booking was confirmed and Judith sat back with a faintly nervous smile. The deed was done: one 'arse' would be delivered to Soho as ordered. For treatment that was yet to be specified. She had better pack at least a change of underwear.

She left at lunchtime and returned in the afternoon with a small shoulder bag that would not look as though she was presuming on an invitation for the whole weekend. Time dragged while she tried to interest herself in a history of legislation relating specifically to female sexuality and she found herself replaying those scenes with Gwen from the time of her first encounter with the rumoured dominatrix and her institution of ill-repute of which she was now a central part. It was all nearly three years ago, but both good and bad had a spark that kept the memories sharp in her mind. Particularly vivid was the occasion of their meeting in the park where Judith had faced down the girl who had been badmouthing her to all and sundry and then later meted out retribution, Archive-style. From her first message Gwen remembered it well and the thought gave Judith heart that she could call the shots again, if need be.

At twenty to five restlessness got the upper hand and she clattered her way down in the new pair of heeled boots that were getting their first outing. She would be early for the train but the pretence of working had become intolerable. Through the connecting door she found Sandra bent over a paperback that she quickly tucked into the space under her out-tray.

'Oh. I didn't hear you coming. I, er, finished all the correspondence half an hour ago.' She picked up a piece of mail and held it out. 'I'm sorry, this was here this morning but it got into the wrong pile. I only just found it.' Judith looked at the slightly flushed face: who was she to worry if a secretary had her nose in a novel when the day's work had been done. Now Miss James, on the other hand . . . She had better deliver a word of warning next week.

'OK, no problem. I'll look at it later. See ya Monday.' Judith took the black leather jacket from its peg by the lift and eased it on, tucking the letter into an inside pocket. Out in the quad a chill wind was blowing from the east so she zipped the collar up snug round her neck and set off at a brisk pace towards the station.

It wasn't until she was settled by the window at an unoccupied table that Judith took the letter from the coat she had thrown off on to the seat beside her. It was addressed by hand under an institutional logo that was difficult to make out, faint as it was and half covered by a heavily inked post office stamp. There was a *The* and something that could be an *R*, or was it a *B*? She made a hole in the corner and tore the envelope carefully open with her little finger. Inside was a plain white card that read: 'My boss is sore her letter had no response and she will make me sore unless you give one. (In-joke, yes?) So, please, Judith . . .' That was it, the whole thing, and the other side was blank. As blank as the look she gave the two items as she set them down side by side in front of her. What letter? It seemed she had ignored one and that had prompted this enigmatic little message. Which implied it was something she had received a while back – a few weeks, months, even. Of course, it could be boringly just something that had gone astray, and she would never know the answer. And maybe that was no great loss.

34

Judith picked up the card and as she looked again at the brief message it turned itself into a voice, one that said her name in its German form. And with it she saw a sweet face that smiled wryly and joked about the strict mistresses they both had. That was the 'in-joke' she and Helga had shared the summer before in their brief encounter at the establishment that called itself The Program. At once it all fell into place. She saw in her mind's eye the Chief Officer hand it to her, asking that she not open it until she had returned to her computer at the Archive. *That* was the letter, and she had not given it a single thought from that day to the present. The fraught business with Grace that had followed and their turbulent relationship had put the thing entirely out of her mind. It must be still where she had stashed it in the side flap of an attaché case bought for the trip that had not been touched since. And here she was, heading in the opposite direction on the London Express, probably for the whole weekend. Oh shit. Shit!

For a space of time Judith considered jumping off at the only stop en route and catching the next train back. Damn that temp: if she'd only given her the mail when it had come in she would already know what was inside. But then, as the station approached, she thought again of Gwen and what this meeting seemed to promise. Postponing it would give out all the wrong signals, whereas the letter had been unopened for more than six months and would keep in the back of her closet for another few days. However intriguing it was to have a communication from the *Offizier* – memories of whom she was discovering still had the power to make her tingle – she would have to curb her impatience. And, as the carriage moved out of the lights and began to gather speed for the final leg of the journey to the capital, Judith resolved to do more than that. She would put the past out of her mind altogether and concentrate on the business at hand. If she lived this weekend wholly in the present, maybe there would come out of it some plan for a future.

4

April 1st

That's me finished my first day at the Archive place in one piece. Some date to start too, but at least nobody tried to make me the Fool. It was supposed to be only for a week but they're having problems finding anyone else and I think there's a good chance I'll be there the whole three. If I want. God, it's weird. Pretty well the first thing I saw was this book lying on the desk with a drawing of a girl in stockings bending over in front of another woman. Old-fashioned looking, it was, with something like 'Correction of the Fair Sex' printed underneath. And all on the cover for anyone to see! I blurted out something silly – can't even remember what now – I was feeling *that* awkward. But what can I do though except give the job a proper try? I need the money now Ginny's business has gone under, and this lot seem pretty laid back, considering.

Well, except for the Director, that's *Miss* James. Her name's Samantha but no one uses it. I could see her giving me the once over when I went in last Friday afternoon but she didn't actually say anything. I don't care – I was determined after the last office job not to dress any more like the secretary who makes tea for the boss and straightens his tie. Or hers for that matter. It's an easy thing to say of course but it would take guts to go against her. Not that she's sarky or anything nasty like that, just that I could imagine she'd get you doing things you didn't really want. Well, me, I mean. And with some of the things she's interested in, it makes me go a bit wobbly to think about it. But that's just me being silly, isn't it? Anyway, I don't think I'll have too much to do with her except the formalities, so it's probably going to be all right.

Judith looks OK, though it stands to reason she'd be way over my head if we really talked. I know she's only young too but being cooped up dealing with all those records and papers is going to make her all intense and intellectual. And Penny says she's actually written things about some of them. Now *that's* a strange one. Penelope, the Director calls her, and she seems to be like some kind of, well, *pet*. In that little black uniform – very short it was – she could have stepped on stage as the maid in a French farce. She's really friendly, but I do get the idea of her being a bit, well, maybe not simple exactly, but sort of naive. She's from the country, up north somewhere, and I don't think she's had much experience of anything else.

I'm going to stop there for now, though I'm not going for my run because it's raining and it's nearly dark. I'll set the alarm earlier and do a circuit before work: got to keep on my toes.

I ran through the park right round to the station and came back on the old by-pass. So now I've got my breath back I'm going to tell what happened today. Oh, that's Wednesday, er, April 3rd. It all started when the woman came from the instruments company. I mean, fancy working for a company that just sells *those* kinds of instruments. Well, I got her in all right through the doors downstairs and when she came up she was really quite normal looking in her business suit. But then she sort of eyed me up and down and made a twirling movement with her hand. I didn't get it first off but then

I twigged: I was supposed to turn round like models do or like I was auditioning for some dodgy film. How embarrassing! But I did what she wanted and she said, 'You can't hide it, dear, not under the oldest baggiest jeans in the world.' Those were her actual words and there was no misunderstanding her. I didn't know *where* to look. Thank God Penny came out at that exact moment and took her into the Director's office.

That was all bad enough but while I was trying to settle down to the mail I realised that the door wasn't quite shut. In fact I would have heard the voices quite distinctly if I hadn't covered my ears. I couldn't work out what to do. If I shut the door properly they would hear and think I'd been snooping but if I didn't then I would have to listen to everything that was going on. And I knew I couldn't stick that. But I just stood there like a ninny and then those – those *noises* started – and, and I –

Sorry, I had to switch off there for a minute. But I've done the breathing and counting thing you had me practise and I'll go on now. Well, what I did was just scram. There was a box file on my desk that belonged in the stacks so I grabbed it for an excuse and nipped through. Judith was running something up top on her PC but it was too far away to make out what *that* was so I pulled the connecting door shut behind me and left the others to it. Whatever it was exactly. I mean I didn't want to know the details. *Don't* want to either.

I saw the place on the shelf where Penny had taken the file from but when I tried to get a proper grip on it the bloody thing slipped and fell onto this table and a few of the papers on top spilled out. Then when I went to put them back a row of paperbacks caught my eye. Green and gold they were and the one I took down was called *The New Mistress at St Bridget's*. I love school stories and used to read absolutely loads of them, so I just had to dip in and get an idea of what these were like. Well, guess what, I was soon engrossed and suddenly came to realise that there was complete silence. The time was getting on and if Judith had finished what she was doing she'd be coming down on her way out. Then it happened. I'd picked up the papers to put them back in the box when there was like a creak and a thud from up the stair that was right beside me. I just went rigid for I don't know how long, hardly daring to breathe. I don't quite know now why I reacted like that, I mean I wasn't doing anything terrible, was I? But the weather was really grey and overcast and it had got quite dark and spooky amongst all those books and those black iron struts everywhere.

But I got a grip of myself in the end. There wasn't a sound now so I managed to put the box file back on the shelf with one hand and tiptoed to the exit. I just kept hold of the papers and my story, they could go back another time. I shut the door as quietly as I could and saw that the one to Miss James's office was properly closed this time. So that was that. I stashed my ill-gotten gains in the bottom drawer and sat down to this card index I'm supposed to be putting into a new database. And I didn't see a soul until it was time to go home, so if that *was* Judith on the prowl in the stacks she must have gone back up to her own area. At the minute I think I might have imagined it, being a bit worked up by what I was reading – about how while everybody adored the gym mistress she was a bit of a stickler about proper behaviour and, er, discipline. In that place everything comes back to the same thing, and I just don't want to talk about it right now.

I just played that last bit back and it sounds really stupid. I mean, what am I afraid of? Thing is, that was the day before yesterday and since then I've been reading more. In fact I got through two of those books and I'm well stuck into a third. I never went to a school like that – just the grubby local comprehensive – but I can see it so vividly in my head, all the corridors and high windows and wood panelling. Trying to think about it, one of the things that really gets me is that it's a complete world with its own rules. It's all ordered from first thing in the morning till last thing at night and the girls don't have to make any real decisions at all. Of course it's not all sweetness and light, there are lots of squabbles and rivalries and so on, but their basic lives are all charted out for them. They don't have to leave at the end of the day to go home to – well, whatever. Heaven!

Miss Carter is the new mistress of the first one I read and she features a lot in the second. What a character – half the girls have total crushes on her and so do I! She cuts such a dash in her white sports clothes and she always has a smile and a word of encouragement. But of course she's firm too, though completely fair. When Sally – she's in the fifth – makes a cruel joke by tying the fat girl's shoelaces together Miss C is *so* cross. And Sally's just devastated to be out of favour, but then she decides to go after class to the office in the back of the gym and make a proper apology. Her best friend waits for her and when she comes out – after quite a time – she's walking a bit funny and her face is flushed but she's looking really happy again.

What happened in there Sally won't say, except that it's all fine now and *she's* not going to be playing any more silly tricks. Later on two other girls get on the wrong side of the sports mistress – at different times – and they each get to visit that room which most of the pupils never see. The author kind of glosses over the whole thing, except to report that one curious third-former overhears the word 'plimsoll' being whispered between two unusually giggly seniors, but then it's plainly written to prick your interest. Of course, *I* know

41

what she means to imply – why else are there copies of her stories in The Nemesis Archive? – but somehow the way it's done links it in with the good order of the school and makes me feel a lot better about the thing. At least that's how it seems right now.

I'm going to finish there: I've gone on too much about these funny old paperbacks and it's too late to run. I don't like going in the dark much. So now I've got to set the clock again for the morning.

I put this week's tapes aside after the last bit because I was feeling OK about the things in them. Well, sort of. But I don't know what I'm going to feel about this one. Not that it's *that* bad. Just kind of odd. You see, Ginny phoned and said I simply *had* to turn up at an impromptu drinks party at her place and meet all sorts of gorgeous men who would be falling over themselves to give me a job. Well, that's the way she talks, but she is sweet really so I had a quick shower and for once put on a dress, for her benefit rather than any of her guests.

Gregor was there, of course, though it hadn't really occurred to me in advance. I know he fancies me – which I don't particularly want – but he is funny and good company, so I don't like to put him off altogether. Everything went well with some of Ginny's girl friends in the group till she took me off and introduced me to this man who she said was looking for an assistant that wasn't the usual secretary type. That turned out to mean one who wouldn't say no, because he got me on my own in a corner of the kitchen and in ten seconds flat was trying to get his hand up into my pants. But he backed off when Gregor appeared though with not very good grace and after that I wanted to escape so I let him walk me home.

Well of course he came in and I got out the bottle of vodka that had been in the back of the cupboard since Xmas and we were soon kissing on the sofa. I don't mind *that*, really I don't, even when it gets kind of tonguey like this was, but of course he didn't want to stop there. So now *his* hand was making its way up my thigh and I just couldn't stomach the thought of it groping about in there, and even less what he would *really* like to poke into me. But what I did next took me by surprise: I suppose I was a bit squiffy by that stage and I must have been thinking he deserved a reward. So I just reached down and opened his trousers and after a bit of fumbling I had this hard thing with a wet end out in the open.

Gregor just gaped for a second then he said: 'You're not –' But I cut him off quickly, guessing what was going through his mind. No way was I going to get my *mouth* near it, not that time anyway. I don't mean the idea of sucking it was horrible, in fact him pushing it between my legs would be much more of a problem to my thinking. I've never felt like doing that – though I have twice – and can't see what girls are supposed to get out of it. Anyway I told him to give me his hankie and lie back and I set to working my fingers up and down the shaft. I must have been doing it right because it got even bigger and wetter and he was going 'yes, oh yes' over and over again. I wasn't ready for the first real spurt which went right up my arm but then I got the material kind of cupped round the end and watched while it pumped out a positive *pool* of the milky stuff.

And that was it, really. After a minute I zipped him up and we kissed a bit more, then I manoeuvred him to the door and out. Telling it like this makes it all sound very, I don't know, slutty, but that's not how it felt. Having him go off in my hand like that, *I* was the one in charge – quite the opposite of having a bloke on top of you grinding away. Just saying that makes me go 'ugh' inside, but I'm actually quite looking forward to Sunday when Gregor's coming round again.

* * *

43

What with the bloody card index taking up hours and those stories getting under my skin I forgot all about those papers I shoved away in my desk drawer till this morning. Er, that's Friday the fifth, by the way. Turns out they are all about first experiences of, well, since this is the Nemesis Archive, guess what? One of them really got to me though and we're back in school again in the 1950s. Maybe I was born in the wrong age.

It doesn't explain very clearly the background to what happened, just that she has cheated in a test with the result that another girl gets a bad mark she shouldn't have. Well, this preys on the first girl's mind until after three weeks she can't stand it any longer and goes to the headmistress. By this time it seems the other girl has easily made up her overall score, so the head decides no good will come of publicising the evil deed. But she says the event calls for extraordinary measures if the culprit will go along with them. Well, of course she will so a cushion is placed on a clear surface of her desk and the girl is told to lift her skirt and lie over it. Then the head takes a key and unlocks a cupboard in the corner, saying that what she is going to do must be kept strictly between them, since the cane has been outlawed from the school for the past three years.

According to the account it hurt more even than the girl's worst fears and that she was really sore for the rest of the day. Sitting on the hard wooden bench for the duration of double maths was an ordeal. But she didn't mind any of that because after three weeks of torturing guilt she had paid her debt and it felt wonderful. It turned out that she went back three more times in the course of her final year when there were things she wanted to confess, and each time she was able to leave with the feeling that she had a clean slate. The body was in pain but the conscience was clear.

How I wish *I* could have a clean slate, but I know that's silly. It isn't as simple as she makes it sound, I mean for a start I haven't actually done anything bad like cheating or deliberately hurting someone else. But even so . . .

I'm maundering here so I'm going to switch off while it's early enough to do a couple of circuits of the park.

5

Manacles

Judith made to roll over, the groan already rising in her throat. After a long night in The Phoenix she might wake early and nuzzle lasciviously into the bed-clothes until the foggy aftermath of drink began to clear. But this time there were no pillows to be found and cold metal encircled her wrists and ankles. At the realisation she reared up wildly in the dark only to provoke a clatter of ratchets that dragged her first to her knees then brought her face down, spreadeagled and gasping. There was a fruity chortle from somewhere behind her and she strained round.

'Neat, eh? And be warned, Jude, this machine is mean. Fight the sucker and it pulls *real* fucking tight.'

A light clicked on, but before she could take anything in a leather hood was drawn down over her eyes and buckled under the chin to leave the mouth clear. A firm hand to the back of the neck kept her still and when Gwen's voice spoke again it was close to her ear.

'Go with the flow, sister. You know you want this.'

It was true of course. She'd come down to London with the intention of submitting to her ex-lover-turned-dominatrix. In the pub amidst talk of exploring limits that had been last night's clear resolve. But the morning had leapt up at her: she felt ambushed and her head hurt. And to make matters worse her bladder was painfully full: there was one flow that would have to be attended to, and soon.

'Look, Gwen. Let me get up and have a shower. Or even just wash my face. And I'm bursting for a pee.' Judith tried to make it a matter-of-fact request, but she was uncomfortably aware of the wheedling tone that had crept in. Not that she should have worried for the sole reply was the crack of a whip across her legs just below the buttocks, and before she could catch her breath it was repeated, excruciatingly. The way this scene was unfolding it seemed reasonable demands were not going to get a look in. Six more cuts burned the tender flesh then she felt a hard rim push under her belly.

'You got ten to start, right? That's one – and two – and –' Damn the girl! But there was no space for resentment to be indulged and Judith tried to squeeze her mind empty of emotion. At last, at the count of nine, there it was: a trickle that swelled into a stream that splashed noisily into the metal pan. A cloth dried her while she allowed herself to bask in the relief, holding the moment like a talisman against what was yet to come. It was brief indeed, for fingers pulled her open and gripped the folds of her cunt. Two hard pinches to the left and another two to the right had her yelping with shock.

'Ow! Ow! Jesus Christ, what the fuck –'

'Nice little trick, this one. You won't feel too much just now, girl, but when they come off . . .' The sentence tailed off into a dirty chuckle that made her irritation flare but the first tightening click that answered her pull on the bonds stopped Judith dead. *Go with the flow* – she said it to herself and repeated it over and over in her head – it was the only way. She willed herself to lie flaccidly subservient while the lash continued its decoration of her thighs, and in the pause that followed breathed deeply as the pain gradually eased.

Then the mattress at her head shifted under the weight of a body and legs crossed her stretched arms. The helmet was jerked up and damp coarse-haired flesh pressed against her mouth. Suddenly her nostrils were full of a fishy reek that was laced with sweat and urine.

'I ain't washed neither, girl. And I can feel a piss coming on, just like yours. So get to work.' Judith gagged, bile rising in her throat, but a flick of the whip against the labia clamps made her force down the wave of nausea and set her tongue in motion. When it came she was almost glad to swallow a little of the hot jet that sprayed over her face, and it was mercifully not long before her tormentor was engulfed by a frenzy of deep-throated grunts.

After that it all happened at once. The tension was gone from the restraints, the nether clips removed and the headgear pulled off. An exiting figure threw the blinking Judith a key. In the grip of an absolute imperative one frantic hand fumbled to free the other so that its fingers could be pressed hard into the sharp stabs of pure agony that seemed to strike at the very centre of her being. It took several – infinitely long – seconds of paralysis for the blood flow to be restored and only after the pain had eased was she able to open the remaining cuffs and inspect the tender ridges that laced the backs of her thighs. From the crotch to the knees it was ouch, ouch, and fucking ouch! Judith slid off the bed and got slowly up on to her feet, drained in the wake of such extremity of sensation.

When the door opened she started and the sight of Gwen with what looked very like a length of rattan in her hand was not a reassuring one. But the young woman shook her head and held out the instrument for Judith to take from her.

'I ain't forgot when you took me in hand that time way back. I know you don't do this, Jude – well, I don't neither – but I reckon you should be mad enough right now. Or you will be when I tell you I spiked your drinks last night. I mean how else d'you think I got you pegged down like that? So tell me I ain't wrong, sister.' Judith stood open-mouthed at the shamelessness of the admission: if ever there was an act deserving of retribution . . . She let her eyes wander over the black girl's curves that swelled deliciously under white latex and felt a surge of lust mix with her anger. Newly invigorated, she took the cane and tapped it on the bed rail.

'OK, get a hold of this. I want you bent down, legs apart. And get that big arse of yours right out.' Gwen did as ordered and Judith took the hem of the dress and peeled the clinging rubber up well clear of the target area. There was of course no underwear and the smelly vulva that had been so overwhelmingly in her face minutes before was slick with further excretions. Judith was not often in the mood to administer a thrashing but this time she felt positively eager to inflict the kind of pain that would bring such blatant lubrication to a halt. She measured the instrument carefully across the centre of the full cheeks, noting with approval the way they quivered slightly as if in anticipation of their fate.

'Two to get my eye in, then six just as hard as I can make them. And I'm considering an extra little something. OK?' Taking the silence as assent Judith drew back a little and swished the springy rod down in two carefully centred strokes. Strength growing to equal her enthusiasm, she rose on to the balls of her feet and lashed her victim three times more.

'Shit. Oh shit.' The utterance was almost conversational though the jiggling of the buttocks before the back was arched again as required told another story. Judith completed the half-dozen at full stretch and watched while the globes seemed to take on a life of their own for a space, although the hands kept their grip of the rail.

'Jesus *fuck*.' It was not a loud response but the word was loaded with such feeling it made Judith tingle.

'Now, if Madam has had her say, I'll finish.' The announcement made, she contrived to lay on two swingeing diagonals that intersected the existing marks to curl, one high and one low, round the opposite hip. It was one of those rare occasions of an idea perfectly executed and Gwen started up, mouth working wordlessly. Judith fell upon her, squeezing the body tight under its rubber skin while the girl kneaded furiously at the source of her pain. When the spasm had passed Judith pressed her mouth on Gwen's, sliding her hands down to enfold the wealed rounds of the prominent backside. Later she wanted a good look; for then it was first things first.

'Shower. That's *now*,' she managed to insist in spite of the tongue pushing against her own, and she steered Gwen in the direction of the bathroom she had vague memories of using when she'd come in the night before. It wasn't that she was obsessive about cleanliness, for God's sake, but there was a difference between ripe and overripe. And in her still rather delicate state (to say nothing of the after-effects of indulgence in whips and canes) she was going to draw the line where *she* wanted it.

In the spacious cubicle they soaped themselves under the hot flow, then Judith pulled the black girl to her and reached down under the thick wiry tuft between her legs. 'Remember that time?'

'In the field, yeah.' Gwen was grinning. 'And my bum was all hot from that strap. But hey, girl –' the eyes on hers had widened with surprise '– what *is* this? What you gone and done?' She snapped off the water and dropped to her knees. 'Jeez, sister, this is smooth as silk. And you got a real special taste, you know that? Judith took a sharp breath at the touch of the exploring mouth.

'I took the plunge last summer, in Seattle. I've been waxed twice more since and they say that should be it.'

'Well I got a treat for these luscious lips if you ain't sworn off the guys altogether. But right now I'm fucking starving and you must be too.' Gwen was back up on her feet, thrusting a towel into Judith's hands. 'Here, grab this and I'll get you a robe. And let's go and eat. These days I got help and it should all be ready.'

The narrow hallway was pleasantly aromatic and when she was ushered into the dining room the smells of the food arrayed in covered dishes made Judith feel momentarily faint with hunger. Gwen popped the cork on a bottle of Cava standing in a bucket on the table and filled two long-stemmed glasses with the fizzing liquid.

'Get this down you first,' she said holding out one of them, 'it'll settle your stomach.' Judith obeyed thankfully, lowering herself onto a padded chair with only passing attention to the soreness of her thighs and genitals. A gas fire hissed and glowed, warming her legs below the hem of the gown, and she sipped steadily, savouring the taste of bubbles on her tongue. After what had passed before, it was a welcome lull in which the two young women drained the bottle then took the places set for them. Gwen removed the lids to reveal steaming bowls of mushroom risotto sticky with parmesan, and fettuccine with basil and cream. They fell to without a word. Eventually Judith pushed away her plate and saw that the black girl was watching her with a grin.

'Good, eh?'

'Fucking brilliant. I could not eat one more thing. So who –'

'Hold the questions for now, OK? If you take another drink with me, you'll find out. A *digestif* I think they call it and it'll put you in the mood for the *afters*, right?' She emphasised the word with a lascivious chuckle and made the bell on the sideboard give out a loud 'ding'. Almost at once the door to Judith's left swung open and

51

with a flourish a bottle and two tiny tumblers were placed on the table. She took in the mop of streaked blonde hair and the dark stubble above a T-shirt that declared its wearer to be GWEN'S, then the apparition had their dirty plates on a tray in a trice and was gone whence he had come. But not before Judith had registered that the trousers were in fact chaps that left bare a posterior quite handsomely streaked with the marks of a whip.

'Girl, you should see your face. Here, you better knock back a nip for the shock.' Spluttering with laughter, she handed Judith a small glass of spirits and downed her own in one after clinking them together. 'It ain't just for the cameras, like, though he's the star, no contest. This guy's for real. And he's kinda *mine*. Now tell me that you ain't envious.' While Judith tried to get her head round these revelations, Gwen poured out two more shots and leaned closer over the table.

'I didn't have you down as a stickler for rules, am I right, sister? I reckon I'm as stuck on women as anyone but that don't mean I gotta pass by a cock going begging. Especially one like the one we got here.'

'Sure. Yeah.' Judith was nodding vigorously. While there had been times she had espoused a separatist line, she had lapsed uncomfortably often. And when friend and confidante Marsha confessed to having intermittent recourse to just such a male member it had set the seal on a more laissez-faire attitude to the whole business. One that allowed her to indulge in a sense of anticipation at seeing rather more of the dishy young man her host seemed to have acquired. Restored by food and drink, Judith was beginning to feel distinctly randy.

'Cool. So let's do it. Hey, boy, come out and show yourself.' The order was addressed to the still open door of the adjacent room and a head appeared round it at once.

'Ms Gwen?'

'Don't come the innocent, Max. Arse over here pronto or I might get tempted to break in that nice new quirt early. Today you get to service a new lady, *if* she likes the look of you. So watch points, kiddo.' At least eighteen and maybe even twenty, Judith estimated, but the figure that sidled in was as reticent as an ill-prepared schoolboy called upon to answer in front of his class. While he stood, squirming slightly, she noticed the handsome tooled codpiece that hung between the leather-clad legs. There was a small padlock in which Gwen turned a key from around her neck and once it had been undone the whole thing was quickly removed.

'Not so easy to do what all boys love doing best with this little gizmo in place. And just to make sure . . .' She opened out the side flaps of the device and Judith saw the cluster of sharp metal points inside.

'Oh God. If he gets hard inside this –'

'Then he quick as fuck goes soft again. Or gets punctured where even the Chinese haven't thought of sticking needles.'

'Ouch.' Judith made a face. 'So that means he only gets to come when you say so. And I bet you're a real meanie, too.'

'Too right, sister. Now Maxie boy, how long is it this time?'

'Er, I think it's five days, Mistress. And I really need –'

'Shut it, slave. We ain't interested in what you need.' Gwen lifted up the exposed penis which began to stiffen and swell in her hand. 'But you did well in the kitchen, so we are feeling generous. And if you can just show us the beastie all primed, maybe my friend will want to give it a run.' Judith watched as the shaft thickened and lengthened under Gwen's manipulations and the thought of it moving inside her pricked her with desire.

'I've had bigger, of course,' she said, feigning the nonchalance her rôle seemed to require, 'but it stands up well. And it's nice and wet.'

'Seems you've passed muster, Max. But it ain't quite the green light yet and I'll tell you why. Now what is it that you never *ever* do when you are allowed into the female parts?'

'Ejaculate, Ms Gwen.'

'Indeed you don't. And how are you gonna keep all that you got in there bottled up? You ain't, boy. In no time at all you'd be giving our guest's insides a right hosing down.' It was hard not to smile at the woebegone face that greeted this assessment and Judith was glad when the stern mistress broke into chuckles. 'But I did say I'm in a good mood, so here's what we'll do. Fetch the oval paddle for my friend and the collecting bowl for me and we'll do a bit of milking. And *then* you can pleasure the lady.'

Judith understood what was expected and while the boy bent over the table she applied the instrument with vigour to his bare behind. After a while, when the earlier weals had taken on a dark tinge against the pink flush, Gwen called a halt. Then, as Judith stroked and squeezed the hot cheeks she watched the hand ring the cock which in the space of a few seconds spurted jet after jet into the silver dish. When eventually it was done she knelt and ran her mouth over the diminished member until it had regained most of its former size.

'Right, Maxie boy, that's us set. Now get down and worship at the shrine you gonna enter.' Judith slipped off the robe and spread her legs, anticipation rising as she felt first the hot breath then the lips pressed into her bare vulva. When the lad's tongue lapped into the inner folds then flicked around the clitoris she had to put her hands on his shoulders in order to steady herself.

'OK, enough.' Gwen had moved the table to one side and pulled a bench out into the centre of the room. In what seemed a practised move, Max lay on his back and Judith guessed she was to straddle the now rampant erection while his 'Mistress' stood facing her with his head between her legs. She rocked gently back and fore, vagina filled with his hard meat, while in front of her eyes swayed breasts with the sheen of ripe plums. Judith leaned and took into her mouth, one after the other, nipples that stood out like dark cherries and sucked on them till Gwen cried out for mercy. After that things moved with gathering pace towards a conclusion for the insistent clitoral friction was making Judith weak at the knees. As she began to writhe in the grip of orgasm the black girl gripped her forearms.

'Oh, yeah. Oh sugar, I got to see you come. Oh fuck, sister, yeah, yeah ...' The eyes pierced her and the fingers dug alarmingly into her flesh but the overmastering sensations swept all before them and Judith cried out, jerking up and down on the stiff organ until she slumped used up into the waiting arms. When she eased herself off the boy's body the cock still stood, firm and proud and he raised his head to look down at it.

'Yes, Maxie, you done good. And don't you ever say your mistress don't appreciate you. This, boy, is turning into your lucky day.' Gwen hunkered down at his side with her face close to the phallus that was glistening with Judith's copious juices. She looked on, transfixed, as the mouth closed over the purple head and moved up and down the shaft. As the boy tensed and began to groan, she glanced up at Judith and drew back enough to show the white stuff squirting on to her tongue, then sucked and swallowed voraciously until he was all spent.

6

Password

On the train journey back on Sunday night there was one moment more than any other that would not leave Judith's mind alone. It was when that voyeuristic gaze had fastened on to her helpless in the throes of orgasm: there was an underlying detachment to it the memory of which left her with a chill inside. Other episodes stayed with her too. Only that morning she had been bound to Max face-to-face and hoisted on tiptoe from a ceiling hook while Gwen paced about them landing cuts of her whip at will. Naturally it hurt – and hurt a lot – but that was par for the course. Nor did it trouble her particularly that for a second time she had been impaled on the boy's erection; on the contrary that memory carried a definite frisson. It was – dangerously, said a small voice of lesbian conscience from somewhere within – a thing she could get rather keen on, if not exactly addicted to. No: she was more worried about what came after she had contrived to accentuate her thrusts such that, at the end, she brought him to the point of pumping out his discharge inside her. The breach, as she perhaps should have anticipated, earned him a serious flogging and, while the pitiful cries from the next room when it was inflicted were no doubt all part of the ritual, they still seemed to ring uncomfortably in her ears.

When you added in the fact of the doctored drinks, it showed an unrestrained determination to exert control.

This was a woman with a streak of ruthlessness that made her cut straight through issues of consent in order to grab what she wanted. Coupled with the potent sexuality she exuded it made for an exciting ride, and there was no denying that the sore stretched body Judith was carrying home had been satiated to an unusual degree. On leaving, she had not so much been invited to return as ordered to wait for instructions. Though piqued by the arrogance of the assumption, it suited her to have a space to let her feelings settle about how far she really did want to go with the exercise of 'black power'. Judith shifted carefully in her seat, free to indulge a pantomime of facial grimaces unobserved in the almost empty carriage. The bruises raised by Miss James more than a week ago on her bottom were no longer a problem but they had impressed Gwen and provided her with an excuse to focus on the much more sensitive flesh of the thighs. So, thought Judith wryly, if she had arrived unmarked, the treatment received would have in all probability been less, not more, stringent. As it was, she itched and burned from the unaccustomed whippings to a degree that made her long for the journey's end and the bottle of soothing lotion in the bathroom cabinet. And that was not all that would be waiting for her at home. The intensity of the last two days' experiences may have pushed it to the back of her mind, but as the miles clattered steadily by it was coming once again to occupy her attention. *Haupt-offizier* Sibyl Metzger had given her an envelope that had – quite unaccountably – disappeared from her memory for almost half a year. And before the end of the next two hours she was going to learn what was in it.

The hands of the clock pointed to ten minutes past eleven when Judith emerged at last from the station and, turning away from the taxi rank, she set off on foot to skirt around the town centre. Tired though she felt, the effort was rewarded by the cool night air that freshened her mind as she made her way across the park. It was time to draw a line under the weekend and focus instead on what was coming next. Inside the flat she dropped her bag in the hall and ducked into the bedroom. There at the back of the built-in cupboard lay the attaché case where she had thrown it on her return from the Czech expedition, and the item that had been stashed forgotten in its pocket was retrieved in a trice.

At the kitchen counter she inserted the blade of a knife and sliced neatly through the long flap. Inside there was a folded sheet of heavy, watermarked paper which contained a piece of card whose cut-out centre was occupied by a floppy disk. Wonderingly, she freed the square of black plastic from its packaging and read the terse injunction that had been inscribed on it in a neat hand. *WARNING: Do not insert unless connected to the Internet.* Otherwise there was not a single word to be found anywhere. Bollocks. Judith resisted the temptation to send the article spinning across the room, placing it instead on the table and making for the bathroom. There she took off her boots and stripped herself naked, consigning the discarded clothes to the laundry bin. The full-length mirror on the back of the bathroom door showed her exactly why the train ride back had been less than comfortable. While the buttocks still carried the dull remains of the encounter with her boss's cane, the hips and thighs were decorated with a tracery of lines and curves that positively glowed with fresh, angry colour.

Judith ran a warmish aromatic bath and soaked herself until some of the soreness had dissipated. Then she patted the afflicted flesh gently dry and with equal care applied the calamine lotion that had been laced with a mild analgesic. Much restored, she padded through to the kitchen and picked up the communication from the past that remained so tantalisingly inaccessible. Sleep was never going to come to her while it was lying there in her flat with its contents unexamined. So there was only one thing to do. Late though it was, and however much she needed rest, she would have to take the object to the one place where it could be made to cough up its contents in accordance with the clear-cut stipulation.

It took less than a minute to kit herself out in jogging pants, trainers and a sweatshirt, over which she pulled on a fleece against the easterly wind of the April night. At nearly one a.m. the streets of the old university town were empty save for an occasional passing cab returning to the rank with its sign lit. Coming upon a gang of young men at the door of a club that was shutting up for the night, Judith tightened her fists in the pockets of her jacket and imparted a slight hunch to her shoulders, leaning forward a touch and lengthening her stride. The adjustments were small ones that had become routine since her coaching by the survivor of a tough inner-city upbringing who always insisted on roaming as she pleased. It was not a provocative transformation; that was the whole point. Rather it made the quiet assertion that here was a young woman *with a right to be there* moving through her territory.

That night, as on many others before it, the desired effect was achieved. With little in the way of conscious effort Judith passed by the group seemingly unobserved. Her mind, indeed, was occupied by the question of the disk and what its purpose was. Why did she have to have an Internet connection before loading it? OK, so it must contain links to one or more websites, but they could be activated any time. Unless, unless . . . Suppose it was somehow booby-trapped, with a tool that wiped it clean once the programme had been run. Then, if you weren't online, that would be it, finished. Well she might just be able to do something to hinder the execution of such a scheme.

59

Buoyed up by her thought, Judith swung into the quad at a brisk pace and made her way quietly across the grass by the lights that burned 24 hours a day in the basement laboratories of the Psychology Department. While as Assistant Director she could come and go as she pleased, to crunch loudly over the gravel seemed an offence against the silence of a space insulated by the solidity of weathered stone. At the door of the Archive the dim glow of the panel under its brass flap allowed her to tap in the security clearance that made it possible then to insert a key into the deadlock. Having negotiated the inner door, she was happy to let the lift do the work of carrying her to the third floor where it took only a few concrete steps to admit her to the top level of the stacks. Inside she paused, caught by the slightly musty residue of the books and manuscripts that had been housed within these walls for many earlier decades. While their present contents would no doubt have shocked earlier generations of users, it gave the place a reassuring air of continuity.

At the L-shaped counter that provided study space and housing for her monitor and keyboard, Judith reached for the wall switch and eased herself into the swivel chair. She booted up and in a matter of seconds the system was online, ready. Taking the disk from its envelope she pushed it into the opening in the stack tucked away on a shelf to the right and waited. Nothing. Not a flicker in last week's desktop image of an antique flogging frame complete with victim re-enacting quite realistically its original function. So far, so good. Obviously the thing wasn't set to autorun and in that case she would have the chance to try out her little idea.

Judith clicked on her shortcut to the drive and a window opened that showed the disk to contain a single file. Still nothing happened so with bated breath she clicked on the name 'AOC.exe' that was displayed and then on the toolbar icon for 'Copy'. At once a black-barred panel filled the screen and the words *RIGHT TO DUPLICATE DENIED* flashed on and off in a menacing fashion. But there was more. *File delete in 30 seconds* appeared below the pulsing letters and at the same time a webpage began to form itself in front of her. A new panel instructed the viewer to enter a username and password – each alpha-numeric and of six to eight letters – that would make her real identity plain. And to do it before the countdown took itself to zero. Fuck. What was this about a real identity? Did she want to 'make it plain'? It was no time to dither yet she felt her brain numb. Then suddenly it came. Alpha-numeric yet short: it had to be *jud1th*. And the password should surely be the name of the Archive, similarly modified: *nemes1s*. Ha! It was keyed in and entered before she could think better of the whole thing. She sat back and after a very small hesitation the whole screen turned a deep magenta while a superimposed message in pink declared *ACCESS GRANTED. WELCOME JUD1TH TO THE AOC*.

A moment later the colour faded into white and the restrained black lettering appeared:

Our *raison d'être* is the induction of *ingénues* with potential into the theory and practice of corporal discipline, in other words, the Art of Correction. Your increasingly noted expertise in this field would be a great asset to us. Please consider it. We have logged the URL of your institution and will direct future mail to *jwilson@nemarch.com*. If you do not want to receive this or if the address is inaccurate, please respond at once.

Hmm. They seemed to have her taped. But of course the domain name of the Archive was public anyway, so the format 'jwilson' could be just a lucky guess. May as well go with the flow. It was becoming something of a motto.

Judith counted the elapse of two seconds before the screen shrank to a pinpoint of light which then expanded into a small square.

Thank you for your support. We shall be in touch.

Before she could react it had gone. Jesus, that was brief. No more by way of explanation and no opportunity for dialogue. A check showed that there was no record of the site left in her browser: all traces of the visit had been eradicated. Frustrated, she put some obvious keywords into her favourite search engine but all it came up with were resources for editing text. And the miserable disk was now totally blank, or, what amounted to the same thing for present purposes, no longer contained any files she could access. So there she was, already waiting for 'orders' from Gwen, consigned to further passivity at the hands of the AOC. Who the fuck were these people, anyhow? 'The Art of Correction', she had to suppose, was the name from which the acronym derived. It was a new one on her, yet they had connections with The Program and, it seemed probable, with her own institution. But that would be no help. If Miss James knew anything, on past form she was unlikely to pass it on, believing that her employees were best left to solve their own problems.

Judith shut off her computer and stomped down two flights of spiral stairs feeling thoroughly out of sorts. She crossed to the opposite side of the stacks and went though the connecting door to the main office. With the clock showing twenty to two it was, of course, deserted and she checked the racks for any late mail without much hope of finding them anything other than empty. She sat on the secretarial chair that used to be occupied by Grace and swung it to and fro listlessly. It was only ten days since her lover had gone and yet she seemed to have moved into a different world – so far not one that was taking a very appealing shape. Judith banged on the wooden surface with the flat of her hand in a gesture of exasperation. Get a grip, she told herself. She was tired – overtired – after a strenuous couple of days. In the morning she would find ways of taking charge of things again.

She pulled at the large desk drawer on the left and it slid easily open in her hand. Moving forward to close it she saw a small pile of books tucked inside and leaned over to take a better look. *The New Mistress at St Bridget's* was the title of the top one and Judith recognised at once that the three other paperbacks with the distinctive green and gold border were all stories in the same series by one G. R. Marshall. Author of nothing else in the Archive's collection that Judith could recall though it was possible, even likely, that she – he? – used more than one pen name. As she remembered, they were diverting little tales of teenage girls whose emotions ran high (and why not?) but what distinguished them from doubtless many others of the 1950s was the role of physical punishment in their lives. It did not occur frequently, nor was it described in detail. There were no salacious particulars about knickers or – God forbid! – bare flesh. In fact, so discreet were the episodes that someone new to them might not understand on a first reading quite what it was the gym mistress had done to leave her pupil so hot and flushed and at the same time with such a welcome release from guilt.

There was a certain charm to all this decorum, but a young woman who seemed to be ploughing her way through the whole series could hardly fail to have understood exactly what was going on. These were narratives that pivoted on remorse for wrongdoing and retribution, though rarely involving more than the application of a plimsoll to the appropriate (if unspecified) parts. All about *correction*, in fact, to deploy the word still fresh in her mind. What was the phrase she had read from the screen? 'Ingénues with potential'. That was it. Maybe their new temp – plainly drawn by the subject – was just the kind of girl the AOC were looking for. Suddenly a picture popped into her mind of white pants stretched tight over a bottom that bounced under blows from a rubber sole while a ponytailed head jerked in protest. There was an instant response in her groin that was intense enough to give her a shock.

God, no. Judith got to her feet and shook her head in disbelief. She couldn't be getting the hots for the awkward and naive Sandra on the basis of this pile of mushy twaddle, could she? Rose-tinted memories of youth laced with a little spanking. More than likely the girl just liked soft-centred school stories with teachers you could have a crush on. She was just a bit immature, that was all. Jesus. Judith banged shut the drawer and stretched, wincing at all the aching muscles. Then she walked slowly down the stairs and put out the lights before letting the door clunk shut at her back. Time to go home. It was too late altogether – well past the bedtime even of a mature twenty-two year old.

7

Amends

It was a bleary-eyed Assistant Director who made her way into the Nemesis Archive at almost ten-thirty on the Monday morning. No more did she have to fear the penalty for late arrival that had once been a condition of employment, and she recalled with a wry smile how it had taken almost two months before she had been able to return the first time to face the music. If that was the word for the sounds the cane had made inscribing red-hot lines into her arse. She said a cursory 'Hi' to Sandra who was bent over a pile of papers. Sandra mumbled back around the chewed pencil in her mouth. God, with that cap jammed on the head round the jaunty angle of the ponytail she did look rather fetching in a juvenile sort of way. It made Judith feel all the more guilty for poking about in the girl's things and she carried on quickly through to the stacks. There was an article she had promised to write for *Strictly Fetish* and Wednesday's deadline was getting uncomfortably close. It was intended as one of a series in which the author explained how it was that a properly brought-up young woman found herself engaging in highly improper sexual pursuits. The memories just awakened would make a good start: how she had presented Miss James with a yard of prime Malay rattan brought back from her travels and requested to be reinstated. She had not needed to ask twice, and the first ever beating she had in effect asked to receive was administered with such zest that the feel of the strokes burned in her mind as if it were days, not years ago. Mix in some experiences that summer in Brittany and it could add up to a readable paragraph or two.

Once she had wrestled the opening couple of sentences into shape the words flowed freely and she was startled out of her absorption by the buzz of the intercom. Only one person made a habit of its use to contact her and fresh from her efforts to set down the Director's rules on – among other things – time-keeping she felt a twinge of guilt at the voice.

'Judith, it's Samantha James here. I don't want to interrupt your work, but if you're not involved in anything too important, perhaps you could come down for a few minutes?' Instead of the direct instruction Judith was accustomed to, the phrasing was unusually circumspect.

'Er, yes, Miss James. No problem, I'll be right there.'

In the wood-panelled office stood a small whipping horse with a tooled leather top, over which was draped a split tawse. From the young PA's flushed face it was a fair guess both items had been put to use, though the sparkle in her eyes told of more than a punishment strapping. The Director's eyes also were bright as she rose from her desk.

'One of the new batch of instruments, and a pleasure to apply. Be so good, Penelope, as to show Miss Wilson its effects.' The girl hoiked up her short black skirt and stuck out a knickerless rump for examination. The deep cherry-red of the plump little cheeks extended on each side to square imprints of the tails vivid against pale flesh. The 'application' had plainly been a thorough one.

'A fetching sight, I'm sure you'll agree, Judith. Now I have it in mind that the person of our Assistant Director could – ah – assist in a similar fashion, if she were so inclined. To be recorded, subject to her approval, for possible use in a small promotional effort.'

'Well, um, yes. I mean, of course. Er, if I understand you right, Miss James, I'd, er, be pleased.' It was an awkward little tumble of words that mirrored the confusion of her thoughts. The last – indeed the *only* – leathering she'd ever received from the boss had been a lascivious affair of strokes aimed to arouse as much as they caused pain. Very different from the brutal welting at the remove of a cane's length that had been her most recent experience. In fact that hot licking whose memory was making her prickle had come soon after the American woman had engineered her an undeserved beating. It seemed to have been a way – the way of an unusually committed disciplinarian – to make amends. Judith chanced a little smile on the strength of her supposition and the Director visibly relaxed.

'Thank you, my dear. I do believe you have understood so I shall, as they say, come clean. I'm afraid I was guilty some ten days ago of a palpable overreaction: not so much in the fact of caning you but in the manner of it. In effect, I apologise.' She paused to silence Judith's demurral with a gesture, then continued. 'I let a past grievance or two get the better of me – quite wrongly – and as you know I do tend to get carried away when I have you in position over the desk. So I propose to make a little occasion for the three of us in a couple of days. I take it any traces of my excesses will not stand in the way?'

'No sweat, boss. As long as the canes stay in the cupboard.' Miss James flinched slightly, whether from the burst of familiarity or the allusion to her transgression Judith didn't know or care. She was feeling euphoric at being back in the fold where limits were dependable or at least negotiable.

'That's settled, then. I should add, of course, that for future reference I pretend to no rights over our new secretary.'

'Miss James! I haven't so much as looked at Sandra.'
It was almost true.

'I didn't mean to imply that you had, Judith.' The uncharacteristically mild reply was disconcerting. She had better stop pushing her luck before it changed. 'However I did want to quiz you on how the girl is getting on. I have received no word at all of another candidate, so if there were a chance she might graduate in time to a permanent position . . .'

'I think Sandra could be fine. I mean, she's made a couple of mistakes –'

'Remember she forgot that card of yours, Miss Judith.'

'Well, if there are important reservations, I should like to know about them. Speak freely; I shall not take anything said back to the girl.' The Director looked from one to the other, waiting. Judith went first.

'I'm not sure how serious you'll think it, but there is one thing. She's been taking stuff from the stacks. On the quiet. The point is, she could have asked.'

'Ah. Can you tell me what exactly?'

'Well, I think it started with a novel from the fifties that featured a sports mistress rather fond of using her gym shoe on naughty bottoms. All rather veiled, of course. And now the whole series has gone from the shelf.' It didn't seem necessary to explain that she had come by this information from rummaging in Sandra's desk. 'And then I'm pretty sure she's been into a box file of reminiscences about first spankings – seen later as a kind of initiation.'

'Hm, interesting. Initiation, eh? That gives me an idea. The girl plainly has an interest – exactly the interest that could suit her for the post – but we wouldn't want to force anything, would we? So I think I shall have a quiet word with Mrs Rowleigh at the College. She was very good in filling our gap sooner than expected and Sandra is one of hers. If I were to send the girl over on Friday afternoon, with a note –'

68

'As in one of her stories, yes!' Judith grinned as the penny dropped: Marjorie Rowleigh was known to take pleasure in the moderate correction of her 'bad girls'.

'Indeed so. Perhaps the application of a firm hand from one she respects might be just what she needs.'

'Or is even looking for.'

'Very good. It shall be done. As to the other matter, how would eleven a.m. on Wednesday suit? I may have a little surprise for you downstairs. But don't be alarmed, Judith, the basement is for the purpose declared – as I believe the current expression goes – a rattan-free zone.' The dark eyes that could bore right through you were almost twinkling and the sight sent the Assistant Director back to her article with a light heart. The mood couldn't last, but she was going to make the most of it while it did.

On the appointed morning, Judith slept luxuriously late. The impending event had lodged itself in her mind such that dreams came and went that left her waking consciousness chasing the fleeting memories of their fierce sensuality. She indulged her languor with a hot bath, after which it was time to dispel the last remnants of sleep with a pot of freshly ground mocha and a brioche. A cupboard drawer gave up a pair of white shorts in tailored cotton together with a matching top. Intended as gear for the odd occasions she went clubbing they had yet to be worn and Judith decided that the present was as good a time as any for an unveiling. The figure-hugging fit of the fine material made even her small breasts jut provocatively and after lacing up a pair of black granny boots she announced to the mirror that she was going to knock 'em dead. Perhaps not, however, on the mid-morning streets that lay between the flat and the Archive, so she found a long black coat that gave the whole an air of rather trendy respectability. Out in the park the sun was shining on trees almost fully in leaf and Judith cut a course through them in a tingle of anticipation.

Divested of her outer covering she entered the Director's lair via the connecting door and found Penny in the briefest of grey tunics making a final adjustment to the heavy silver buckle that fastened together the dark weave of Miss James's skirt. All clothing judged to be in order, the small party swept through the outer office where a startled-looking Sandra raised her head. Conscious of her scrutiny Judith paused and saw the cheek redden as the glance travelled over her bare thighs. Gwen's whip-marks of course – she hadn't really given them a thought. Braving it out with a wink she was rewarded with a rather nervous little grin. That was better. The girl didn't know yet she was, albeit in a minor way, going to join the club if their little scheme worked out. Suddenly Judith was confident that it would and smiling back hurried after the others down the stairs.

In the basement the first thing she saw was a short figure teetering on a step ladder in the process of adjusting the angle of a spotlight. The spiky hair had turned cerise but there was no mistaking its owner and Judith faltered. The last time in the camerawoman's company she had been lectured about fucking her pal Grace around. And now the whole thing between them was kaput. Uh oh. The woman was hardly going to be over the moon.

'That you, Jude? How ya doing?' The question was thrown back over a shoulder while she grappled with a recalcitrant bracket. 'Heard you and Gracie ain't an item no more.'

'Yeah, afraid so. Look, Mo, I just couldn't play along any longer, she was so fucking jealous. Shit, I know I was no angel, but –'

'Hey, don't beat yourself up about it, sister. No skin off my nose and you did give it a fucking go in the end.'

She climbed down and folded up the steps. 'Right awkward customer when you consider it, but I've given up worrying. With those looks there'll be plenty more takers. Though I don't know why we're talking about *her*. Who's the dolly moving the furniture? And taking care to show us there ain't even a thong covering her booty.'

Judith laughed. 'Hands off, lady, if you know what's good for you. She's the PA and that spells *Private* Assistant. Private property of the boss. Not only would you never get another job down here, she'd take the skin off your arse. Strip by strip with her best four-footer.' Mo gave a theatrical shudder but her eyes showed that the idea was not wholly distressing. Judith guessed it would be the kind of extreme experience she was known to seek out now and then. But before she could make a comment they were all called to order by a brisk clap of the Director's hands.

'If everyone is quite ready, can we get to the business, ladies, please? Judith, if you would take up your position, for now, I think just as you are. Penelope can try her hand, or rather this good firm paddle, at a little warm-up. I should say that my staff and I share certain exhibitionist tendencies, so have no inhibitions about where you point your camera, Miss Hollingsborough.'

Jesus, that was a mouthful. No wonder she wanted herself known as plain Mo. Hiding a grin, Judith draped herself over the cool surface of the padded trestle that had been placed strategically centre stage as Penny took up the leather oval by its polished wooden handle. The loud splatting noise of the first slaps took Judith by surprise and she felt the seam of her shorts pulling up tight between her legs with the force of them. Ouch, ouch, ouch! That was quite a swing the girl had.

'Good, good,' murmured Miss James from her side, leaning to take hold of the bare flesh on each side above the waistband. 'Keep it up, my dear.' As the strokes fell

71

on one cheek then the other in rhythmic alternation the sting of them soon merged into a smarting heat under the cotton covering. With the contact of those hands that gripped her squirming figure – hands more commonly employed in the dispensing of severity – and the chafing of the cloth against her clit Judith's loins were liquefying. No doubt the lens that was sure to be trained on her nether regions was collecting the visual evidence. Then a flurry of smacks that made her gasp out loud brought respite in which the Director moved round to pull the shorts down and off over her boots. Again there was the touch, this time of cool palms against tender burning skin.

'Penelope, the straps please, and make them tight. A restrained body allows one to concentrate the stimulation. That's it, spread the legs and take them well forward – good – and now the waist. Hard down.' So this is how it was to be. Rump jutting with cheeks splayed: obscenely open with every fold and wrinkle of cunt flesh exposed to the camera's pitiless gaze. And the thought of it sent her lubrication into overdrive.

'A little weekend experimentation, I see. With quite an accomplished pattern of marks.' Delicate fingers were tracing the residual effects of Gwen's whip, then they moved up from the thighs and there was a sharp intense pain in the underside of both the buttocks that made her yell. Jesus, pinching was one thing but with sharp fingernails . . .

'I'm glad to find you so responsive, Judith, and to see that the bruising has subsided so nicely. Your hindquarters are perfectly ready for a good beating, and that is exactly what I shall supply. Penelope, I'll take the Lochgelly first, the one with the three tails. I intend to see that Miss Wilson earns her pleasure.'

And she was as good as her word. For the next several minutes Judith reared and lunged against the bonds as the heavy leather scorched her flanks. When respite came she clung, panting, to the rough wooden frame, bathed in the sweet relief that was the cessation of pain. A hand cupped the oozing purse of her genitals, sending a renewed shock of arousal through her feverish body, and when the paddle slapped lightly into the base of her behind she began to come almost at once. When the spasms had done with her she became aware of the form of Miss James to her right and turned a bemused head. Legs apart, she stood straight-backed with her skirt unfastened on the floor while two figures crouched in attendance. At the far side the digital eye performed its silent scan while in the front of her field of vision lips closed on that monstrous protuberance at the apex of the bared labia. Senses stretched to breaking point, Judith appeared to see not one but two jets of a milky ejaculate splash off the busy chin as the hands clenched and unclenched on the girl's shoulders. A wave of giddiness engulfed her and she closed her eyes.

When she opened them again it was to glimpse the Director's parting back and see Mo's hand lift Penny's tunic to squeeze a chubby little buttock.

'Don't you get your jollies then, sister?'

'Oh, that's her nibs's privilege. After a bit when I go up, she'll –'

'Look, kid, why wait? How's she ever gonna know?' Mo put down the camera and began to undo the buttons one by one. Penny looked doubtful but allowed the skimpy garment to fall around her feet and stood naked with the damp pubic curls matching the brown of her pageboy cut. The camerawoman went over to her bag and took out a strap-on together with another black shiny dildo with prominent ribs.

'Jude's come alive again, so you go and untie her, there's a good girl. Then we are both going to give you a bloody good seeing to. And this one ain't for the record.'

* * *

73

It seemed an age apart when Judith pushed open the back door into the deserted bar of The Phoenix, though it was only the space occupied by a long bath and a short nap. Marsha was wiping down tables with a distracted air while a horde of dirty glasses jostled for space on the counter. She lobbed the cloth over the bar into the sink. 'Too many fucking students. I need a break. But hey, honey, you're looking in the pink.' The American bar manager took Judith's shoulders between her hands and held her eyes for a moment. 'OK, I get it. Can we surmise that there's a glow in places we can't actually see?'

'Jesus, Marsha. Is it that fucking obvious?'

'Don't knock it, girl. Your openness is a quality to be prized. At least you seem to have got over the other week.'

'The other week?'

'I hear Samantha was a little heavy handed.'

Judith stared, briefly at a loss. But there was really only one possibility. 'Marsha,' she said severely, 'have you been chatting up Penny? You've got some bloody nerve.' The scandalised tone was only partly assumed.

'Well, don't ya love that haircut, Jude? And she's not blabbing your secrets all over town. She only told me because she knows we're pals.'

'OK, OK. How about I agree not to be cross if you can rustle up some tasty leftovers from lunches. I'm fucking starved.'

'Right, honey, it shall be done.' She uncapped a Pils and plonked it down in front of her visitor. 'Why don't you suck on this beer while I get things together? And then you can tell me all about your new temp. Sandra, isn't it? A little bird tells me she's quite a dish underneath the baggy clothing.'

'*Marsha*. You are completely impossible.'

74

8

In Hand

When I got handed that thick envelope I made myself
come all the way back here before I opened it. If it was
going to say I'd been given the heave, then I had to be
home before I read the message. Er, sorry, this is Friday
and that was yesterday. But when I looked inside what
I saw didn't make any sense at all to begin with. There
was another envelope that had Mrs Rowleigh's name on
it – she's the deputy at the Business College who'd got
me into the Archive in the first place – and then there
was this note for me. I'm going to read it out 'cos I have
it right here. 'Sandra', it says, no 'dear' or anything,
'Sandra, I want you to deliver this note on Friday
afternoon' – that's *this* afternoon of course – 'at
2.30 p.m. In order to do so you may finish work for the
week at lunchtime. I wish to take this opportunity to say
that in the main we are well satisfied with the work done
since you joined us. However, there are one or two
points needing rectification and your old mentor has
kindly agreed to take the matter in hand. Then I hope
we can move on to consolidate your present status in
our establishment.'

Well, that's it. I thought straight away, wow, that
doesn't sound like the sack. In fact it sounds like the
opposite, like I might be in the running for a proper
contract or something. And I still think that, but the

75

more I stare at the rest of it the more it makes me feel all wobbly. It's things like 'needing rectification' and 'taking the matter in hand'. Whatever it is I'm supposed to have done is going to be dealt with and by someone who's been a bit like a mother to me. I mean quite a formal one in some ways, but definitely with a parental sort of attitude. And that must be why she's being called in. Or rather that I'm being sent over to her. For – for – oh, I'm not going to say what I'm beginning to suspect, it'll sound just plain silly if I'm wrong, as if I've lost my grip on the real world with all these school stories. But it helps to say this much out loud, even if I don't ever actually send any of these tapes.

OK, right. I'm back and it's nearly four in the afternoon. I know what I said, I mean what I wouldn't say, what I was half thinking, but I just couldn't believe it. Still can't.

I've only been to the house once before and that was for some small college do for Mrs Rowleigh's tutees. This time we were downstairs in a kind of study den sort of place curtained off from the rest of the room. It was dead silent and closed in with a huge desk. Well, she sat me down in this big armchair and quizzed me about the Archive and how I was getting on – all the stuff you'd expect a tutor to ask an ex-pupil who's got a new job. And she wanted to know particularly what I felt about being upgraded to a full appointment. Miss James was really quite keen on the idea, she thought, but there was this one thing that was maybe holding her back. Nothing to do with the usual secretary things, nor was she bothered about how I dress – though I can't really believe *that* – no, it was to do with unendorsed staff use of the material in the stacks. Of course then I realised: someone must have come across my small stash of books and papers.

What was bothering them all, it seemed, was why hadn't I just asked if I could borrow things I wanted to read. Why sneak them out and hide them in my bottom drawer? I would have thought the explanation was all too bloody obvious but I didn't say that of course. Just went red and mumbled something lame about not liking to. And that was my chance for constructive intervention out the window: from that point Mrs R just took charge. She had, she said, been authorised to react appropriately to the deceit. That was the phrase and it was said in the plummy voice that comes on when she's being all official. So then she stood up and I did too and she took this thing out of a drawer and put it down on the desk. It was like an oblong ping-pong bat but in leather and we both just looked at it in silence. She said she preferred the term 'tapette' though most people would call it a paddle.

'But you know what it's for, don't you, Sandra? And I'm afraid those jeans of yours are rather going to get in the way.' That was how she said it exactly – I can still hear the words in my head – and they made the whole thing all at once seem inevitable. I mean I know I wasn't compelled to go through with it but somehow I just did. So I took the jeans off and just stood there in my pants – at least they were clean on for the occasion – and it all happened really fast. In a moment I was bent over under the crook of her arm and she started to spank me. There: I actually said it. Mrs Rowleigh was *spanking* me, whacking away with that, that tapette, on my seat and it was stinging like hell. Unreal. Un*real*. I was wriggling and crying out and all that but I just kind of basically took it. I mean even though she's a strong woman, well built and all, I'm sure I could have got free if I tried. But I didn't.

When she stopped it was almost worse. I couldn't look her in the eye and I don't think she could look at me. I scrambled back into my denims while she made some remark about giving Samantha a favourable report. Then I was up the stairs and out that bloody door.

I mean it wasn't extreme or anything. I've just had another look in the mirror and the red has gone down a lot compared with when I came in. I'm not even that sore, I mean I can sit down no bother. But this time I noticed that I'm damp down there. Sorry. I know these euphemisms are horrible. I should say that my pants are a bit wet. Between the legs. In the *crotch*. And it's not, like, sweat, and I don't think I ever ... God, what would Gregor say, I mean this is me being like him, like he gets when ... Oh, that's enough. Too bloody much in fact. There's plenty of daylight left and I'm going out to run and run. Run till these thoughts stop going round.

God, I don't know why I'm doing this, it's late. Fucking late. I never used *that* word before but it felt good, so there. It's been quite a day and after I played back the last few messages I just couldn't leave it there. You know, it's kind of necessary to set the record straight. Well not so much that, more like I have to do an update. Not that anybody's going to hear this stuff.

Thing is, when I got back it was nearly dark and Gregor was waiting round the corner for me. He was there because he's going away on a field trip tomorrow and can't come on Sunday or the next one for that matter. So of course he came up and I'm saying I've got to get a shower 'cos of how hot and sweaty I am but he's saying how good I look and pulling me down on to the sofa beside him. Well, to keep this short, we're soon kissing quite hard and I'm actually enjoying this more than I ever have. So when we stop for breath I say 'Gregor, you'll never guess what happened to me this afternoon' and the whole thing comes out. And what really caps it is that he's not shocked, more sort of *interested*. So, like I've become a completely crazy slut I promptly pull down my shorts and stick out my backside for an inspection. God it doesn't seem possible now, but that's what I did. And he's got his hands all over, finding a trace of red still left here and a bit of a bruise there and before either of us really knows what's happening his fingers are inside me and I am ready for them. Not kind of moist like earlier, but dead *slippery*. Kneeling on the couch with my arse in the air like a bloody baboon while he strokes my – my – genitals. No, I *can* say it. Cunt. That's the word I want. He's playing with my cunt. And what's more amazing than any of this is that I promptly have my first orgasm with him holding my waist and saying 'Yes, yes, yes' along with all the noise I'm making.

So after all that, there's really only one thing for it. I open up his zip and go for his thing – his *cock* – and when it springs out I pull him up and get down on my knees. There's a big drop of clear stuff that I lick off – it's kind of a bit salty but not bad – and I put my mouth over the end. He's kind of gasping and saying 'San, San, if you keep on –' so I stop sucking long enough to remind him I've *seen* what happens, then carry straight on. I manage to get my tongue sort of up against it so the stuff doesn't hit me in the throat but now I'm determined to see the thing through and swallow it all down. Salty *and* sour this time and definitely a bit of an effort, so as soon as it's decently possible I find some vodka and give us both a stiff one with some tonic to cut the taste. I suppose you could get used to it, but then I'm not planning a career in cock sucking, am I? *Am* I? God only knows. I'm going to leave it there for now and haul myself off to bed. Alone, of course. Why ever did I say that? What else would I be?

PART II

9

Suited

From: thechemist
Subject: viagra really works!
Received: April 15, 09 45:32

Fucking *spam*. Judith allowed her mail screener to bounce it back to source before she shut it down and tried to return her mind to the task at hand. Since eight a.m. she had been at her top-floor station sketching the framework of a new project, but as the days passed since her brief encounter with the AOC she found herself checking the mail more and more often in the hope of some further communication. She couldn't contact *them* and it was, to say the very least, irritating. It was possible it wouldn't come to anything, but the fact of the link having originated with the *Haupt-offizier* of The Program suggested otherwise. If nothing else, though, that line about the induction of ingénues had coincided with her own train of thought. Now the article about her own first experiences had been dispatched, she was becoming beguiled by the idea of writing something more wide-ranging on the same subject. Perhaps a series of pieces or even another NemArch title, if she could get her act together.

Absorbed in thought, she was aware of a door opening and closing below. Fine: if some new materials had come in to be catalogued she would go down for them later. But then footsteps crossed the floor and there came the distinct sounds of someone climbing not only the first but the second spiral stair. Judith swung round in her chair in time to see a head appear over the bottom rail with an apologetic cough.

'Can I come up? I won't disturb you for more than a moment, Judith.'

'Oh it's you, Sandra. Yes, of course. I don't get many callers up here.' The figure emerged fully from the opening and came towards her.

'I just, um, wanted to apologise for taking those things without permission. I've put them back where they came from.'

'You – er – what, sorry?' The words had passed Judith by as she goggled at the sight before her. It was Sandra all right, and the ponytail was intact though it had lost the baseball cap once fixed to it. Gone too were the shapeless sweatshirt and jeans: now there was a visible swell of breasts under a white halter-neck and snug grey suit trousers tapered down to heeled boots. The matching jacket swung loose over it all from the shoulders.

'I came to say sorry. About the books and the papers.'

'Yes, OK. But there's no need, really.' Judith tried to pull herself together. The girl had always looked rather cute, but this . . . She pulled out a stool from under the counter and patted it. 'Here, have a seat. Look, in future take anything you fancy reading – just two things though. If you leave a slip, on the off chance someone else is looking for it they'll know where to go. And if it's something dead rare or old you had better check with me first. You'll understand that we don't really want an eye-witness account of the practices of flagellant nuns in seventeenth-century Bohemia disintegrating into fragments when the air gets to it.'

84

Sandra laughed and leaned back displaying an enticing curve of hip. 'Right. I get the point.'

'Good. You know, Sandra, I should show you around properly if you're going to stay on. You are, aren't you? I heard the boss is quite keen.'

'Er, well, I *think* so. I mean I think she is. She was all smiles to me this morning. In fact I'd better run – I'm due in her office in five minutes and I'm told that with Miss James late is not an option. But I'd like a tour some other time.'

'You need one really. We've collected quite a lot of stuff and it's not always obvious what's what. My brilliant cataloguing, I'm afraid.' The visitor stood up and smoothed the creases from her sheathed thighs in a way that made Judith feel distinctly warm.

'Hey, you've got some view from this window.'

'Yeah. Look out there and it seems to say age-old stability and order. Can be handy if you're feeling a bit frazzled by some of the madness on these shelves.' Judith watched the retreating form and was rewarded by a glimpse of material stretched tight over two neat buttocks as the secretary turned to clang down the steps. 'Oh Sandra, there is one thing. You don't have any languages, do you?' The head pushed back up into view.

'I suppose German. I did it for years at school and I can read quite a bit.'

'Right. Now I think of it, I've got this thesis from the University of Leiden that might be important for something I'm working on. All about initiations. If you've got the time to have a look at it for me, I'd be grateful.'

'Initiations?'

'Yeah, into s/m and stuff. I think it's mostly just spanking . . .' Judith's voice died away as she saw the colour flood into the face in front of her. Fuck, what was she saying? Her own preoccupations had put Miss James's plan out of her head, but if it had worked

Sandra had been very recently exposed to exactly such an initiation. Then she realised the implications of it in time and choked back the apology that was rising to her lips. 'Er, anyway, it was just a thought. Here, I mustn't keep you back. Speak to you later, OK?' She turned away with what she hoped was a cheery wave and sank down into her seat.

Phew, that was a close one. It was a fair guess the girl would be mortified if she thought they were all in on a plot to have her chastised. Maybe she would think that, even did think it already, but at least Judith hadn't let the cat out of the bag. When the noise of the steps died away and the door shut two floors beneath with a soft thud she breathed a sigh of relief. If the boss had been 'all smiles' Marjorie must have done the business and Samantha could be really charming when things were going her own way. It looked like Sandra was going to be around for a while and if the new look stuck she was going to be quite a teasing presence. Judith sighed and turned back to her outline. But first one more look at her mail. If she was giving up on the AOC coming through, maybe an invitation was waiting from Gwen to a weekend of nasty and deeply gratifying sex. You had to hope.

'So Jude, is this going to be another hot session in the red-light zone?'

'The only ones I saw last time were stopping traffic. But we managed.'

'I'm sure you did. Though I have to say I never got a full briefing on the occasion.' It was the American bartender's night off and they were ensconced in a basement bar along the street from her own establishment. 'But I do seem to recall something about a guy on a leash wearing leather chaps and not much else.'

'No leash, Marsha, you made that up. Max is a pretty boy though, no mistake. But did I really omit to tell you

86

about me and the handcuffs and a big bed? Now if you just add in a plain *dirty* black girl and her whip . . .'

'OK, you win, honey.' The hands were held up in mock surrender. 'You'd better stop right there before ears start flapping all around. But you're quite right: go for it while you're young, I say. At my age I have to settle for a juicy poppet hanging on my arm.'

'Or three at the same time.'

'Jude as long as I can get away with it, I shall do exactly that.' Marsha smirked slightly at the reference to the magnetic attraction she appeared to exercise over certain young women of the town. 'But to get back to your sex life, girl, what's the score this time round?'

'Well, Max is out on loan as chef for another party, so I have been instructed to eat beforehand. Then, once I've, er, settled in, we're out to some pub or club the lady has recently discovered. And, of course, when we get back from there, I don't suppose it'll be quite time for the Horlicks . . .' Judith stood up with a chuckle. 'OK, don't walk out on me, Marsha. I hate heavy-handed innuendo too. So stay where you are and let me get the beers in. And we'll try a small chaser.'

When she came back from the bar Marsha pulled her down into her seat and leaned forward. 'Don't look straight over, but isn't that eye-catching creature by the stairs getting some serious chat-up treatment actually your temp?' Judith cast a surreptitious glance around her companion's shoulder to confirm the identification.

'Aha. Yes and no. What you see there is no temp but a full member of staff since Monday. However, get this: the startling transformation came first.'

'Remember what I said about the potential? But if she's not dressing up to the job, what the fuck *did* set this off?' The pale eyes fixed on her, narrowing. 'Judith Wilson, you are holding out on me. Exactly what is it I am not being told?'

'Well, from what I hear, *ma'am*, there was another event at the weekend that might have some connection to the newly tailored appearance. Though the precise logic of it rather escapes me. I mean, why should an encounter with a heavy hand bring on an attack of dress sense?' She giggled and took a careful sip of vodka followed by a deliberately drawn-out slug of beer. The face across the table from her was a mask of barely contained impatience. Judith leaned over and put a hand on her friend's arm. 'It's not often I get to wind *you* up, so don't be cross. But you will have to swear on all that you hold sacred not to breathe a word. To a living soul.'

When I saw that American woman looking at me and Judith with her and all I just made out I was wrapped up in the guy spinning me a line. I mean they could just be talking about my clothes, but I don't think so. That would be fine, I'm getting quite a buzz out of the change. Not that I really know what I'm doing, I just broke open the piggy bank and went to Ginny's friend Tamsin who's got that trendy place in the Close. And she took charge. Somehow after Gregor it was time for a change. Not that I'm going to carry on like that with *him*, it was all kind of too much. Well, not too much exactly – I mean I don't look back with horror or anything – but not sort of *right*. I dunno. But anyway, what was making me cringe was the thought of them all talking about what happened earlier, in the afternoon, as if the details are being passed round.

Well, I just played that back and so it was yesterday and now it's Thursday the, er, eighteenth. It was nice after work, quite warm really, so I set out for a good long route through the park and right round. But I just couldn't shake off the stuff that's preying on my mind and before I knew what I was doing I'd taken a detour down the path that comes out in Mrs Rowleigh's cul-de-sac. And when I got to the house it was just getting dusk and there she was down at the desk with a light on. So of course I sort of hesitated and she looked up and that was me taken inside. As soon as we got downstairs I said how pleased I was to have the job and she said she was pleased too. Then I blurted out what was bothering me and she went dead serious, in fact she looked a bit hurt. She had said *nothing* except to tell Miss James I had accepted reasonable discipline – that's how she put it – and to recommend she take me on. She told me not to worry because they were all only guessing. If I just faced them down it would stop before long.

That was great. It kind of put the boot on the other foot, making them into idle gossips I could shrug off no bother. But Mrs Rowleigh was still looking solemn and said she had something to own up to. If she was going to be honest with me I ought to know that she did take pleasure in giving a good old-fashioned spanking to an attractive girl. Or 'gel' as she says it. And she wasn't talking about the satisfaction of giving out something deserved. Well, I kind of guessed as much though I hadn't been thinking about *her*, only about my end of the situation. But once she said it that just sets me off and there I am saying, 'Oh Mrs R, if you'd like to, right now that is . . .' I must be feeling grateful for her taking my side like, but the upshot is her sitting down on a long box-thing against the wall and me draped over her lap. Last time I was dead anxious about it but now I'm the one who has volunteered myself and it actually feels kind of reassuring – almost safe in a funny way – to have those solid thighs under mine and a hand pressing down on my back. But that's me leaving the main element out of the equation and when she starts in on the seat of my shorts I'm soon squirming. That's bad enough, but when they come down – God, does that big hand sting! Before long there are tears and all kinds of undignified stuff I am *not* going to mention but –

and this *is* like before – no way am I going to make her stop until she has decided she's done.

When she does let go I shoot up and rub at the smarting bits – like a complete ninny in only my singlet – and she's telling me to go and take my time in the bathroom at the back of the hallway. Rather than trying to say anything – how *do* you go from being spanked like a kid to adult conversation? – I just grab my shorts and scarper up the stairs. There's a nice big mirror and I'm standing there looking at this totally red backside thinking what the hell am I doing. And it's really tender too. But that's not the big deal; what *is* is how wet I am. *Wet* wet. If the shorts had been on they would be soaked. OK, I remember you tried to talk about masturbation, and I did try to get into it once or twice. But it always felt kind of rubbery and *ugh*. Now it feels all slippery it seems right to have my fingers in there. It only takes a few seconds of stroking and there I am hanging on to the washbasin with the other hand to keep upright. Like with Gregor but this is more so. So intense it almost hurts, but I am hooked and I know it.

After that I tried to come down a bit with a quick shower and when I got back downstairs we have actually turned into grown-ups again with glasses of wine and a plate of sandwiches, *and* we talk about the College, for God's sake. But after a bit Mrs Rowleigh says she has something to show me and draws back the curtains that go right across the room. The other side has a parquet floor and the thing that strikes you straight off is this trestle all made of rough wood with a flat black top. It's got straps hanging off it all over and I suddenly get a bit panicky. She doesn't, surely she doesn't think that I . . . But she must have seen the look on my face 'cos she lets out a laugh and says 'Not for *you*, dear, for *me*.' And then she explains that she has a requirement for ritual punishment, one that has not been met now for two months. It is, she says, difficult

90

to find the right person but she has at last made an appointment for a young woman from the town – an expert she trusts apparently – to perform the service. I'm trying to take this in – after the wine my head is spinning slightly and it's like I've been shipped to another planet. A far out one. What it is about – why she's telling *me* – is because she needs someone to be with her *during*. Like a second or something at a duel, can you believe? And then she says she wouldn't expect me to watch, though I'd be very welcome of course.

Well, that was it. I made my excuses and beat it back here. I said I'd give her an answer tomorrow. It's all left me a bit shocked. I really don't know what I'm going to say.

10

Sign

Judith came out of the station and, shouldering her bag
with a swing, set off on foot in a southerly direction. It
had been a good plan to pick up a couple of the
delicatessen's 'gourmet' sandwiches for the journey and
one agreeably topped off by a half-bottle of wine to
wash them down. She skirted the edifice of the British
Library with scarcely a thought of the treacherous Rare
Books man she had dallied with until the previous
summer. Instead, as she crossed the busy thoroughfare
and made to thread her way through the collection of
University buildings, her mind was becoming occupied
by the weekend ahead. In the eagerness to be abroad
again in the city, she had let the reservations generated
by the first visit drop out of consideration. Now,
however, as her steps were bringing her through
Bloomsbury towards the Soho destination they began to
regain some of their earlier force. If she could only do the
sensible thing and strike up a steady relationship with a
'nice' girl she would not have to worry about coming
round handcuffed to a bed. But then a nice girl wouldn't
turn her on like the bad – and very possibly dangerous –
Gwen did. As Marsha said there was plenty of time for a
quiet life later on. And besides, she could surely expect to
have more say in future games: once deployed, the
spiked drink was not a tactic easily repeated.

By the time she turned in through the narrow brick arch just off the square, Judith had managed to convert her doubts into a rather keen anticipation of exactly what might happen in the next couple of days. And first impressions were scarcely a disappointment. No sooner had her finger been removed from the bell than the shabby inner door was whisked open and she was pulled inside. The bag was taken from her grasp with a 'Just come with me' and Judith followed meekly after her host down the short passage, eyes wide at the sight before them. For, with the exception of the brown bowler hat jammed at a rakish angle onto her head, Gwen was entirely nude.

'Right, girl, you too. Strip. I got gear there for later, but first we do an exercise, OK?' They were in a small anteroom Judith had not seen before. In the corner was a contraption like a sawing horse whose upper arms had been swathed in padding and it gave her an idea.

'OK to all that, but first you do something for me.' She pulled the device out from the wall and pushed the bare young woman down over it. 'Now you be good and *stay*, right?' Judith stroked the cheeks that undulated so deliciously from the wide hips when Gwen walked and pressed one hand down on the back. Then she raised the other and brought it down in two sharp rapid slaps.

'Ow! Ow! What the fuck you doing, Jude?' The voice was complaining, but the body was making no attempt to resist, so she stroked some more and began to spank in a steady rhythm. 'This (*smack*) is for (*smack*) knocking (*smack*) me out (*smack*!). In future (*smack*! *smack*!) you tell me (*smack*! *smack*!) what you're (*smack*! *smack*!) going to do (*smack*! *smack*! *smack*!).'

'Ow-ow-ow-ow! Right, sister, I promise. But you whacked me last time for the same thing, remember? So just stop it, will ya?' Judith massaged the brown flesh that was beginning to show a distinct blush, observing the telltale glistening between the legs. So she continued until the sting in her own palm said enough then delved into the juiced vulva. It took mere seconds for the writhing figure to gasp out: 'Yes – oh yes – oh fuck yesss.' When the spasm had passed Judith put the dripping fingers into her mouth and sucked at the tangy juice until her partner got to her feet and replaced the hand with her tongue.

After a while Gwen said: 'Now you stand there just like that. You wanna know what I'm going to do? Well, this is me telling you. I get to strip you bare-arse naked and then, courtesy of yours truly, you get to come. Deal?'

'Deal.' Judith decided that if that was the result of it, being assertive would have to become policy. She stood still while the black girl carefully unbuttoned her grey shirt and sucked on the nipples until they stood out hard from the small breasts. Then she removed the garment altogether and ran her tongue up and down Judith's spine in a way that made her shiver. The boots and socks came next and when the trousers had been unzipped Gwen eased them down from behind so that she could knead the uncovered buttocks. Last came the thong and it clung wetly to her for a moment before it was round her ankles and off. Then arms clasped her spread thighs and it was as if there was a burrowing animal with snout and teeth between – inside – the engorged lips. Judith rocked and steadied herself on the shoulders of the woman kneeling before her as the orgasm came sharp and fast. 'God, oh God – that – is – good,' she breathed, crumpling gently into the thick pile cushioning her feet. After a few moments she twisted her neck to look up at the figure beside her.

'So when's Max coming back?'

'Later on, if he knows what's good for him. The boy don't get to stay out nights.'

'You keep a tight rein, you know.'

'He needs it. And we've had his cock all locked up for a week.'

'That's plain cruel. But I suppose we'll get a good show.'

'The whole point, Jude. But he'd better fucking behave himself this time.'

'Look, Gwen, last time was mostly my fault. I did everything I could to make him come when I knew he wasn't supposed to. Pure devilment and I'm not proud of it.'

'You saying *you* should get whipped, girl? I can always oblige if your conscience is bothering you. But not right now, because *we* –' she stood up and pulled impatiently at a hand '– are going out.'

In the shower Judith soaped between her partner's legs then took the shower head down and held it in close. First she said, 'Sister, you trying to tell me something?' and they both laughed at the memory of the first morning after the night before. But then the chuckles became aroused squeals and they were once again rocking together in a wordless embrace as mutual fingers found and explored genitalia still primed from the recent climaxes. Outside Gwen threw over a large towel.

'Girl, you can't be getting enough sex in your working week.'

Judith stuck out her tongue. 'Don't see you holding back, lover. But to be honest I have to admit there's something in what you say.' Swathed in white fluffy cotton she let herself be steered over and seated at the dressing table while the black girl studied her face in the mirror.

'Ain't ever seen you made up, Jude.'

'Nah. I suppose I was always the tomboy type and just gravitated to kind of mild butch. But, sometimes, y'know, I wish I could do sort of femme now and then.'

'Hey, Jude, you always look great. But if you'll allow me just to jizz it up a touch ...' She fished out eyeshadow and a blood-red lipstick and applied them with a flourish. 'There! What d'ya reckon – hot, eh?'

Judith had to admit there was a frisson in the tarty edge her features had acquired and watched while Gwen painted her own lips a wondrous deep bluish-purple. On the bed lay two sexy little numbers in a shiny stretch material: one black and one white. There was plainly no need to ask which was which and Judith reached for the first and eased it carefully over her head.

'We'll leave out the knickers, OK?'

'OK.' There was really no option. The dresses clinging from a high neck all the way down to mid-thigh were a buttock fetishist's dream and even the wispiest of thongs would have marred the line of the rolling curves of flesh. Judith grinned delightedly at Gwen and at her reflection, then the black girl lifted the hem of her dress and planted a kiss just at the apex of her bare labia.

'Shows someone's laid a claim to the goods, right?'

Judith thought that the imprint of a perfect cupid's bow was more likely to provoke than warn off, but forbore to say so. What the hell. If they were going to the sort of establishment where pubic messages could be expected to become visible, then it promised to be an interesting evening.

Not to be encumbered by coats they hailed a cab, although in the Friday night traffic it would have been quicker to walk the short distance. Dropped at the end of a narrow side street, the two young women headed in the direction of the only visible light. When they reached the stout double door beneath it looked very firmly closed, and through the narrow pane of reinforced glass could be made out a burly figure whose pose did nothing to invite a caller to knock.

'Bugger it.' Gwen drew back and looked up and down the ill-lit lane as if for inspiration, but Judith's attention had been caught by the illuminated board hanging above their heads. The more she looked, the more curious it became. Painted in the manner of an inn sign, it showed on the right a face with big blue eyes gazing up between flaxen pigtails from what was plainly a sheet of proof-reader's marks that lay beside a pile of papers. The left-hand side had the rear view of a sleeved wrist, the hand gripping a piece of split leather that hung down in a line at the edge of the frame. The style was mannered with a foreshortened perspective that emphasised the anxiousness in the girl's expression and Judith stared, feeling herself to be on the verge of some insight. But at that very moment there was a blaze of light as a limousine swung into the street. They flattened themselves against the wall and it drew up just ahead of them at the forbidding doors which were at once drawn back.

'Hey, Jude, this is our chance. Grab my arm and do what I do, right? And for fuck's sake look *cool*.'

Ten minutes later they were seated at a table sharing a bottle of Rioja while an official-looking lady gave them a briefing. 'It's good to see young women like yourselves venturing in,' she was saying, 'and you will of course realise that we do not allow entry to single men. Too much trouble altogether, though some gay couples are welcome.' It was sounding as though they had not needed to attach themselves to the mixed – and obviously expensive – party to get through the door. 'We make a point of avoiding names, the whole idea is for people to feel anonymous and, we hope, inclined to, er, experiment. So I was wondering if one or the other of you might be up for a degree of participation. I'm sure I don't need to say that either would make a most attractive subject.'

'Well, um . . .' Judith faltered but a pressure against her thigh made her turn to see Gwen mouthing the words 'Go on'. 'Could be,' she said trying to sound positive. 'Perhaps you can tell us a bit more.'

'Sure. We're just talking about some minor restraint and a little s/m play. I take it that's the kind of thing that brought you along.'

'Er, yes.' Judith glanced sideways at her companion. In fact Gwen had said almost nothing about the place, but obviously it would be why she had been taken there.

'Good. Then if you come over with me I'll show you what's involved.'

Up to that point the surroundings had made little impression for they were in a large lounge bar with the furnishings and buzz of conversation that could be found in many others. Only the music differed from the norm, consisting of the kind of subdued melodic thumping that one might have heard from a DJ next door. Its effect though was not so much to stand out as to give a background pulse that ebbed and flowed in a slightly unsettling manner. Now, however, their guide drew back a curtain at the side of the room and showed them into a place not quite so run-of-the-mill. The small room was painted black and in its centre stood a waist-high cube top-lit by a spotlight directly above. On its cushioned top lay what Judith surmised was a kind of head piece, in black, together with a length of white rope.

'We think generally the wrists tied and sight and hearing restricted is a good start. I shall personally select a few women from our customers, and remember you will not be tied down and, though you won't be able to see her, your friend will be at hand.' Then she stopped and a puzzled expression crossed her face. 'Wait a moment here. Are you not a member – a full member – already? I mean with a password. Well, of course, you would know if you were, but . . .' She was staring into Judith's face and it made her look down uncomfortably. Her eyes dwelled for a moment on the lapel of the woman's jacket where she saw was sewn a monogram of three intertwined letters. They were ornate but easily decipherable and understanding came in a flash. 'AOC' was what they read: The Art of Correction, the website from which she had been waiting for a call. And the girl in the picture outside – correcting and about to be corrected. Ha! But the woman was talking again.

'I'm sorry, you'll think me rude. I must be confusing you with someone else. So if you're ready, shall we carry on?' Judith nodded in agreement and she ducked out through the thick folds of material.

'What was all that about members? The word I got said this was a fun place, sexy but nothing, like, heavy.'

'I haven't the foggiest.' Buoyed up by the discovery Judith shrugged to mask her excitement. She wasn't going to find it that night but there was more about the place than 'fun'. It was not the time to give Gwen any explanations and she pushed her hands out behind and turned her back. 'OK, lover, tie me up. But not too fucking tight. And when that thing goes on over my head you'd better be watching out for me. Right?'

'Sure thing, sister. Count on it.'

Her wrists were fastened with an efficiency that betokened practice and, though she was firmly held, the soft cord was not uncomfortable. Judith looked at the mask with more misgiving but once it had been pulled over and secured round the neck the padded leather enclosed her in a kind of cocoon, with external sounds dulled and vision completely removed. The ball, though, caught her unawares: a real intrusion that forced open her mouth as it was zipped into place. The patronising 'Good girl!' that accompanied the operation didn't help any, but Judith made herself compliant as her dress was folded up about the waist and hands bent her forward over the block. The knees rested on a padded step and her bare behind was at the mercy of the selected punters.

The position was scarcely unfamiliar to her, give or take the gag, but it was one she associated with bracing herself for a beating. The sting of cane or strap she could handle – *had* handled – albeit with difficulty; but what was to come in her present situation was uncertain and it was making her nervous. Then she became aware that other people were in the room and she twitched as a hand applied pressure to her left buttock. It began to stroke and squeeze and was joined by one on the other side that kneaded more vigorously. Snatches of speech drifted in and out of audibility and from what Judith could make out her characteristics were being assessed as if she herself were not there. Which, of course, in a sense she wasn't.

'. . . ooh, she's a real cherry . . .'

'. . . see how her arse moves . . .'

'. . . this one just can't wait . . .'

'. . . begging for a red bum . . .'

And as if on cue the spanking began. Not hard at first, but fluttery little smacks that made her shiver, interspersed with caresses that moved now and then in between the thighs. She was already wet when the slaps started in earnest and she realised that she was moving lasciviously in rhythm with them. Oh God, talk about up for it. At this rate she was going to come before she was even properly sore. Then a voice came into sharper focus, an accented voice that declared: 'I saw this one before,' at the same time as fingers inserted themselves confidently into her vulva. She pushed back in a pure reflex of sexual appetite and after that events moved swiftly to a conclusion.

'Hands *off*, lady!' came in a yell from behind and there were sounds of a brief scuffle as Judith straightened her back, still kneeling at the block. By the time her headgear was off and her arms free, the event was over and the room had been cleared by its organiser. Except for Gwen who stood glaring at her while Judith, aching with frustration, massaged her jaw and glared sullenly back.

11

Three's Company

They were arguing their way back to Gwen's flat, at
times with voices raised to a level that caused passers-by
to turn and stare.

'You being jealous, Gwen, I just got out of months of
that shit and I don't fucking NEED IT!' The words were
underscored with the stab of an upthrust finger at a man
who had dared to frown in their direction.

'That was too much, Jude. Hell, she was gonna bring
you off there and then – a fucking *stranger*.'

'So what the fuck were we doing there, eh? I mean
that could have been you at the centre of attention if
you'd wanted. I thought it was the whole idea. Look,
can we please change the fucking record?' For the first
time there was no comeback and they rounded the
corner into the last street in a merciful silence. To
Judith's mind it was plain that Gwen had overreacted to
a bit of semi-public play, and the green-eyed exhibition
was distinctly unsettling. Not least because she thought
the voice and hand both to be Helga's, though she had
not been able to see any sign of her before they left. If
the place was all part of the AOC it was entirely possible
that the German girl could be there and, on recognising
Judith, she just acted like the former lover she was and
maybe it showed. That could be why Gwen was acting
up like this. Judith shook her head and stole a glance at

the set features of the young woman walking beside her. She was the last person Judith would have suspected of harbouring a jealous streak and it did not bode well for the future.

In the hallway they were met by a Max fetchingly clad in a leather waistcoat and calf-length boots in addition to the infamous codpiece. He managed a smiling acknowledgement of 'Ms Judith' but she could see anxiety in the face that was turned to his 'Mistress'.

'You do right to look worried, boy. I ain't in the best of tempers. So you can fetch me that ace new whip. I reckon I'm gonna call it my cat of many tails.' Judith watched her with a sinking heart: she did not want to witness her taking out her feelings on Max, acquiescent though he might be to it. However, when he came back, Gwen tossed her the small brass key and she carefully removed the enclosure, noting that while the spikes had left red marks the skin had not been broken.

'Boy, I am going to hurt you, and I am going to enjoy it.' She was dangling the multi-thonged black instrument over the unsheathed organ and it sprang at once to life. '*You* will not, but it will do you good. And you *need* it.' Now the erection was as full as she had ever seen one and Judith took it in her hand, wondering. Its state amounted to a declaration that a disgruntled mistress was not a wholly bad thing. 'And to show you I ain't really mean, our visitor seems to have taken a fancy to that magic rod you got there. So, if she was of a mind to . . .'

That was better. Gwen's mood seemed to have lightened and Judith was more than happy to participate as indicated. Perhaps she was filling a role performed by others, for Max went at once to a tallboy against the far wall and leaned on it with arms folded and body arched. Positioned in that way his bare behind was presented for the lash while there was room for a figure to sit on the floor below. So Judith stripped off her dress and, when the whipping started, found herself at close quarters to the shaft that swung before her face with each pained jerk of the attached body. It occurred to her that to suck a cock so engorged in the approved porn-shoot manner was likely bring matters to a premature conclusion, so she contented herself with a little finger manipulation while running her tongue over the glans, tasting the salt of the pre-ejaculate that oozed from it in clear drops.

Thus they continued, almost suspended in time, while the thongs slapped and the boy grunted. Then, wincing at their impact, she heard three hard strokes in quick succession and the end came fast. Max cried out, the beast reared up and a jet hit Judith full in the chin. Spurt followed spurt, spattering breasts and shoulders until at the last she took the final gobbets from the shrinking shaft into her mouth. When the boy sagged down to the floor, Gwen was upon her, lips on her lips, tongues meeting coated with the copious flow. Then Gwen was down, head bobbing as, slowly and deliberately she licked Judith's body clean of every trace of the discharge, for all the world like a cat lapping up spilt cream. Half in a trance, Judith let the operation run its course, by which time the penis was once more swelling in her hand. Aching to come, Judith brought it stiff with a few brisk strokes and straddled Max, kissing him on the mouth. As she lowered herself on to him the touch to her clitoris was an electric shock that travelled up her spine and stopped her breath. Rocking ever so gently back and fore she felt a blob of jelly between her buttocks and something cool and smooth pressing into the ring of muscle. She was aware of a voice over her shoulder saying, 'This once, Maxie, just this once,' and then there was nothing but a tidal wave of sensation that rose inexorably from the centre of her being to engulf all consciousness.

* * *

The soft quilt moved with her as she stirred, wrapped in an erotic glow. That was what you call a dream; now if she could drift gently back into it and . . . Judith turned over and the memories clicked into place, one after the other. Oh God, the club, the row and then the threesome on the living-room carpet. No dream, that was real. Fucking brilliant. Well, actually, brilliant fucking. She giggled to herself and stretched out in the massive bed, then sat up, wide awake. It was where she had woken that first Saturday morning but this time there were no handcuffs. Nor, however, were there any signs of the others. Judith frowned but, try as she might, no clear picture would come of how she had actually got to the bed, though it seemed obvious she must have been assisted. Sitting up on the edge she saw that her bag was on the floor and in a side-pocket she found a small travelling clock.

Jesus, what was this? Ten minutes past twelve. OK, so it must have been late last night – though she could not even make a stab at the time – but still. That shattering orgasm must have really knocked her out. Smiling at the thought of the potent sex life that seemed to be coming her way, Judith found the tiny adjoining bathroom and showered briskly under the near-scalding flow of water. The long sweatshirt that doubled as dressing gown and bathrobe on nights away came readily to hand and, thus clothed, she peered out of the door into the passage. The muted commotion of city traffic filtered through the walls but inside the flat there was not a sound to be heard. At the living-room door Judith realised she was creeping on tiptoe like some kind of intruder, so she forced herself to open it in one movement and march in. On the floor was the little black number just as she had discarded it, but otherwise the place bore no marks of their orgiastic doings of the night before. To the side was the small anteroom and beyond was the kitchen where Max was master, but it lay bare and gleaming with no indication of recent occupation.

That was the extent of her acquaintance with the rambling collection of rooms and Judith retraced her steps to see where else she might look for signs of life. Off the passage was a spare single bedroom – empty – that exhausted the total number of doors, so she returned and stood wiggling her toes in the thick pile of the carpet. Then she saw through the adjoining space where their gear had been laid out there was a curtain that hung from rings along a wooden rail. A quick inspection revealed that it concealed a door covered in green baize from which protruded a heavy brass knob. A rubber surround made its fit snug and – Judith guessed – soundproof, and the sight of it made her reluctant even to try the handle. In addition, it opened outward and if someone was on the other side of it then someone else must have drawn the curtain closed after them.

It struck Judith that the possible implication of that was something she did not want to explore, and so she went back to the room she had occupied during the night. Taking out a sheet of paper from a folder in her bag she wrote:

Guys – I'm going to creep off back to the provinces while no one's about. You've worn me out. Only joking, but I can't see topping last night straight off.
    Be in touch, Gwen. More, soon, yeah?
    Jude xxx

She read it through once and put it in a prominent position on the hallstand. Then, as if to mark the end of another erotic escapade in the capital, she pulled an old pair of jeans up under the baggy top and folded the smart coat over the bag before hoisting the strap on to her shoulder. As the lock snapped decisively shut at her back, blinking in the sunlight she came out of the archway and merged into the Saturday bustle to make her way to the station.

* * *

It was early evening before Judith was installed at her machine in the stacks, drumming impatient fingers as the list of incoming mail started to itemise. At last, there it was: the AOC had deigned to send a message. Of a kind. There was no greeting and no sign off; in fact nothing but a URL, albeit one that ran to two whole lines in the browser window. Mindful of the disappearing act staged the last time, she pasted what was on the screen into a new file, and activated the link with bated breath. The window that opened was similarly lacking in content, containing only a panel with blank spaces for a name and password. She typed in 'jud1th' and 'nemes1s' carefully, pressed enter, and waited. The screen went blank and then against a purple background there appeared a heading THE ART OF CORRECTION below which lines of text loaded slowly, one by one.

Coming so well recommended a new entrant to our group could expect a warm welcome: one that, sadly, cannot be extended here. The present candidate it seems saw fit to pre-empt the proper channels of invitation by an impromptu visit to the outer rooms of one of our premises. The error requires rectification by returning within 48 hours to present a copy of the authorisation at the foot of this page. Please note that should the applicant not attend, the penalty incurred by the lapse will be borne by a young woman of her acquaintance.

Judith read and re-read the paragraph, indignation growing. It was Gwen's idea for God's sake, she had gone along with the suggestion, having no idea the place might be connected with the AOC. And here was this frostily formal rebuke that assumed she had been trying to sneak into their precious organisation through the back door. So to speak. It might have been enough to make her take umbrage and forget the whole thing, except for that last sentence. Knowing what she did of the outfit left no doubt about the nature of the 'penalty' and there was only one 'young woman' to hand that she knew. If Judith didn't show, Helga was going to get it in the neck. Well, not the neck exactly, she thought with a grim little smile. But it was the clincher, and she would need to be on a train in the morning to take her there before the deadline ran out.

The 'authorisation' referred apparently to a string of characters that she guessed were Japanese and she duly selected it and printed it out. Below them was the comment that the viewer would be wasting her time to bookmark the page since it would cease to exist once she had left. With a sour expression of defeat Judith shut down her machine and made her way across to the top exit. At the foot of the first flight of stairs her eye was caught by a strip of light under the office door and she turned the handle. Inside a startled face looked up from the open box-file on the desk.

'Oh, Judith, it's you. I'm sorry, I didn't leave a note on the shelf, I was going to put it back today and with no one about . . .'

'OK, Sandra.'

'I didn't expect – I mean – I thought you were away for the weekend and –'

'And you didn't reckon on me coming around snooping. Don't worry, I am away really, this is just me flitting back for five minutes, as it turns out. So I'll leave you to read in peace.'

Out of work hours Sandra was back in the sweatshirt and jeans and looking very young, quite the ingénue. There was that word again. The grey-blue eyes, though, seemed a little perplexed and Judith hesitated at the door.

'Everything all right?'

'Yes. Er, I went to see Mrs Rowleigh again. Oh, I

don't think I should be saying this.' She looked down at her hands.

'Sandra, I kind of know what happened the other week. It's none of my business, so tell me to keep my nose out if you want, but is she coming on a bit heavy?' Judith thought of the decidedly heavy hand that had been used on her ex-partner Grace.

'Oh no. Well, yes, maybe. I'm having trouble trying to make up my mind about something.'

'Look, I know she has a taste for laying it on a bit thick now and then. I was there myself once.' Judith had the disconcerting feeling that they were getting in deep without first having confirmed they were actually on the same topic.

'Yes, but this isn't *me*. She wants me to, um, *assist*.'

'Well, if you're not going to be in the firing line –' Judith was hoping fervently that she had the right end of the stick (in more senses than one) '– my general advice would be, do it. Otherwise you'll be left wondering, now if only I'd . . . Sins of omission and all that.' Sandra nodded her head slowly and there appeared the hint of a smile.

'Yeah. I think that's a good way to look at it. Thanks, Judith.'

'You could try Jude.' She smiled back, noticing how a wisp of hair that had come free from the ponytail curled round the nape of the neck. In the silence she became aware of holding her breath, sharply conscious of the young woman's bodily presence. Judith cleared her throat. 'Well, I'd better shoot. Just help yourself, you know, to whatever you need.' She waved in the direction of the stacks and opened the door again. 'And if you want to chat about anything at all, you know where to find me.'

'Right, er, Jude. There is one thing. You know you were asking about languages, well there's some German stuff in this initiations collection right here. If you wanted me to make a start . . .'

'Sure. Great. That would be very useful. See you on Monday.' Judith shut the door at her back before she could invent another reason to stay. With Gwen on the go – and jealous to boot – and the adorable Helga coming into view, she had enough to be going on with. After all, Archive secretaries were bad news, weren't they? Either they were off limits, the infringement of which could earn a girl a very sore behind, or they turned out impossible to live with. Besides, odds were on this one being a determined het-case, as Marsha liked to put it.

On the way out she told herself to banish the girl from her thoughts, but it was not so easily done. Try as she may to desist, Judith found her mind tantalised by speculation. Had the girl gone over Marjorie's knee or over a chair? A table, perhaps? And would she have been bared? Surely not, the first time. But maybe there had been more than one occasion – she had mentioned a second visit – so perhaps the underwear had come down for the application of that broad hand or a strap. And what about the underwear: had it been specially chosen for the event? So it was that on the walk home Judith was so beset by images of a Sandra's bare delicious squirmings that she was filled beyond all sense and against her best resolution with a desperate yearning to witness, or even participate in, the actuality.

Back in the flat she went straight to a small shelf of books in the bedroom and took down a plain hardback volume. There was one sure way to defuse the potency of these lustful preoccupations. It was a tale – purporting to be first-hand – of a Prussian girls' academy she had acquired a few years ago, and after reading it once in a state of delicious horror had put it aside for just the present kind of eventuality. The author's lurid yet precise imagination conjured into being each disciplinary episode with a vividness that could take her from cold to full orgasm in scarcely more than a minute. That was one – very occasional – use she made of the text. What she was planning at the present juncture was to indulge in the other: open a bottle of wine, soak in a hot bath and then take to her bed. With a careful perusal that savoured each lascivious turn of phrase – the stripping and ogling, the verbal caressing of rod- and whip-streaked buttocks – she could keep herself on the exquisite brink for page after page until self-control would prevail no longer and the floodgates opened. Judith took a long swallow from her glass and padded through to the steaming tub. This was going to put little Miss Sandra Butler firmly in her place!

12

Whipping Girl

Judith rose late from a deep sleep and made coffee. In the midday sunshine the peremptory summons with its threat no longer made her angry; instead it represented a challenge. She was going to give the AOC a run for their money. Cup refilled, she ate toast and honey, then went into the bathroom. Gwen had given her some eyeshadow and lipstick together with a small bottle of scent which she took down from the shelf. Having washed carefully between her legs, she dabbed a touch of the aromatic fluid on each side of the bare labia. Then in the bedroom she snapped on a pair of silk string briefs and wriggled into the tightest pair of trousers the cupboard would deliver. Black boots and a short fitted white blouse completed the picture after which it was a simple matter to throw a change of clothes into the waiting bag.

Outside Judith turned up the collar of her coat against the north wind and followed a leisurely route into a town centre free of its weekday bustle. There was no need to rush: she was in good time for the next train and that should deliver her comfortably to St Pancras by the end of the afternoon. However, at the station she was greeted with the news of a points failure that had blocked the line half a mile to the south. There was really no choice in the matter: when her connection arrived she had to get on and wait since it could leave at any time once the line was cleared. Settling into a window seat from which she might see any signs of imminent departure, Judith delved into her luggage. At least she had had the forethought to bring some samples that had reached the Archive only the week before from what looked like a hot new imprint based in Japan.

In the package were two large-format paperbacks devoted to the art of bondage. The minimal text was copiously illustrated *hentai*-style, which was just as well since it had not been translated; and the accompanying note seemed to suggest an English version would be forthcoming if there was sufficient interest. Caught by the elegant intricacy of knots against bare flesh, Judith scanned slowly through the glossy pages. She came upon a section where the restrained bodies had plainly been prepared for punishment, as indicated by the red-streaked buttocks and thighs and the instrument fashioned from what looked like strips of bamboo. Out of her absorption, Judith realised with a start that they were moving, though not, as it turned out, for long. Once beyond the perimeter of the town the carriages again came to a halt, and there they stayed. Thus she was reminded that without an explanatory commentary pictures soon palled, however skilful their execution, and she stared moodily out of the window at the nearby road on which people were speeding to their respective destinations.

After a while she fell into a reverie in which a blindfolded Sandra allowed her wrists to be tied and then the clothing below the waist to be removed piece by piece. With a silky cord cinched round the slender waist, she attached another to it above the belly button and drew it between the legs of the compliant girl. Following an unhurried inspection of the surprisingly pert arse, she was just about to pull the cord up hard between the cheeks when a jolt of the carriage jerked her back to the present. At last. Waiting until the train had gathered enough speed to confirm that they were indeed underway, Judith consulted her clock. Five thirty-six. Shit. Even if she were picked up at once by a fast cab, beating the deadline was still going to be a close-run thing.

Rather than wait for change, she sent the driver away with an outsize tip and jabbed her finger at the brass bell-push. The heavy doors were firmly locked and there were none of the signs of life that had been evident on her previous visit, minutes short of 48 hours before. Eventually, though, a light showed within and the hefty form that had given them pause on the Friday night re-appeared in the narrow window. She was aware of scrutiny from a heavily jowled face before there came the welcome sound of bolts being drawn back. One of the doors opened and the man took the paper with the line of characters she had printed from the website. Bidding her wait, he vanished inside and after several seconds the inner door swung back to reveal their host of the night before last.

'I think the time has come for introductions, Judith. My name is Constance.' She extended a hand and they exchanged a squeeze rather than a shake. Judith observed the sheen of blonde hair that fell each side of the high cheekbones, but the eyes were dark and outlined in a way that emphasised their slant. This was a more assertive, not to say alarming, presence than she remembered from their first meeting. 'You will follow me, please.'

On the left the lounge bar with its curtained alcoves lay in darkness and Constance led them in the opposite direction along a stone-flagged passage. At the end was a stair to an upper level on which Judith was shown into a room lit by flickering candles. Her guide threw a switch and the sudden illumination of a spotlight picked out a figure hanging naked by its wrists against the far wall. On a low table was coiled a heavily thonged martinet, but while the bottom was flushed red that did not appear to be the cause of its colour. Constance moved a stool over so that the body's weight could be taken on the feet and Judith saw the familiar profile as the head turned. 'Yoodit,' it said, and the German pronunciation of her name coupled with the palpable relief in the voice brought a lump to her throat.

'You arrived with not a moment to spare. I was warming her up to serve as the whipping girl for the absent offender. But I am pleased – as I am sure is she – that the culprit herself has now come forward.'

Judith bridled at the designation but held her tongue. No way was she going to launch into the rigmarole of explaining that her transgression had been unwitting. Punishment was going to be meted out and she may as well get it over with. Eyeing the drastic-looking instrument on display, she attempted a matter-of-fact tone.

'OK. Shall I strip here and now?' Constance shook her head while she occupied herself with freeing the bonds.

'Oh no. Helga's keeper sent word that she is to be treated with maximum severity during her stay here. Your case, Judith, is rather different. The important thing is that you obeyed the instruction, though of course there will be a penalty.' She consulted her watch. 'If you report to me at nine o' clock that will give time for the girl to acquaint you with the premises. I take it you intend to stay the night.' With that she left the room and Judith reached out to the young woman still rubbing her wrists and gave her a hug. It was returned but then Helga pulled away with a sudden awkwardness and turned her back to haul on jogging pants and top followed by trainers.

'*Komm*, Yoodit. I must give you the tour or I shall be in extra trouble.' She put on a centre light where they were and waved an arm. 'You see this is the big

punishment area.' Indeed, besides the hooks to which
Helga had been attached, there was a sizeable whipping
horse and a ladder hung with ropes that was fastened at
an angle. Beyond that stood a rack of canes and whips
and with the heavy drapes on the other three walls the
space felt airless and filled with gloom. Judith breathed
more easily next door in a brightly lit study room that
housed a small library where she was pleased to see a
copy of the first title from their NemArch imprint. They
passed by two offices to enter a classroom that was set
out with a blackboard, projection equipment and tables
arranged in a semicircle with maybe a dozen stacking
chairs. A lectern stood at the front and to one side of it
a tall desk of the sort that graced Samantha James's
office at the Archive. There seemed little doubt that it
was intended for the same purpose.

'That goes down to the bar where they come for a
demonstration,' said Helga, indicating the stairs as they
exited by a different door. 'But we go up to the sleeping
places.' On the top floor she took them into a room with
a sloping ceiling that contained two sizeable bunks. The
trim blonde turned down the duvet of the lower one and
plumped up the pillows. 'This is yours, Yoodit. I think
it is time now for you to go to *die Herrin*. She is in the
office that is marked DIR.' She sat on the bed with a
little bounce. 'I wait, yes?'

'Come in and shut the door, if you would.' Constance
came round from behind her minimal cube of a desk
and perched on it with one leg swinging. The silk dress
was slit to the thigh and the glow from the desk lamp
highlighted the oriental cast of the face. Beside her lay
a stiff-looking rectangle of leather mounted on a
wooden handle while her hands toyed with a length of
cord. 'I thought I might indulge myself with a simple
one-point restraint. With your consent, Judith, of
course. Are you acquainted at all with the art?'

Judith explained that she had been dipping into two new volumes on the journey down, but had been hampered by her inability to read the characters.

'Ah. I should like to see them, if I may, before you leave. I was myself raised in Japan and could perhaps help communicate the gist of the text. But to return to the matter in hand: would you oblige me by putting your arms behind your back?' Having done so, Judith felt the rope coil around both wrists and a deft piece of knotting had them held fast together. Constance flicked the cord upwards over a hook fixed in the ceiling, caught the end of it and pulled. As her arms were lifted back and up, Judith was forced to bend at the waist at an angle chillingly appropriate for what was about to happen.

'You understand that the trousers will need to come down, don't you?' It wasn't really a question and Judith submitted silently to the unsheathing of the buttocks from the clinging material. At least she was being allowed to keep the minimal cover of the briefs. Then the instrument was measured against her and there was a disconcerting weight and roughness to its soft smack.

'Brace yourself, Judith.' There was a rush of air and the *crack*! of impact was unnervingly loud in the small room. Then a bolt of sheer white-hot agony blotted out all else. Judith howled and jerked and howled again as the rope wrenched her. Oh God. Oh God.

'Intense, is it not? I thought that might surprise you.' There was a barely concealed relish in the quiet remark. 'I am going to give you six more, and the whole is to be repeated first thing in the morning.'

Six more like that one. Jesus fucking Christ. She was going to have to get a grip or her arms would be out of their sockets.

'After that we shall be square and your young friend no longer under threat of stand-in duties. So Judith, you will be quite free to walk away for ever. But I want to

116

stress how much we hope you will see fit to return with a novice of your choosing.'

Talk about timing: it could make a girl in a less dire predicament chuckle. She was being asked back to put herself in line for more of *this*?

'Ready, Judith?'

'Uh huh.' As ready as she ever would be. Trying to plant her feet firmly on the floor, she willed herself to stay down *whatever* and waited with clenched teeth.

'She has used the paddle-strap, yes? Oh she is wicked. You are bruised and it will be worse after the second time.' Judith screwed round her head to see Helga frowning as she dabbed at the burning flesh with a cold wet cloth. When she had done Judith let her unbutton her shirt, wincing a little as it came off over the shoulders. 'And your arms are hurt too.'

'Yeah, a bit. But I'll live.' She managed a grin and the German girl's face broke into a cheeky smile.

'OK, the lady is tough guy. *Gut*. But now I make her forget the pains.' She led Judith over to the bed, lay on it and pulled her down on top, facing away. 'Now the hips up so, and I have the special view.' Judith felt warm breath then the tip of a tongue insinuated itself between her bottom cheeks and she arched her back with a delicious shiver.

Later, when they lay still, Helga said, 'I must go soon to the big room. I get blamed for the trouble in the bar.'

'That's not right. Jesus, Gwen was out of order. We rowed about it all the way back.'

'I should not have touched, so it is me, really. But you take care with her – to me she appears dangerous. What happened to the other, the one who was a little crazy? I think you have the unsuitable girlfriends always, Yoodit, and you change them too often.' Judith looked sharply across but the blue eyes were earnest.

'And what about you, Helga?'

117

'Oh, I do not have the girlfriend. There is only my mistress.' What they had been doing obviously didn't count but Judith let it pass without comment. She was more concerned that her sweet lover was going to be chastised in the middle of the night.

'Helga, that was two days ago, when Gwen lost it. Why wait till now?'

'I know the idea – it is to build up the, er, how do you say?'

'Anticipation?'

'*Ja* – anticipation.' She gave a heavy sigh. 'It is all part of the same idea of the *Haupt-offizier*. She believes she has too much concern to discipline me as she should, so I am sent to one who does not care. So that she can be truly harsh.' Judith listened, more than a little shocked by the bald assessment.

'But you'll be going back – to The Program?' She wrestled with the urge to fold the young blonde in her arms, to protect her from these calculated cruelties. But of course it was absurd: what was happening was the result of a clear-headed choice.

'I go back, *ja*. When my lady wants me again.' That was all she would say and ten minutes later she pulled on a cotton shift and left. Judith rolled over and stared at the light that filtered in under the door. She would stay awake to do what she could when Helga came back.

When she next opened her eyes the illuminated strip was gone and in the gloom she could just make out the rectangle of the skylight suffused with the glow of distant streetlamps. Damn it, she must have dropped off. Then there was a faint noise above her and she strained her ears. There it went again and this time there could be no doubt: it was a stifled sob.

'Helga,' she hissed, 'Helga, are you OK?'

'*Ja*. Go back to sleep.' But the quaver in the voice made her sit up and throw off the covers. She pulled two tissues out of a box in her bag, stood up and thrust them at the huddled form in the top bunk. An arm came out and then there was the sound of a nose being vigorously blown.

'Helga, please, come down and come in with me.'

'I cannot, I am too sore.'

'Look, you can lie flat, to the side. There's plenty of room. I won't touch you. Please.' She stretched out close to the wall and after a pause the German girl slid in beside. Judith felt a breast and a thigh against her own and put out a tentative hand. 'How about the back?'

'Low down is not so bad. *Ja, das ist okay.*' A head nuzzled gently into her neck and Judith began to relax. That was better. 'Thank you, Yoodit. You are kind to me.' Eyes pricking, Judith lay in the dark until the breathing at her side had become soft and steady, then she too drifted slowly off.

In the half-light of early morning they made love with a controlled passion. Helga's marks were not as bad as Judith feared and she guessed that the tears had been shed more for the auburn-haired Sibyl Metzger from whom the girl was forcibly separated and plainly adored.

While she dressed to go and face her parting ordeal Helga lay watching her from the bed. When they kissed goodbye she said, 'You are going to come back with a new one, yes? Like the people who come up to see things from the lounge, they are novices too. But remember, Yoodit, that this place is also about us. You understand? We are here to learn also and to change.'

The odd little speech stayed with her downstairs as Constance secured her to a small horse by wrists and ankles. She examined Judith's behind with her hands, lifting and fondling the cheeks, before suggesting that the trousers could perhaps stay in place. 'Such a lovely snug fit. They will help the instrument build up a good heat, providing, of course, I have your approval to double the number of strokes.'

'If you must.'

'Don't be so grudging, Judith. While I admit freely the pleasure I shall take in this, you too are part of the occasion. And I have no doubt you will rise to it splendidly.' Tied as she was, it was difficult to do much rising, but she pushed her bottom out as best she could and was rewarded with an appreciative pat. Then came four hard blows delivered with a grunt of effort that had her panting. Another four and she was squirming uncontrollably against the burning pain.

'Settle down now, young lady.' A hand rested on the small of her back while another cupped the blazing globes. 'Warming up nicely and with your permission I should like to remove the cords. Your taxi is waiting and I want you to leave directly the punishment is over. It will make a little exercise in public deportment.'

Damn the woman! But she was determined to live up to expectations so Judith found the words: 'Go ahead.' She could – would – take four more without leaping up; it was just a question of a bit of self-control.

Once they had begun to move, Judith dived into the lavatory with a huge sigh of relief. The stop-start jolting of the cab had tried her sorely as she perched on a left hip that had escaped the brunt of the right-handed action. Then the unexpectedly crowded train had scuppered the plan to lower herself very carefully into a window seat. It was out of the question to squeeze her throbbing rear end into one of the few spaces left unfilled, so she had been obliged to lurk at the door as if waiting for some last-minute arrival.

With the lock turned Judith stood on the seat and eased down the garment that had become perceptibly tighter as a result of the recent treatment. Craning her neck she saw in the mirror a right buttock that was a lurid reddish-purple, already turning black, with the edges of the infamous 'paddle-strap' clearly delineated. It was too late for bathing to do any good and, in any case, the after-effects were beginning to call for attention. Squatting over the bowl was not really an option, so Judith stripped down her briefs and leaned against the wash basin, spreading her legs as far as the clothes bunched round her knees would allow. One, then two, fingers slipped with ease into the well-primed opening; she had something to thank Constance for.

As the sensations built to their inexorable end she thought of Helga's fair bush and the silky lips that nestled beneath. But when the climax came her mind's eye fixed on something rather different: a pumping phallus, close-up, that was drenching her in its milky goo. Judith leaned back, drained, and let the contractions die away. Shit. Oh *shit*. What on earth was happening – what *was* she turning into?

13

Hearts to Heart

'*Cumslut* is the term you're looking for, honey. And they are all over the Internet these days, I think you'll find. Porn-addicted men love them to bits. So I'm afraid we are talking the lowest of the low. The sisterhood may just tolerate the use of a hard cock for the purposes of clitoral stimulation but to bathe in its, its . . .' Marsha leaned back and laughed with an abandon Judith had not seen for a long time. 'I'm sorry, Jude, I couldn't help seeing the funny side. It seems both of us have become rather poor examples for the next generation of women-loving women.'

'Marsha, I think you're forgetting something here. I *am* the next generation, give or take.' The older woman clutched at a point below the belt of her faded denims and pulled out a white handkerchief which she flapped in the air.

'Ouch. OK, I'm not going to dispute it. When the age card is played, I'm resigned to the fact that graceful surrender is the only option left me. Though I'll accept a drink to smooth down my ruffled pride. But to get back to your stud for a moment. He sounds quite the catch: polite, dishy, submissive *and* impressively equipped.'

'Well, I'm no expert –'

'Honey, don't do yourself down. I can recall quite a session in your basement last summer. But I won't press the point. I'm going to lock up and then you can pull up a stool and tell me all about the latest one.'

When she returned Judith slapped a ten pound note on the bar. 'Mine's the usual, please, but I'm going to decline the offer of a seat.'

'Ah-hah. A busy weekend altogether, it seems.' She opened two cold beers and pushed one of them over. Judith took a long swallow.

'You could say it reached a cracking finale – at seven o' clock this morning, no less – that's leaving me decidedly tender. No, on second thoughts, *tender* doesn't begin to get close. But I did make it down in time to save a lovely young German girl from a much nastier encounter with a heavy-duty bundle of thongs.'

'Impressive. And you'll notice I'm not asking for the full story – yet. But I take it that event was all part of a foray into the – what do they call themselves again? – the AOC. I have to say it's a new one on me.'

'I think it's new full stop. Their thing seems to be about putting experience and inexperience together. Before the lady set about blistering my arse – for the *second* time – she gave me the big come-on to bring along a novice before two weeks are out. In fact, I think there's a special demonstration planned we could both take part in.'

'Do I get to guess who could be in line for this role?' The bar manager was scrutinising the label on her bottle as if it might hold the answer.

'Short list of one. Unless you know someone I'm overlooking.'

'Not anyone that *you* know, honey. And I guess it wouldn't be politic to invite a stranger. However, is your new and highly fanciable secretary up for no-holds-barred whipping? I mean I know that Marjorie has big strong hands –'

'Don't mock, Marsha, and remember you are sworn to secrecy. Of course she isn't.' Judith grimaced and drank some more beer. 'I'm worried that she won't want to go any further at all, and especially not at the bidding of an unknown organisation.'

'I'm not quite sure how to put this, Jude, but sayings about irons in fires and eggs in puddings come to mind. At the last count the players number a potent black girl, her slave/lover and – I'm guessing here, so feel free to correct me – an intimate of last summer's trip now installed in-house. Some might call that a potent brew on its own, yet we find the lady at the centre of it proposing to stir into the mix one delectable more-or-less innocent. Were I involved I think I might want to stand well back.' The bar manager tilted her cropped head and Judith shrank a little under her gaze.

'Well, Helga isn't *really* a lover and it's sort of Gwen 'n' Maxie, like an item, and I wasn't thinking of Sandra *that* way, honest . . .' She came to a stop and made a face. 'That sounds fucking pathetic coming from one who – if she would just be honest about it – has been screwing around and loving every minute.'

Marsha took her hand across the bar. 'Jude, I'm sorry. Maybe the maxim we need here is one that talks about glasshouses and stones or pots and kettles. If there's anybody up there watching, she'll know how many times *I* have had to make a quick exit. So pay no heed to the cluckings of a mother hen: I'm sure you can look after yourself as well as I could. So let's have another beer and you can bring me up to date on the ravishing young German.'

Early Tuesday morning Judith was at her station above the greening grass of the quad with the low sun casting odd angles of shadow across the roofs. It had been her intention to compile a list of the sources she might draw on for an in-depth study of initiations and at first it had gone well. A lot of material had surfaced in the previous year or so (not to mention her own NemArch title) and

124

some of it was quite promising. There was, for instance, a diary kept by the daughter of a large house in the 1920s who, neglected by parents, had learned to love the birch of her governess, to say nothing of the lady herself. Bang up to date was the manual from a Californian collective for the training of teenagers in the arts of what they called 'feminist discipline', but intriguing as these materials were, she could not stop her mind wandering to the specific case on her doorstep. Would Sandra want an initiation of her own? Or if she didn't want, or didn't know she wanted it, might it be something she would be glad of later? And how was she going to broach the topic in time for the schedule the AOC wanted to impose?

There were no easy answers and if it all came together it was going to be the result of luck rather than judgement. Judith got up and made her way down in the direction of the office. It was nearly eleven and maybe there was coffee on the go: she could do with something to kick-start the brain into more efficient operation. But when she opened the door from the stacks the machine was dead and there was no sign of life. OK, maybe a turn round the precincts in the crisp April air would do the trick just as well. However, as she turned to head for the exit her attention was caught by the sound of running water coming from the direction of the bathroom. The door was ajar so she pushed it wide, leaning on the handle – an action that produced a disproportionately dramatic effect. With a shriek the figure that had been propped on the counter over a full wash basin lost its balance and sat down with a splash that slopped water out over the floor.

'Ow! Lord, Miss Judith! Oh bugger, pardon my French, look what I've gone and done. What a mess.' She struggled up and jumped to the floor, bare save for a lacy bra. There was a moment's silence in which the PA looked down at herself, then at Judith. Grabbing a towel she let out a giggle, then another and they both collapsed in helpless laughter.

'Sorry, Penny, I didn't mean to startle you. But, hey, what's this?'

'That's what I was trying to do something about. Her nibs kind of lost the rag this morning, I don't know why, it's never happened before ...' After the fit of merriment she looked suddenly close to tears.

'Well, you stand there while I mop this up –' Judith took a cloth and swabbed the tiles quickly '– and then you come with me. I've got just what you need.'

In her own office she bent Penny over the desk and examined the damage with mounting anger. Instead of the red glow that was commonly the young woman's due, the plump little cheeks bore a grid pattern of angry purples that had plainly been inflicted with a cane. Judith stood shaking her head. 'This is out of order, girl, way out of order.'

'She had me go over this low stool, then she got my head between her legs. And after that she did it like you'd expect, from the side. If I moved she said she'd boot me out, there and then.' There was a real catch in the voice and Judith hurriedly opened her drawer of potions and salves.

'I'll give you a spray with this first: it'll take the edge off. Just give it a moment. It's not so long since you were doing the honours for me, remember? I reckon this director of ours is getting out of hand. There now, how's that?'

'Oh that's much better, thanks.' The girl made to get up but Judith pressed gently on her back.

'Not so fast, my girl. I haven't forgotten that your treatment was a little more comprehensive. You're not expecting the big bad boss back soon are you?'

'Er, no. She may not be in tomorrow either, she's gone to London to sort them out. It's some kind of organisation. That's what upset her in the first place – what came in the post from – from – oh, it's some initials or other I can't recall.' At the word 'initials' Judith was struck by a thought that she found oddly disquieting.

'It wouldn't by any chance be an outfit called the Art of Correction, known for short by the letters AOC?'

'Well, blow me, it is. Though I never heard the name you said. But that's it – the AOC. How on earth did you know, Miss Judith?'

'Ah-ha. Too long a story, Penny, but I had wondered . . . Anyway, that's neither here nor there. We've got a job on for now. Let me give you this cushion under the hips, like so, and while I give you a proper go with the witch hazel we are going to try out this little egg-thingy I got hold of the other week. You spread nice and wide and I'll just ease it in . . .'

'Ooh, go on then, I'll have a vodka, but make it lots of orange.' When she came back from the bar, Judith put the drinks down and looked at the still-flushed PA. Rather than submit to Marsha's inquisitiveness they had installed themselves in the basement bar along the road from The Phoenix for a spot of lunch.

'Is that seat OK for you, Penny?'

'Yeah, I'm fine now with all that stuff you put on. And that whatsit – phew! That would take your mind off anything.' Judith laughed.

'Well it's all yours, girl. Courtesy of the Archive management. Once you get the hang of the remote it'll keep you going nicely until the return of she who must be obeyed. Have you any idea what was making her upset?'

'Well, she don't tell me much, Miss Judith, but she does sort of think out loud sometimes. And from what I could gather these AOC people were going ahead to do something without her say-so.'

'But, Penny, how long has this being going on? She's never said anything about them to me.' Judith put her bottle to her mouth and drank, trying to get a handle on the situation. If Miss James was involved with the group – albeit in a less prominent role than she desired – then was she in on their recruitment plans, which, of course, included herself?

'Now don't you rely on what I say here, but I reckon it's a new thing. She goes all over, as you know, on the continent and to the USA, but I never heard about any place in London before.' Good. It sounded like their Director was jockeying for position in a new – for her – venture and while she might have had a hand in the postcard reminder she had received, the original invitation that had lain forgotten in her bag was not of her making. Judith found that deduction comforting, although she was not sure why. Maybe she just liked the idea that the striking Sibyl Metzger from The Program was still pulling strings somewhere off-stage.

'But you won't say anything to her, will you? I mean about this morning. I'd hate her to think I'd been running to you complaining.'

'No, of course not, girl. Let's hope it was a bad-tempered one-off and things will sort themselves out. Now you are going to take advantage of this unexpected break and have another. I am not going to take no for an answer.' It took in fact two more rounds and a plate of rare beef sandwiches before Judith felt emboldened enough to turn the talk to what was really on her mind. Brushing a crumb from the sleeve of her silk bomber jacket she said casually, 'So, Penny, what do you make of our new acquisition in the office?'

'Well, since you're asking, I'd have to say she's a bit of a rum 'un. Don't you think? I mean the way she started off in those sloppy old jeans then one morning she's flipped right over into the sharp suits. Either way, it don't really fit with the plain old secretary behind a desk, do it?'

'I suppose not. But what she has to deal with isn't exactly plain and ordinary. What do you think she makes of all that?' Judith picked at the single crust that was left on the plate in front of them. Jesus, why couldn't she just come out with it?

'You mean all the spanking stuff – and worse?'

'Er, yes.'

'Why, don't you think she's coping? It's not for me to say, of course, but the boss seems happy enough. And the lassie went to Mrs R, like we talked about, didn't she? Not that she's said owt to me about what happened there.'

'Nor to me, Penny.' Judith steeled herself to spill the beans. 'You see, I've got myself involved with this AOC crowd too, and they have a thing about each full member introducing a novice. Someone who might take to the s/m stuff but doesn't have much experience.'

'You're wanting me to say if Sandra'd be game? Lord, why don't you just *ask* her?' Aware of a rising flush, Judith looked away from the inquisitive eyes. 'Oh my. If I don't mistake the signs, you're sweet on the creature.'

'I am *not*. No *way*.'

'If you say so, Miss Judith.'

'Well, um, I might have looked at her a couple of times lately . . .' Judith gave a sheepish grin in acknowledgement of the overemphatic denial. 'I'm sorry, Penny, I shouldn't have snapped at you.'

'Don't bother about it.' The Director's PA stood up and reached for the empties. 'I'm going to buy you a drink this time – we may as well make a lunchtime of it while her nibs is gone. And then I'll tell you what I'm going to do. After that last one, it's time you were sorted out with a nice *quiet* girl.'

14

Big Pants

I said a whole bunch of stuff when I got back in last night and I've just wiped the lot. All it was was me ranting about how sick this business is, over and over. OK, I suppose that *is* what the average person might say who walked in to find this respectable middle-aged woman being beaten black and blue by choice. But one thing I did learn from those sessions last year was how going on and on disgustedly is a dead giveaway, more likely than not. Especially if sex is involved. Like the rabid anti-gay who's terrified he's one himself. It was just so bloody obvious this morning and I'm going to come clean. Try to, anyway. Try to think the thing through. I mean, when it comes down to it, whatever I may *think* I think or ought to think, what happened turned me on. *Right* on. So I'm going to go through it step by step.

Naturally I was really uptight about the whole thing by Friday and couldn't concentrate properly on work. So much so I nearly chickened twice in the afternoon and phoned the College, but of course I didn't because it was too late. I couldn't let her down at the last minute. When I turned up we went straight downstairs where this time the curtain was drawn back and the trestle all lit up. Mrs R was in a long black thing and introduced me to this woman in a short yellow dress called Nancy who runs a high-class massage parlour place off Market Street. She was all petite and demure-looking and explained how she owed a favour for all the help in getting a licence. Some favour.

Then Mrs R lifted her robe showing a pair of full knickers and got in position over the trestle. Obviously we were going to get underway without more ado, but it was strangely a case for me of so far, so good. My stomach had even settled a bit with the polite chat and that big covered bottom on display looked, well, even a bit *homely*. But then Nancy came right up to me saying 'May I?' and suddenly she's got my head between her hands, staring. She's kind of Asian-looking and whether that's the reason or not I don't know but I can't make out her expression at all. I can't see a thing in her eyes, but I'm feeling that she's seeing *all there is to see* in mine, and that includes things I don't know are there. What a weird feeling – not scared exactly, more frozen, rabbit-in-headlights sort of thing. But then she breaks the spell and says I'll do with a funny little smile.

Out of her bag comes a clothes brush, a wooden thing with a flat back and it's not going to take many guesses to get what it's meant for. But she's handing it to me – *to me* – and next she's outlining the whole area of the black pants and telling me to give it my best shot. We need to get a good blood circulation, she says. Well, I get going – what else was I going to do at that precise point – and it's all so unreal that I kind of forget that I am actually spanking this mature woman who only recently spanked me. Twice. I didn't think so at the time, but that seems quite appropriate whereas what's happening now is just bizarre. But I somehow get caught up in the activity: the brush is heavy and makes a loud noise and I get lost in bringing it down and watching the knickers stretch and cling as the behind bounces. After a bit Nancy comes and puts a hand down inside the elastic – to check the temperature, I suppose – and says it is good. So I follow instructions to pull the pants right off and do up the knee and ankle straps on both sides. The skin is deep, deep pink and I can't help noticing the dark hair in the cleft. That's all you can see really, but it makes me think of how gooey and prickly I'm feeling there. I mean there's no escaping the fact: this stuff just gets to me. Nancy's looking at me again and I'm sure she sees this because the next thing she does is to nod at the brush I've put down and tell me to take it with me when I go. For a souvenir.

I know I said I'd spell out what happened in detail but I really don't want to dwell on the caning. I wasn't being asked to take part in it, thank God, though it was obvious I was expected to stay around. But first I got the low-down on what Nancy was going to use and that was enough to bring the butterflies right back. It was a straight black rod with a greasy feel to it, not very nice to hold. I forget what she said it was made of but it didn't swish like a cane's supposed to. Instead when you brought it down hard there was this nasty sort of hum like it really meant business. Ugh. That was bad enough but then came the cruncher. Nancy was going do the job, of course, but she wanted me to keep a tally. And she wouldn't say how many beforehand, only that we'd take them half a dozen at a time and see how we went.

Well, that puts me in some state. The welts are *horrific* – dark purple from the word go – and I'm trying not to look yet not lose count of the current number and how many sixes we've had already. So my head's spinning and my guts are churning by the time – eventually – it's over. Six times six in all is what it comes to. Thirty-six strokes and leisurely with it, every one savoured. There's not a millimetre of unmarked skin on her bum and she's hardly made a sound. What a trouper – it makes me totally ashamed of all the squirming I did with a few smacks.

Mrs R's just lying there as if the stuffing's been knocked out of her (no wonder!) and Nancy takes one look at me and says to go and get some air. I can leave the rest to her and she thanks me for my help. So I'm out of there just as fast as I can but something makes me remember to pick up the brush. So that was it: I took a long way back here, jogging to try and clear my head but I was still shocked when I got in and just sounded off on tape. Just let it all out. That was yesterday and now it's a different story. It's still kind of awful but spelling it out has made me so wet. My cunt – yes, *cunt* – is dripping – *fucking* dripping – and I'm going to switch this thing off and masturbate. It's what I should have done last night and then I wouldn't have had to lie awake tossing and turning till I could see the dawn.

Now I've gone and done it and I reckon I want to get this down too. Stop it going round and round inside. Maybe. Last night Gregor was due to appear and my head was still just full of the night before. So what do I do but dig out a pair of big pants and an old pleated skirt and put the clothes brush out in full view on the coffee table. He's brought a bottle of gin with him so I get busy with ice and lemon and tonics. It's just what I need to give me a bit of Dutch courage. Well after a couple and some small talk we start kissing on the sofa so in a bit I remind him of the time I first went to Mrs R and he searched for the traces, and so on and so forth. Right, I say brightly, now it's your turn, and I go on to tell him that if he's horrified (though I'm betting he won't be after his reaction before) he should just leave and I promise I won't ever mention the subject again.

He does look a bit taken aback I suppose, but he goes along with my little scheme. So there I am with my skirt up over the sideboard waiting for him to whack my seat and after a couple of timid pats he starts to get into the swing of it. That wood really stings and I'm going 'ow-ow-ow!' and at the same time trying to keep my voice down so as not to bring the neighbours banging on the door. I've told him to take no notice till I say 'OK' very clearly then he's to stop. Talk about organisation and I'm just a bloody beginner.

Well, of course, when I do make him finish what happens then is kind of predictable. Or rather it would be if it wasn't *me*. Which is what makes it such a turn-up for the books. When the knickers come down I just stay there bent over while he pets me then I can feel his erection just pushing a bit between the cheeks. There's a pause and it dawns on me that the boy's not sure it's OK. I mean it hasn't been before and he must be a bit thrown by the crazy reception he's getting, so I go, 'Yes, yes, yes.' Then he's pushing again and I'm all ready for him and I really really want him inside. It's all over pretty fast – one minute his hairy thighs are all tingly against my tender bum and the next that's me coming like a steam engine.

Hot stuff. And I've got all hot again just telling this. Hot and wet. So I'm going back under the covers – it is Sunday morning after all – to have a good long wank. So there!

It's Monday night now and I thought I would just tack this bit on the end here. It kind of rounds things off. Today Penny came and sat on my desk when the others were out and we had a long chat. A lot of stuff about her background and how she didn't dare own up for years to what she liked. In fact, she didn't own up at all, she was spotted by this guy who thought she might be suited to Miss James and that's how she ended up at the Archive. Then she asked had I guessed that Judith was trying to get up the nerve to ask me along to this place in London for the weekend. Well, I hadn't, of course. What Penny said was that they call themselves 'The Art of Correction' and they're looking for experienced people to take along a novice. Well, that's it, isn't it? What could be more appropriate? That's exactly what I am. So I am going to find Judith – I mean Jude – first thing tomorrow and *invite myself*. That sounds super-confident and I'm just saying it really. It's not how I feel. Not at all. But I've got to make myself do it. I only hope Penny isn't way off beam or anything.

15

Conflict of Interest

On the Friday afternoon, while Sandra resisted the temptation to duck out of her date at Marjorie Rowleigh's, Judith was sitting in the top corner of the stacks in a condition of irritation. However she dressed it up, the invitation to a weekend *à deux* in the capital for certain pain and very possible humiliation played in her imagination with but one outcome: the mutual embarrassment of asker and asked. Leaving a note seemed a cop-out; broaching the topic of real-life s/m was surely something that had to be done face-to-face.

'You've got mail!' Smack. '*Ow!*' The cheeky little announcement from her speakers started Judith out of her preoccupied state and she turned her chair to open the message and bring it up onscreen. The header identified it as being from the AOC and her pulse beat faster as she read the short paragraph.

> Judith – can you come to play? It is short notice you will say but I say PLEASE. One night only is good if you want. I believe Constance will be happy that you visit too (and not for punishment this time!) Do not reply. See you I hope. Helga

God, it was after four already, but there was a train – if she remembered right – at six fifteen. The plan had been

136

to hang out at The Phoenix later but Marsha would understand. OK. It was time to go home and get ready. And then on the Saturday she could maybe drop in on Gwen instead of waiting for the next invitation. Take the initiative: it had paid off before.

On the way down Judith paused on the carpeted landing. Here she was jaunting off boldly at the drop of a hat when she couldn't find it in herself to ask the Archive secretary a simple (if awkward) question. Before there was time to think better of it, she turned the handle and marched in – to an empty office. Spick and span and deserted. Well, it was just half an hour short of five at the end of the week. In the continuing absence of their Director what did she expect? Judith went out, leaving the annoyed bang of the door echoing down the stairwell at her back.

The bear of a doorman nodded in recognition and patted her behind as he waved her in. Judith simpered through gritted teeth: better keep in with him if she could thus avoid the rigmarole of printed passwords. She was hesitating inside, unsure which way to turn, when Helga herself came bustling out of the crowded bar lounge and guided her up to the accommodation floor into the room they had shared before.

'Thank you for coming, Yoodit.'

'It's good to see you, Helga. You're looking great.' Judith took in the plaits that had replaced the customary ponytail and the very short flared skirt. When she pulled the girl in to put a tongue in her mouth she found there were no pants underneath the already revealing article. After a minute Helga slipped out of her fondling grip with a giggle and twirled around showing all.

'It is hot, *ja*? I have another here for you.' She held out a diminutive strip of material. 'And then I have the idea for a game down below. You will like it, I promise.'

It might have been called a micro had it been straight down and clinging and on a shop-window dummy it could have been made almost decent. As it was, the slightest movement made the pleats bounce, and the airflow over the genital region in the descent of the back stairs gave a clue as to the display the seated clientele was going to get. Efforts to move with decorum would be a mere waste of time. However, when her partner in crime pushed open the door the scene did much to dispel Judith's qualms. There was an active buzz of talk at the nearby tables and a flurry of staff service amongst them, such that no one seemed particularly interested in the two outrageously clad young women who had just entered. Furthermore, in the centre of the room, a pole dancer wearing rather less than they were themselves was writhing to the background thump of music in a way that held the eyes of those otherwise unoccupied. Judith felt a tug on her arm and she was pulled into a nearby booth from which they could peer out round the curtain.

'There, see the one who sits by herself. With the slogan.' Judith followed the line of Helga's gaze to a broadish back that said in bold black letters: MUFF DIVERS UNITE! The owner was leaning on folded arms to peer up through a shaggy fringe at the near-naked performer but when they pushed their way through she looked round and grinned. 'It is good, the shirt,' said Helga, 'but does it mean what it says?'

'Well, I guess.' As she leaned back, Judith saw that nestling between an imposing pair of breasts was the image of a hairy pink vulva. The girl looked from one to the other of them, then down at the ultra-brief skirts. 'Are you, um –'

'We are the believers in your text, so you should come with us. To play a game, yes?' No more persuasion seemed necessary for the stranger got up and followed them into the small area they had just come from. Once they were closed off from the main area Helga reached for the fastening on the girl's Bermuda shorts. 'May I?'

'Sure thing. That's what I came along for.' She lifted her arms from her sides to allow the skin-tight garment to be peeled down.

'Hey,' said Judith when she saw the close-cropped yet thick black bush making a neat inverted triangle, then she said it again as she moved round to get the rear view. The provocative jut of the buttocks was accentuated by the narrow waist and there was a residue of puppy fat in the folds and creases. Helga took a cane from the shelf and Judith watched the girl raise an eyebrow, though she looked more curious than alarmed.

'We do the cunnilingus, *ja*? My friend you make come then me. Then we put you on the couch. But there is – you call it I think – a catch. It will be done from here.' She patted the horse beside her in the small room with a mischievous smile. There was no mistaking its intended function.

'Ah, got you. The technique's on the ball and the arse gets off lightly. Otherwise ...' She put on an exaggeratedly rueful expression and Helga laughed.

'It is so. But we do not use the long stick. And after it is your turn to come.'

'OK guys, you're on.' So saying she settled herself over the square leather top and Judith stood so that the young woman's head was at the level of her own crotch. The cool, slightly quizzical compliance was a real turn-on and she could feel the juices beginning to flow. There was no safe bet on the tally reaching even a classic six. In the event Judith wasn't counting, for their new acquaintance was good. After a few preliminary slurps of the tongue well into the vaginal folds, she located Judith's clitoris in a movement that made her gasp out loud, and when the mouth pushed in hard and teeth nibbled it was all she could do to stay on her feet.

'Jesus fuck,' she breathed as the impossible peak fell away and she released her grip. 'Oh God, your shoulders. I'm sorry.' Below her she could see the shape of two sets of fingers imprinted red on the white skin.

139

'Don't worry about it. I'll take marks like that as a compliment.'

When she changed places with Helga, Judith saw there were four vivid red lines crossing the pale cheeks. Whether she was trying to delay it she didn't know, but the German girl's orgasm was long enough in the building for her to be able to add another good dozen. The target was one of those behinds – as was often remarked of her own – that simply begged to be beaten, and she took a delight in slicing hard into the fatty underfold. When they were done, the new girl jumped up and clutched at the striped parts for several seconds, before taking the face cloth offered to wipe her bedewed chin.

'Shit a brick. If that was the wee cane, no way am I volunteering for the one the big girls get.' With some token wincing she was positioned on her back on the floor carpet where, with Helga bent double, feet astride, and Judith squatting on her face, they were able to complete a rather unstable triangle. Fortunately, the newcomer was well enough primed to reach her climax before they toppled and fell into a giggling heap.

'Is it by invitation, or can anyone join in?' The trio scrambled self-consciously to their feet. Exactly how long Constance had been standing quietly by the curtain was not clear.

'We were making a game with our friend, er, er . . .' Helga gestured helplessly towards the participant who had been drawn from her table.

'Niamh. And it was fun.'

'I'm sure,' said Constance drily. 'But tell me, young lady, have you not submitted a form? I seem to recall –'

'Yeah. I used to do stuff at Safflix, you know, on the other side of the square.'

'A good training ground, if regrettably named. Well, Niamh, if you're keen for more, Magda's in the next room raring to go and grab a few greenhorns. Tell her I sent you.'

'Great.' The new recruit climbed quickly into her faded denims, smoothed down the eye-catching top and made an exit with a wave to her recent partners. 'See you guys.'

'See you.' Judith turned back to see that Constance had fixed Helga with a stern look.

'Initiative is a good thing, of course, but I should like to be consulted before you invent any more games. Is that clear?' The German girl nodded with downcast eyes, the very model of demure obedience. But it was not going to be enough. 'And while Judith is always welcome, can I take it that she is here tonight at your bidding, Helga?' Again came the silent acquiescence and the older woman clicked her tongue. 'Pass me the cane, girl, then bend over the horse.'

Watching the tiny skirt ride up to leave the cheeks quite bare, Judith found herself speaking. 'Um, I was involved too, Constance. I don't think Helga should suffer alone.' To volunteer for a dose of the thing she'd enjoyed using had not been part of the plan, but what else could she do?

'Very well, I won't argue the point. I'll take the two of you side by side.' Judith lowered herself carefully into place: with her arm round Helga's waist, the square padded top was just wide enough to support both of them, hip tight to hip. The strokes were applied in strict rotation and while the cane was not full length, Constance had a vigorous arm. So it was that once the allotted dozen each had been delivered, both young women were on their feet, hands clasped to stinging behinds, while she put away her instrument.

'Helga, you will go to Magda next door; she can use some help with the *official* sessions. Judith, would you be so good as to come with me? There are things I think you should be aware of.' Judith followed her out of the bar area, past the entrance where the substantial figure stood guard in his vestibule, to the end of the passage

141

where the stairs led up to the higher floors. In front of them was a door she had not noticed before and Constance inserted a key in its lock.

'You know, I expect that Samantha, your Director, was not pleased to receive an outlined programme that had been drawn up without consultation. Her reaction was hardly surprising, since the scheme for the AOC was first mooted between herself and Sibyl together with two others I don't think you know. Following her representations – in person – there have been amendments to include events staged by the Archive; doubtless these will be discussed with you next week. But for now, there is something you should see, which has come about as a consequence of Samantha's recent behaviour. It's true – is it not – that she has been a little, shall we say, erratic?' Judith was suddenly uneasy. What gave Constance the right to raise questions about the woman who was, when it came down to it, her own boss? But it seemed her disquiet had been anticipated.

'I'm not asking you to break employer–employee confidentiality, Judith. Samantha has told her version of things in some detail when requesting the arrangements we have made. I would like simply to have confirmation.'

'OK. It all makes more sense given what you say. Yes, she went overboard on me a few weeks back, though she did sort of apologise later. But then there was poor Penny – her assistant. I mean she gets spanked all the time, but last week . . .' While she was trying to find the right words to convey just how over the top it had been, Constance put up a hand.

'That's all I need, Judith. It confirms the overall picture.' She turned the key and the door opened on to a flight of steps disappearing down into the gloom. As her eyes became accustomed to the meagre light Judith saw the worn flagstones of another passage that showed a dull grey ahead. The air was chill and a little dank, a far cry from the warmth and hubbub of the bar they had left. In front of them were two doors and she followed her guide through the one on the left into a narrow space in front of a long window. On the other side of it in a dazzling spotlight stood a long, low apparatus equipped with wooden stocks at head and foot. It was plainly a punishment bench and Judith saw that it was occupied by a blindfold figure, face down, whose bare back was streaked with red. Below the waist the form was clothed in breeches which she recognised with a shock that stopped her breath.

'Yes, Judith, it *is*. The penitent, and in *my* hands. It will be a long night, in many parts, with intervals for reflection on what is yet to come.' Constance had moved closer and Judith stiffened as a hand fondled the bottom cheeks it had recently made tender. When the voice came it was low, in her ear. 'I should so much like to do to you what she did. And more, much much more . . .' Judith shivered but the words stabbed straight into her loins and she shifted uncomfortably.

'You are well aroused, I think.'

'The cane, it always – afterwards –'

'Of course.' The supervisor squeezed her bottom and moved away. 'Perhaps one day I shall have the privilege. For now I am going next door: it is the turn of the buttocks. Watch if you will, and while you watch there is something I want you to do. Stimulated as you are it should not present any difficulty.' Below the window there was a waist-high counter and Constance turned to it, unfastening and lowering a flap. Once she had manoeuvred Judith in front of it there came a shaft of light from below, warming her thighs and belly. 'There is a camera now running: indulge me by masturbating while your Director is punished. I shall value the addition to my collection.'

Judith tried to still her whirling thoughts but there was no need for a conscious attempt. Constance was right: by the time the silk knickers had come down and the many-tailed whip began its work her arousal was fierce, demanding satisfaction. With one hand she parted the labia to expose the oozing folds while the index finger of the other circled the bud of flesh at their apex. That should give the lens something to be going on with. As the white flesh on display reddened and darkened, Judith slowed her movements to draw out the climax for as long as she could. And when, in the end, it broke, in synchrony with a final crescendo of lashes, it was not that scene that gripped her so much as another: one that as yet existed only in her imagination, in which she submitted to Constance for the thrashing of her life.

It was mid-morning before Judith slipped away from the AOC building, leaving Helga fast asleep in the top bunk. She had been happy for the diversion of some light-hearted spanking games in the side booths of the bar but afterwards sleep had come late and uneasy, haunted by images of the cellar and its occupants. It had been in mind at the outset to call on Gwen and now the prospect was positively appealing. Bad girl she surely was, and probably dangerous with it, but there was an earthy spontaneity about her that would be the perfect antidote to the rather cold calculation that seemed to drive the establishment she had just left.

Judith ducked through the street traffic and turned in under the archway with a sense of anticipation. But when she reached the doorway and knocked sharply on its peeling paint there was no response. A second attempt had no more effect so she tried the handle and the door opened.

'Hallo! Anybody there? Gwen, it's me, Jude.' She hovered uncertainly in the hallway then went to the door at the end and called again. There was no one in the living room or kitchen so she was left with only one more possibility: the curtained opening in the anteroom that she had balked at before. This time there was a glint of brass in the lock and Judith made herself turn the key. It was no time for faint-heartedness. The rubber surround squelched unpleasantly when she pulled the heavy wood away from it and she peered into the darkness with some trepidation. There was a switch inside so she flicked it quickly before her nerve could give out. The light came on and there it was – what she had half expected – but still her stomach gave a lurch. The small draped room, scarcely more than a cubicle, contained a ladder-type frame at an angle to the wall and fastened to it was the familiar form of Max, clad in waistcoat, boots and nothing else. He turned his head, blinking in the brightness.

'Miss Judith.'

'The very same. I take it that Gwen is out.' It was not as bad as she had momentarily feared, for the visible skin was virtually unmarked. 'Looks like you've been having an easy time of it, eh?'

He explained, she thought a little tetchily, that his Mistress had business at the studio and that he was to be whipped on her return. That, he stressed, would be soon. Looking round, Judith spotted two canes on the side counter that looked like recent acquisitions. She took one up and flexed it; it felt good to hold and she held it out for the young man to see.

'Do you think I could, Max? Just six to warm you up?'

'As you wish. It's not for me to say, is it?' Oh dear, petulant indeed. She must be interfering with the rules of the game and ought to back off gracefully. But instead a sense of devilment got the upper hand.

'That's OK. I'll take the consequences when your domina gets back.' After some trial swishing of the new rod she laid on four beauties, perfectly parallel, then finished them with two diagonals as hard as she could manage. Not a sound escaped his lips but the way the muscles knotted in calf and thigh spoke volumes. Judith put the instrument down and ran her hands over the welted flesh, admiring the firm roundness of the narrow-hipped cheeks. Then through the slats of the ladder she found the full erection she was expecting and knelt before it, taking the head in her mouth while pulling down her own trousers and pants. With one hand on her wet cunt she sucked and licked, tasting the pre-orgasmic secretion. Max groaned and it was good to get a straight response.

'Miss Judith, please. It's been days and days, and I can't manage –'

'I told you I'd carry the can, right?' She looked at the distended pole leaking its lubricant. 'So there'll be loads and loads of the white stuff. Yum. Don't worry boy, that is *exactly* what I want.'

Somehow during the spasms that shook her, Judith managed to keep swallowing and she was about to come up for air when in the distance a door banged. Sod it. But she was not going to be caught shame-faced so she focused her attention on the task of tonguing the flabby organ back to its previous stiffness, aware that they were no longer alone in the room. Judith at last looked up with her heart pumping. There was the longest second of silence she could ever remember followed by a hearty guffaw.

'Jesus fuck. Jude, you don't waste no time. I step out for five minutes and you've milked the boy of a week's spunk.'

'I'm sorry Gwen. I sort of couldn't resist Max all tied up like that.' Be brazen, it was the only hope.

'I know, girl. He gets you that way. And I like the pattern in his bum.' She was outwardly ebullient, but Judith could sense an underlying irritation.

'So am I forgiven?'

146

'I suppose. He'll spurt again good as new later. What I'm more pissed off about is they wouldn't fucking let me in. Last night, to that club place, you know –'

'The AOC. Oh, I was . . .' Shit. It was out before she could clamp her mouth shut.

'Jud*ith*. Say I got this wrong. *Please*. You were inside while that bastard on the door turned me back. You were fucking *inside*.' The strength of emotion turned the word into a snarl.

'Um, 'fraid so.'

'And little Miss Wandering Hands was out to play too, no doubt?'

'She was there, but, er . . .' Uh oh. Talk about digging holes.

'Right.' Gwen went to the figure on the frame and traced a cane-mark with her finger. 'OK, Maxie boy. Your Mistress needs to get something out of her system –' she squeezed the penis that was still hard from its recent manipulation '– and then I can give you the attention you deserve.' Judith followed her out of the room and waited while she closed and curtained the door. It was not the time for protestations of innocence that would in any case be a tissue of lies.

'You wanna square this, sister? I'd better let you know the way I'm feeling, a "no" is going to be your exit line.'

'What do you have in mind?' Judith tried to sound calmly curious in the face of the angry ultimatum while the inner voice of reason was telling her to cut and run. Gwen opened the chest under the table, took out two coils of black leather and passed one over, handle first. As it uncurled in her grip Judith saw maybe a metre length of tapering braid that ended in a short splay of narrow strips.

'You up for a contest? We strip and go at it. Nothing but the whips.'

'But you'll cut me to ribbons.'

'Nah.' Gwen shook her head. 'You take a thirty second start to get your eye in and we'll make a time limit. And it wouldn't be squaring nothing, girl, if we was evens.'

'How long, then?'

'Ten minutes total. And once it starts that's it. Until then, you know where the door is if you want out.'

She was still there staring at a neat pile of clothes when a similarly naked Gwen emerged from the kitchen with a clock. Somehow she had removed the garments one by one without it seeming to amount to a decision to stay. But it had come to the crunch; if she didn't head off there and then she was signed up for the ride. Which of course she was. Judith made a wry face at the recognition of it: to leave was too much like admitting defeat.

'I'm as ready as I'm going to be.'

'OK.' With the sinking feeling of having made a move she was going to regret Judith watched the black girl lock the only means of escape and put the key through into the anteroom. She gave her whip a trial jerk and saw how it curled back on itself with a snap. A second and third try produced a dramatic cracking sound and her spirits lifted a touch. She wasn't going to come out on top, but maybe she could put on some kind of show.

'That's the idea, sister. It's all in the wrist; like one of your swishy canes only more so. So you better get a good grip.' The clock was already set and when Gwen pressed the button the large red digits flickered and jumped from 10:00 to 09:59. She faced Judith, legs apart, slightly crouched, bizarrely like a tennis player waiting to receive a demon serve except that she was naked and her hands were empty. For the present. Judith swung her arm back and brought the whip forward but at the last minute pulled the stroke so that the cracker did no more than graze a knee. The next two attempts fared little better and she saw the dial already down to 09:48. At that rate the half-minute would be gone without a decent cut. There was something unnerving about the face-to-face situation: when you were caning a girl's behind she wasn't staring at you – hard. With an effort Judith focused on the rounded hips and thought of the luscious arse at the back. On the next stroke the braid snaked out right on target but her opponent was too quick on her feet. Two more – at last – made the connection to buttock flesh but it was a case of too little, too late as the time passed to 09:29 and Gwen picked up her weapon.

'Now, girl, you gonna pay.' Quick as a flash there was a fierce sting to the back of her leg and before she could respond in kind another that made her yelp. As the time remaining shrank to eight then seven minutes she managed to land three or four good ones on the dancing body that was glistening slightly from its exertions. But her own thighs and breasts – seemingly singled out for action – were a mass of discolorations that stung as if she had been under attack from a horde of angry wasps. It was no use: six long minutes left to run and she was hopelessly outclassed. As she had known she would be, for Christ's sake. For all the chance she had of defending herself, she might as well be tied to a flogging rack for this vengeful creature to do with as she pleased.

Judith endured the passage of two further minutes in which the best she managed was to block a few cuts from the instrument that darted at her almost faster than she could see. Then the lash caught her square between the legs, nipping excruciatingly into the bare labia. The scalding pain was like nothing else and it drove her howling right over the edge. Fury with herself for the arrogant miscalculation, for not having had the bottle just to walk away, and exasperation with Gwen's hair-trigger jealousy boiled over and she snapped. Leaning forward, low, she contrived with a swing to coil the leather right round the black girl's ankle and jerked

149

it with all her strength. Her opponent thudded heavily to the floor and in a trice Judith was kneeling on her back with the whip round her neck.

'Now you listen to me, girl. You *fucking* listen to me.' She yanked the loop of leather tighter, the voice sounding harsh and strange as she yelled into Gwen's ear. 'You don't own me, right? Max is one thing but what I do outside of here is something else. Got it? You wanna breathe again you'd better fucking get it.' As the flood of emotion dwindled and died she released her grip and Gwen wriggled free. In the shocked silence the two young women looked at each other and Judith saw with a surge of guilt the purple line she had raised on the other's throat. She struggled for words but the attempt was forestalled by a hand over her mouth that proceeded to push her gently but firmly until she was on her back. Weak in the wake of the adrenaline rush Judith put up no resistance. The dark eyes that scrutinised her were intense and they held their gaze when the lips were pressed to the abused breasts.

'Fucking hell, Jude, you got some temper. Wow. Come here and see what you done.' She got up on her knees and stuck out her pelvis so that the crotch was inches from Judith's face. The black hairs were matted and a glutinous seepage oozed from the mouth of the vagina. A potent waft drew her head closer, but her partner had other ideas. 'Uh, uh. My turn. I know for sure you're every bit as ripe, sister. So lie back, get those legs apart, and I promise you ain't gonna be thinking of no England.'

16

Demonstration

The outer room was empty and Judith let herself into the Assistant Director's office with a sigh of relief. Sandra must have taken an early lunch break. She hadn't consciously intended it, but the way that washing the kitchen floor and cleaning all visible surfaces, to say nothing of vacuuming under the beds, had become imperative on a Monday morning was a dead giveaway. Without the necessity of a decision, she had earned a stay of execution before she would have to pop the question. That was what it felt like – as if she were about to put herself on the line and risk humiliating rejection – when in fact she was just going to ask her to do what she was pretty sure the girl was already into. Sort of, anyway. Shit, she needed to get things back in proportion. It would be a controlled situation that was unlikely to go any further: after all she was hooked up with Gwen good and proper now, wasn't she. Wasn't she?

Judith sat down and eyed the small pile of unopened mail, trying to bring her thoughts into focus. In the aftermath of the weekend she felt oddly dislocated. Explosive anger had in an instant slammed into gear as explosive sex – the last orgasms like that she could remember were with, well, Gwen – but her attack was not even mentioned later. Such violence may have turned Gwen on but the fact that she had been capable of it now weighed on her. At the time when they had run out of steam – eventually – on the living room floor, Max was released and dispatched to the kitchen. Food and drink taken, Gwen insisted on instruction in the use of her new canes after which she returned the favour with a whip. Then afternoon shaded into evening as the two young women retired to the super-kingsize bed with the young man between them and a jar of cream to soothe his exemplary welts. It was a potent combination that kept them awake well into the night and was far from exhausted after sleep and a massive breakfast had revived them all. In the end Judith had dragged herself to a train that delivered her home and into her own bed before ten p.m. It was little wonder she was spaced out yet.

A tap on the door brought Penny into the room, who angled her head in the direction of the Director's office. 'Miss Judith, her nibs wants a word while you're in.'

'Oh God, you mean she's here? I thought . . .' She had been wrapped up in thoughts of Gwen; now memory flooded back of a chill basement and a figure fastened to the bench.

'Got back yesterday.' The PA bit her lip, looking upset and indignant. 'What a state. Oh, my big mouth. What am I saying –'

'It's OK, Penny, I know what happened. It was of her choosing, and I don't suppose you'll get any thanks for tut-tutting about it. But how are *you*? I mean, things between you and the boss?'

'Well, I've been that busy with the herbal lotions I didn't give it a lot of thought. Now you ask, though, I daresay I'm back in favour.' The smile and the perky tilt of the pageboy cut as she spoke seemed to signal a return to business as usual. 'But I won't be if I don't get on. We need more supplies.'

'OK, Penny, you do that and I'll go in and have that word right now.'

* * *

152

Samantha James was seated stiffly upright behind her desk and pointed her visitor to an upright chair opposite. She pushed over a sheet for Judith's inspection and at the movement a look of pain crossed her features. The face was pale and the eyes appeared deeper set than usual.

'It is a preliminary listing of demonstrations for a select audience at the Art of Correction's premises. I'd be pleased to have any comments. You will see your name included with a partner for Saturday of this week, Judith. Penelope seemed to think that had been arranged.' While speaking, the Director had risen rather carefully and was rustling some papers on a side table.

'It will be, er, settled today, Miss James.' Maybe Penny knew something she didn't. But if Sandra turned her down, she was going to have to find a naif for the event, whatever it took.

'You saw a little, did you not?' She was still turned away and the voice was quiet but the words were perfectly clear.

'Yes.'

'That is what I wanted. Constance was very – ah – thorough.' Miss James turned back with a file that she placed on the desk. 'Take this with you. It's a draft review of our first title scheduled to appear in the second issue of *Sexual (Per)Versions*.' She marked the brackets in the air with her fingers. 'It seems to be acquiring something of a cachet, as does the new journal itself, and they are inviting the author to reply to critical comments.' Clearly the topic of the penance – if that was what it had been – was closed.

'That's great.' Judith took the document and scanned the first paragraph. 'It was refreshing,' noted the author, 'to find an analytical case history which did not consider its subjects to be in the grip of a regressive pathology. And if this one is any indication of what the NemArch imprint has in store, it is set to make a major impact on the field'. A little pink, Judith remarked that there didn't look like much in the way of criticism.

'No, my dear. As I expected. However, it will give you a platform to expound your arguments. Now, as to the weekend's activities, I shall not, I fear, be quite ready to attend in person –' there was the hint of an ironic smile '– so I should appreciate a verbal report on your return.'

'Yes, of course. Right. I'd better go and finalise the arrangements.' Judith closed the connecting door behind her and placed the papers on her desk. The time for shirking her duty was at an end. She opened the door to the main office with a firm turn of the handle and found, as expected, that the secretary was back in residence.

'Sandra –'

'Judith –'

'Go on.' They had both spoken together and the Assistant Director found herself happy to take what might be an easy way out.

'Judith, I mean Jude, you know we were talking about inductions before. Well, I heard that there was something kind of, er, practical coming up.'

'Yeah. It's a double act with a school theme, like those stories that took your fancy. Are you interested? I was meaning to ask but –' But I was too bloody chicken, she added in her head.

'Oh yes, please. Well, I mean, um, if I understand it properly. It would be the two of us, and, and –' Judith sat down on the edge of the desk and looked the blushing Sandra straight in the eye.

'I get the cane and you get spanked with something that won't be too bad. That's respectively by a Head-master–Matron duo who specialise in these roles. All in front of a small invited audience and complete with commentary.' The girl's eyes had opened wider but she was nodding, albeit slowly.

'OK, I see. Though it's a bit of a step. I hadn't realised it was, well –'

'Going to be in public? Is that the problem?'

'Uh huh.' Judith leaned closer.

'Thing to remember is it'll be closely supervised – it's a very select few who get asked, and they'll all be into it. Just a bit inexperienced, like you.' The details she was plucking out of the air seemed to be going down well. With a bit of luck the event would follow the lines she was laying down. 'But look, Sandra, if you have any real qualms, I daresay I could dig up someone else at a pinch.' Intended to be a clincher, it worked a treat.

'Oh no. Don't do that.' The secretary looked suddenly determined. 'Count me in. And that's definite. I'd not be able to forgive myself if I missed the chance.'

The rest of the week crawled by. Judith tried to concentrate on fleshing out the scheme of her analysis of perverse initiations but the impending reality kept intruding. Would Sandra have second thoughts, perhaps at the very last minute when the action was on the point of starting? And anyway, how did she feel herself about bending over to have her bare bum meticulously caned in front of a bunch of gawping spectators? It wasn't going to be punishment with its dynamic of retribution and remorse to focus the mind; this was a demonstration of technique where her part was to keep the buttocks presented while the stripes were laid on one by one. Perhaps she should join in verbally with a 'Well hit!' or 'Tight, sir, tight!' if the stroke warranted it. Judith frowned: this was all getting a bit silly. If the man did his job she would have quite enough to do to stay down and she was determined to achieve that, whatever else. And maybe the secretary would rise magnificently to the occasion too.

In the meantime things were awkward around the office. Having made the arrangement for the weekend, Judith didn't know what to say to her would-be partner, and it seemed Sandra was equally ill-at-ease in her presence. On the Thursday she found a message that the secretary was going down on the Friday night to stay with a friend and could Judith please give her instructions on how to get to the place the following day. With relief that she was spared an uncomfortable spell on the train, Judith drew a map of the AOC's location and added the suggestion that she arrive for about eight and tell the doorman – who would be primed – that she had come from the Nemesis Archive.

Eventually the time passed, together with a rail journey that seemed to take twice as long as before, and Judith found herself once more climbing the narrow stairs to the top floor accommodation. There she was met by Helga who announced that her usual lower bunk was being occupied by Niamh. Clothed in nothing but a short singlet, the Irish girl gave her a cheery wave from inside the room. Judith raised an eyebrow at the plaited German but her pretty face was deadpan.

'Her mouth is very popular with the women and Constance plans a class she will teach. So, Yoodit, you will go in here.' She opened the next door along and led them into a similar space that contained a double bed. 'I do not think you will mind sharing with your girlfriend, yes?'

'She's the Archive secretary, Helga, not my girlfriend. But I daresay we can rough it.' Judith grinned at the puzzled expression. 'Joke. We'll be fine. I must say your new roommate looks well settled in.'

'You make the hint. Why not say it?' Helga wagged a finger. 'Yes, we fuck. It is nature. And you are welcome to join us with your friend when she arrives.' The slight frown dissolved into a smile. 'Nevie is nice and I think it is not wrong to want you too – with the special bare kitten.' After a moment's incomprehension Judith chuckled.

'You mean pussy, Helga.'

'Pussy, *ja*. What you have inside here.' She squeezed the crotch of Judith's trousers and the shock of desire

156

was instant. Damn the girl! It must have been a hot week with new find 'Nevie' and she felt left out. But the sentiment had to be endorsed.

'Of course you're not wrong. The more the merrier, I always say.' Privately, however, she suspected that Helga's breezy assertion was more of a cover than anything else. And underneath it would be found much the same jealous susceptibilities lesser mortals were prone to. 'But for now, girl, you can get back to your friend while I go and scout out for mine. OK?'

It was as well she did since Sandra had turned up in baggy jeans and cap and was having trouble convincing the bouncer of her status. If the old-style gear had been seized upon as a comforter to ward off stress it didn't seem to have worked, for the face was pale and tense. Judith put an arm through hers and steered her along the corridor to the foot of the stairs.

'We'll dump your stuff, then we'll go and get you ready, right? Once it's all underway I guarantee you'll feel better.' Alongside the space for the evening's show was a dressing room where the waiting Constance shook hands formally with the Archive secretary. Judith had come sheathed in snug black trousers over string briefs, topped with a white shirt fitted at the waist; should the session begin clothed she planned to present an appealing target. Sandra, on the other hand, was to be kitted out in schoolgirl fashion and allowed herself to be divested of her denims with a less-than-convincing nonchalance. But when the organiser stooped to circle a tape measure round her waist and hips she said something that made the girl go the deepest shade of pink Judith had ever seen, then take a fit of the giggles. It was preferable to the furrowed brow so she left them to it and devoted herself to examining her own appearance in the wall mirror. With the short cut of her dark hair and lack of make-up it was suitably androgynous; even though the buttocks were full and well dimpled, the hips were narrow enough to pass for male at a pinch.

She was just thinking that they would make a good couple when Sandra emerged from the changing room and did a twirl that flared out the black pleated skirt to flash a glimpse of pristine white knickers beneath. Similarly shirted she passed over one of two identically striped ties and they knotted them solemnly into place.

'Excellent. With such appealing candidates for correction, our demonstration promises to be a success.' Constance's enthusiasm seemed to have rubbed off and Sandra looked for the first time almost eager. 'If Judith will excuse me for repeating what an old hand knows well, I'll simply say that while our event is staged that does not make it false. Whether intended to punish or not, the implements will hurt, and in both cases the onus is on the recipient to bear her pain without undue fuss. But don't be alarmed, dear –' there was a touch to Sandra's arm and Judith was sure she detected a wink '– I'm sure you will find aspects of the lady's technique quite stimulating.' Again colour flooded the secretary's face and there was the sound of a stifled snort. What had established the rapport was a mystery but it was making her job a lot easier. Which was as well, for she needed a few moments to summon up the right frame of mind for the part she was shortly to play. From what Judith had heard of the canings her demonstrator typically handed out, the word 'stimulating' was not going to do justice to the experience she had in store. Not by a long chalk.

Then, as the noise filtered through of an audience assembling, Constance pointed through the doorway at a side bench they should occupy while she fetched the two guest performers. 'When I return we could begin at once, if you are ready. I think it best to skip introductions: there is nothing personal in the discipline they will mete out, so I recommend you both keep a formal distance from the agents.'

She disappeared and Judith scanned the gathering that was spread around the array of plain wooden forms that would not have been out of place in a spartan public school of a half century past. It consisted of about fifteen women, some in couples, some single and one partnering the lone male member of the group. Out front there was an oblong box attached to four sturdy legs; the padding on it was thick and she noted with approval that it looked sizeable enough to provide good support for the upper body. The horse's properties would be put to the test soon enough, though its comfort or otherwise was hardly going to remain the focus of her attention. She shot a glance at Sandra who was sitting quietly to her left and wondered what was going through her mind. For Judith's own part she felt an excitement that more than outweighed the dread of those near-unbearable peaks of pain to come; in fact the fear was an essential part of the thrill to which she was avowedly addicted. The girl beside her had been spanked twice to her knowledge and here she was ready for more. Perhaps she too was becoming in her own way hooked on the experience.

Then the door opened to admit a tall grey-haired man in a tweed jacket and flannel trousers accompanied by a younger rosy-cheeked woman in a blue uniform. Headmaster and Matron, indeed: they certainly looked the part and when he opened a travel bag to take out a pair of crook-handled canes Judith's skin began to tingle in earnest. She settled back as he welcomed the spectators and introduced his colleague as a confirmed advocate of the therapeutic benefits of a soundly spanked bottom. She, he went on, would have the floor later; it was his opening task to throw some light on the more severe form of corporal punishment whose employment had been once widespread in the education system. If a little pedantic in its use of a version of English common to the newsreader of half a century before, the manner was authoritative and when she was called out as the first of the two volunteers she found herself content to follow the instruction to place herself well forward over the quilted surface. After a moment's silence, there came the sound of a dry cough.

'I have to say, young lady, that you present us with quite a sight. My experience of applying the rod to the clothed and unclothed backsides of boys, girls and, latterly, men and women seeking correction has, over the years, been rather extensive. Yet in the course of it, I have rarely encountered such a combination of the best anatomical features of both sexes. Here we find a female weight of flesh that is ideally braced by a male muscularity: as you can all see, I'm sure, these buttocks are quite splendidly firm and full.' Had the words been directed to her face, Judith would not have known where to look. As it was, the audience was spared the sight of her blushes and she was able to enjoy the expert manipulation of the hands that squeezed and moulded the cheeks under their clinging cover. When she arched her back and spread the legs a little further she was rewarded with a sharp slap.

'Ha!' He chuckled and a titter ran round the room. 'You observe how our subject responds. We must not spoil her with too much admiration. There is business to attend to.' Turning her head Judith saw the self-styled Headmaster move to the side table and take up the instruments lying there, one of which was perceptibly thicker and longer than the other. In the light of his remarks there was really only one way the choice could go.

'I won't bore you with a lot of detail since there are copies of an explanatory brochure you may each consult at leisure. Suffice it to say that I brought two canes with me. One of them is the standard article, three-eighths of an inch thick, which would serve most people's purposes well. However, given the nature of the material we have

160

to work with tonight, I believe that only the full half-inch item, associated in the past with reformatory use, will do justice to the occasion. These days, as anyone who wishes to purchase a similar item will discover, we are regrettably obliged to specify dimensions with a foreign set of numbers.' It was as she had suspected. Judith shifted a little to make sure she was well balanced and tested her grip on the wooden legs. The next several minutes were going to be trying ones. 'I'll say just this before we begin. The rattan is a very flexible wood that requires more than a simple swing of the arm to give of its best. The secret lies in the action of the wrist, a technique which is well worth the small effort it takes to acquire. For, properly used, these canes can achieve a bite unequalled by that of their more rigid rivals.'

There was a tap to her seat and Judith lay still, resisting the urge to shrink into the padding of the frame. 'I shall begin with six strokes just as we are. Please observe the motion of the arm.' The first two stung, though not badly, then three, four and five made her catch her breath. Six slammed into the base of the buttocks and brought a noise from the back of her throat.

'A good one, I judge, and our young lady's reaction confirms it. Now if she would oblige us by lowering the trousers and returning to position, we shall proceed.' Judith did as bid, rolling the garment down to mid-thigh. Back over the horse she spread her legs safe in the knowledge that, thanks to the diminutive briefs, she was not giving a genital display to a bunch of strangers.

Six strokes followed to show varying degrees of 'wrap-around' containing one long cut right into the dimple that made her yelp. Next came six with the left hand, every bit as testing, in order to 'spread the damage'. Then there was a pause in which Judith tried to marshal her resources. Her behind felt huge and hot, and achingly tender, yet she was certain that the worst was yet to come.

'So far so good. You see we have here a bottom already well scored with the double-edged lines that are the trademark of the instrument. Many recipients would be, if not unable, certainly unwilling to take further punishment, but I believe our subject tonight to be made of sterner stuff. So I should like to end with a further dozen, if, that is, I have her permission.'

Judith cleared her throat. What the fuck could she do – get up and say, 'No thank you sir, I'm off to soak my arse in a tub of iced water'? There was no way out with dignity except to say, as clearly as she could: 'You have it; please continue.'

'That is good. I shall count aloud. When we are finished, feel free to rise at once.'

Thank you, kind sir. Let's see first if we actually make it as far as that. But she stifled the urge to say it and contented herself with a silent grimace. Then she hugged the horse as tightly as she could and they were underway. A distant part of her mind registered that it was like some strange ritual sequence of sounds paced by the numbers at intervals of ten seconds or so.

'One.' Swish. Thwack! 'Uh.'

'Two.' Swish. Thwack! 'Uh.'

'Three.' Swish. Thwack! '*Uh*.'

And so on, each group punctuated by a line of white-hot pain that burned through the interval until the excruciating delivery of the next. Please God, let it be over. But the strokes continued, measured and relentless, as she clung in increasing desperation to the hard wood. At ten he cut her low but with an agonised growl she willed her hands to stay put.

'Eleven.' Swish. Thwack! 'Uh!'

'Twelve.' Swish. Thwack! 'U-UH!' Judith leapt up and jigged wildly, clutching at the intolerable hurt, oblivious to the spectacle she might be providing. But when, after several seconds, she was able to remove her hands and look round there was no one laughing at her antics. The man faced her still holding the cane.

'I hope you don't begrudge my severity. It was a privilege to beat you, my dear.' Judith took the proffered hand and shook it, and the gathering burst into unsolicited applause. Blushing, she made a little bow and eased her trousers up with care.

'No, I don't resent a thing. Though if that was a demonstration, I would hate to appear before the Headmaster for real *punishment*.' There was laughter and more clapping and Judith returned thankfully to where Sandra was sitting. She was looking worried.

'Jude, that was *awful*. How did you bear it? And are you OK? Can I bathe you or something?'

'Woah, girl. Slow down.' Judith touched her arm. 'I'll be fine, don't worry about me. I think the idea is to get right on with your part in the proceedings. If you're not having second thoughts, that is.'

'Oh God, no. After *that*, if I can't take a little spanking I'd never hold my head up again.'

'I wouldn't bank on the little, kid, but whatever you say.'

In the short space of their interchange the frame had been turned on its side, legs away from the spectators, to create a bench seat. Matron took her place at one end of it and the low buzz of conversation died away.

'Well, my dears, that was quite a show we were just treated to.' There was a distinct West Country burr to the voice that gave a homely feel after her predecessor's clipped diction. 'Quite a show indeed, though I doubt there will be many here with the taste to be so strict in practice –' at this there were nods and murmurs of assent round the room '– and maybe none at all to follow in the young lady's footsteps.'

'I would.' It came from a chubby skinhead at the back with freckles and a nose ring. All heads turned and she went instantly puce, obviously wishing she had bitten her tongue. But the lady in the uniform came to the rescue.

'No, child, don't be embarrassed. You did well to speak up. I'm afraid the Headmaster has a very taxing schedule at the minute, but the good people here should be able to accommodate you.' Constance nodded vigorously from her place in the front row and Judith guessed the girl would soon have the opportunity to discover how deep her masochistic streak really ran.

For the present it was Sandra's turn. Matron emphasised that while not matching what a cane could do, the hand alone was capable of making quite an impression, especially, she added to laughter, if it was one as practised and leathery as her own. So the secretary was called over and allowed the older woman to unfasten and remove her skirt. Then she was positioned carefully over the ample lap, elbows supporting her upper half on the remainder of the frame. The thin cotton pants were stretched across the rounded cheeks in a way that made Judith all too aware of her own decidedly damp crotch.

The spanking began and continued in a steady rhythm; the smacks falling to the left and the right, higher and lower, until the skin around the white material had become perceptibly pink. Then Sandra was on her feet and, when the knickers came off, there was an audible gasp at the rich red glow thus exposed. Patently there was more – much more – to come and, rooted to the spot, Judith watched the colour deepen and spread to the accompaniment of the girl's increasingly sharp cries. Matron, it seemed, had the bit between her teeth, and slapped with undiminished vigour, until all at once there was a loud wail and a flood of tears. Whether she had planned to produce the effect wasn't clear, but it served to bring the affair to an abrupt halt. On their feet again she gave Sandra a hug and gently moving the hands aside made a gesture to the purple-hued rump. Applause broke out again, and the sniffling secretary acknowledged the clapping with a curtsey and a watery smile.

The effect on Judith was as dramatic as that of a bolt of electricity. The hot throb of her ill-treated behind combined with the sight of the bare bottom so thoroughly spanked had inflamed desire to fever pitch. But the image of the chastised girl with flushed face and downcast eyes turned lust on the instant into passion. Judith had to have her, and have her right there and then. She strode to the front, took Sandra by the arm and led her in short order to the dressing room, paying no heed to the startled faces left in her wake. In a trice the Yale lock had been clicked shut and the open-mouthed girl was pushed face down over the table. Without more ado Judith slid a hand over the blazing buttock flesh and curled her fingers into the – yes! – slick labial folds.

'Jude, what *are* you doing? No, stop it. Don't! No, oh – oh – oh. Oh *Jude*. Oh yes. Oh yes. Oh *yes*.'

PART III

17

Love, Love, Love

Unreal. Just completely unreal. I mean my dreams are never that vivid but now I get what people are on about when they say something's so amazing you think you'll have to wake up. One minute I'm standing there nursing my sore bum – and God, was it sore, you wouldn't *believe* a hand could sting that much – and the next I'm over the table with her fingers in me. In my cunt. Jude's fingers in my cunt. If I keep saying it, it has got to sink in.

Of course I fought it at first, but she knew just where to touch and I was wet and ready. So bloody ready I came off in three seconds flat. And then we were kissing like crazy – sloppy and deep, all tongues. I always knew there was something funny about me, but I can't stop at getting a buzz from being spanked. Oh no. I have to go and have sex with another woman. Wild sex like I just couldn't get enough. So there we are: welcome to the confessions of a lesbian masochist.

Well, no one's invited really. I realised with the last one that I'd lost any notion of sending these off. Probably that was the whole idea anyway – to get me talking, trying to put it into words. If I can say exactly what it is, then it's supposed to stop being scary. Or something. OK, maybe. But it doesn't go away. I mean, it looks like I *am* a lesbian masochist. Phew!

Lesbian should be all right though, shouldn't it? Given there are loads and loads of out gay women. But one who goes for being put over the knee? I mean I know I howled but that was all part of the thing: really I loved it right from the start. Now that's a real no-no. A grown woman being turned into a little girl – it's not even an adult punishment like Jude's horrific caning. And it's not like those school stories which get you picturing a young miss bending over to take the well-deserved gym shoe all stoically on the seat of the pants. Red-faced, red-bottomed and squirming about showing everything, that was me! Just plain bloody infantile – and I'm getting hot all over again just thinking about it. Basket case, that's what I am. Far too far gone for any fucking therapy.

But I just can't get it out of my mind, the way she looked at me. Since I came back – *she's* not here of course but down *there* planning the next weekend – I do all the running I get time for and it just doesn't work. Before, once I got warmed up that was it. Straight into a different world full of pounding feet, straining muscles, bursting lungs and that thudding of the pulse in the ears. And nothing else – no hang-ups, no anxieties, no thoughts at all except to keep on going. And what happens now? Now I keep coming round to find that I've stopped and I'm staring at the water or a tree. Well, staring into space, really. All I'm seeing is how her mouth goes when she's working me with her fingers.

OK, scrub the middle bit of that: I'm not a proper masochist, am I? I mean I don't get a thrill from real *pain*. Well, I don't think I do though I've never tried. I'm sure I wouldn't – the whole idea makes me feel a bit sick. No, what it is is I get off on having my bottom smacked. Pure and simple. And I got off with a bang when Gregor did it – *and* fucked me – so I'm not exclusively gay either. Bi, that's the word: a bi spanker. Er, I suppose that ought to be bi spank*ee*. Tan my bare bum and I'm anybody's. Oo-er, what a slut.

I'd better face up to it. All this wittering is just in aid of avoiding what I'm really strung up about. Friday – that's only the day after tomorrow – I'm due back at the place and I'm terrified. I won't have to *do* anything, though I suppose there are bound to be games and stuff. No, it's not that: it's Jude. When I get there she'll have had a whole week with Helga and that Irish girl and I know there's a porn star or some such in the picture too. I mean with all that, odds on she's forgotten all about little me and our moment of passion. And what do I do then? Oh God, I can't bear it.

18

Diversions

'Yoodit, you must open wider. And bend your knees –
so – that is *gut*.' The oiled head pushed easily into her
vagina and Judith choked, nostrils filling with the
resinous tang of the pinewood bar beneath her chin.
Since the equipment essential to Constance's address on
the founding principles of the AOC had arrived with
only a day to spare, the young women were engaged in
urgent preliminary trials. The two sturdy frames standing side by side were hinged at waist height so that the
upper half of a fastened body could be bent forward to
present the whole area from shoulders to knees for the
application of whatever instrument was deemed fit. So
far so commonplace amongst aids to systematic flagel-
lation; what distinguished the items under scrutiny –
and what had caused their delayed arrival – were the
special features located in the region of the occupant's
groin. From a moulded pad protruded a joystick-like
stud which could be shifted and angled to suit individual
anatomy. Equipped with one of a variety of attach-
ments, the device provided for anything from full
vaginal penetration to exclusively clitoral stimulation
while corporal punishment was in progress.

Now that Judith was positioned securely on the
bulbous phallus she had selected, the German girl raised
her hand and delivered a series of hard slaps to the bare
cheeks held in place to receive them.

'Ow. Ow, that stings. Ow! Ow! Ooh.' She arched her back and pressed down, mouth wide with the intensity of it all. 'Oo-oo-ooh, Jee-sus. I swear I'd come before the bum was even warm with this fucking monster. You'll have to give it a whirl, kid.'

'Helg, stop playing with *her*. Come and suck my big cock, will ya? *Puh-leeze*.' The petulant demand came from a second frame where, in the absence of a male guinea pig, Niamh had been kitted out with a strap-on as generously proportioned as Judith's shaft. In complementary fashion to its sister apparatus (though each could be converted into the other), the cross piece had a centre space that granted access to the genital organs from below during the disciplinary process.

'Nevie will wait for her turn. First – like she says – Yoodit gives it the whirl some more.' The next set of smacks notched desire to a new height and a dozen more brought Judith right to the brink. Then she realised with a lurch that that was it: the 'play' was done. No amount of squirming could quite duplicate the reaction of her hips to spanking, so she was stranded on the brink of climax, grinding her teeth.

'Helga, don't be so fucking mean. Helga!' But it was no use: the pigtailed head was bent to the task of securing Niamh's dildo so that its back spur hooked over the pubic mound. That accomplished, the new victim got the treatment with the flat of the hand until she too was writhing in the throes of genital over-stimulation.

'*So, meiner kinder*, it is the time to learn patience, yes?' Helga giggled and clapped her hands. 'We can have nice red bottoms and keep you – what is it? – hanging up.'

'Hanging *on*, Helga. But don't you dare leave us strapped to these bloody things for a minute longer.'

'A little more smacking will be good for you, I think. It is a fine game, *ja*?'

'*Nein*.' The bark of denial jerked all heads in the direction of the door where Constance stood shaking her head. 'However, it gives me the idea for another game, young lady.' She took a cane from the cupboard and bent it into an arc 'One that you may not find quite so appealing. Untie these two at once!'

The command obeyed, the three stood in a row before the stern-faced mistress making, to say the least, a sluttish crew. Not only were they naked apart from their assorted T-shirts and boots, but Judith could smell the secretions smeared over her thighs and her companion looked as though she wanted to disown the appendage that bobbed in front of her.

'Ankles, Helga. Now!' The slim figure bent at the waist and hands gripped below the muscled calves. Constance raised the length of rattan and administered six cuts the force of which had Judith catching her breath in sympathy. But the recipient made no reaction except to straighten, hands by her sides, only the clenched fists hinting at the effort it was taking to maintain composure.

'I seem to have arrived at the right moment to set up a small servicing exercise, and a nicely mutual one.' Constance's gaze moved between the two crotches with a little smile. 'Fetch the sleeping mat from the ante-room, Niamh, if you would. That's it; now lay it out in the space here. And if you lie down on your back . . . Do I need to say more?'

While Niamh unrolled the pad, Helga was ordered to the unadorned frame where Judith fixed in place the leather bands. Then the Irish girl held the strap-on upright while Judith eased herself slowly down onto it. With a little care it slid steadily into the well-lubricated opening and Niamh's 'Right on, kiddo' confirmed that the other end was properly located to do its business.

'Now take your time, girls. We want you both well satisfied. And for the duration I shall do my best to curb

174

my young employee's appetite for impromptu games.' Constance slashed the cane through the air twice and its noise made Judith give silent thanks that for once it was not going to connect with *her* behind. She began to rock gently, eyes on the eyes of her partner below, relishing every nuance of expression in the mobile features. There was a distinct frisson, too, in the repeated sound of supple rattan impacting buttock flesh to her side, and while Judith had no plan to draw it out, neither was she of a mind to hurry the climax already building. When it came it was sudden and brutal, flinging her forward on to the bucking body beneath to grind against its final thrusts. As the sensations ebbed Judith eased up and back, the air between them rich with the scent of their excitement.

She looked up at the purple-barred rump fastened to the frame and the tearful face with a pang of remorse at her indulgence. Constance, however, was stroking the angry weals she had raised with undisguised relish. 'Our Helga marks up beautifully, does she not?' She put the cane back on the shelf and glanced at Judith with a smile. 'Don't feel bad, I should have found some excuse in your absence. Though you could of course assuage any guilt with a little aftercare, if you liked? There is lotion on the shelf and –' she tossed aside a sheen of blonde hair and looked down at the glistening object that sprouted obscenely from Niamh's crotch '– I daresay the phallus can be called upon once more to work some restorative magic.'

It could indeed, and to such effect that the post-orgasmic Helga took charge of further games on the declared assumption that Constance was gone for the night. It proved correct, with the result that the frames were thoroughly tested by sweating bodies that writhed and jerked in all manner of blends of pain and pleasure. At last, with their energies spent, Niamh's stash of cold white wine was like a gift from heaven.

That was then. Now, as Judith fumbled in her bag for the mobile phone that was doing duty as a travelling clock, it seemed more like something that had been planted by the devil himself. Squinting at the small screen, she tried to bring the image of a clock face into focus. Shit. It couldn't be, could it? But however much she willed it into a different configuration, the digital hands pointed stubbornly to twenty minutes past twelve. Judith struggled into a sitting position, memories of the night's excesses crowding back into her aching brain. As if to underline the point, there was a groan from the figure crammed into the bunk beside her which stirred then pulled the covers up over its head. Muttering imprecations, Judith hauled herself up and clutched at the bedside cabinet while a wave of nausea passed. She was hot and sticky and her head throbbed fit to burst. Jesus. It was Friday morning – correction, afternoon – and Sandra was going to appear. Could in fact well be on her way already. Oh fuck.

Bending carefully, she retrieved a sweatshirt and pulled it on, then peered out into the corridor. She heard a snatch of distant conversation and a door banged somewhere below. But on their top floor there was only the sound of Niamh's steady breathing broken by the occasional snuffle, so Judith ducked into the neighbouring bathroom and locked the door. After forcing herself to swallow down a glass of water, she located the number she wanted and pressed the call button. It rang and rang until at last there was a click and a flustered voice came on the line.

'Nemesis Archive. I, um, can I help you?'

'Is that Penny?'

'Miss Judith. Thank the Lord it's only you. Er, I mean, not a proper customer. Oh, you know what I'm trying to say. Sandra isn't here, you see.'

'God, has she left already?'

'No, not quite. I think she said the one o'clock train. Yes, Miss James, I *have* switched it on.'

'Right then: back in place *now*.' Judith winced slightly at the sharp command in her ear: plainly the microphone had just been activated. 'Good afternoon, Judith. I trust you are keeping up the good work in the capital, as I am endeavouring to do here. Now Penelope, I shall finish with the butcher's dozen as we have learned to call it. You will count them out, if you please.'

Thwack! 'Ow. One.'

Thwack! 'Ow. Two.'

Despite the state of her head it was hard not to smile. She was being treated to a live leathering of the sort that premium-rate numbers often promised but rarely delivered. True, it was in audio-mode only, but as she listened her mind had no difficulty in supplying pictures of the plump little buttocks all aquiver as they acquired the square-edged marks characteristic of the tawse.

Thwack! 'Ow! Twelve.'

Thwack! 'Ow-ow! Thirteen.' There was a perceptible pause, after which the Director's tone was a touch frosty.

'I'm waiting, Penelope.'

'Oh I'm sorry, Miss James. Thank you for disciplining me, Miss James.'

'You are not quite appreciative enough, I fear. Perhaps a repeat performance may evoke something more like real gratitude. But our caller will have better things to do than listen to the sound of your bottom acquiring a deeper shade of red. Indeed she may wish to meet our secretary at the station. Judith, I shall be with you next weekend, as you know. In the meantime I shall look forward to being given an account of the proceedings.'

And with that the connection – if not the correction – was terminated. Meet Sandra, eh? Had the boss got wind of what had passed between them or had she sensed the motivation behind the call? Either way, that was exactly what she had in mind and she had better get moving.

* * *

A little early at St Pancras Judith patrolled the concourse, glad of the bustle to divert her from too much self-analysis. After all, there was no point in beating herself up for rampant sexual indulgence until she could discover more of the secretary's state of mind. What was *her* take on their rabid coupling almost a week after the event itself? And what exactly would she be expecting from the weekend?

Then it all happened quickly – too quickly – for Judith realised that the train had actually pulled in while she was pacing about. It was already disgorging its passengers and through a gap there was a momentary clear view of the fair-haired, suited figure striding in her direction. Something about the swing of the tailored hips hit her full in the gut and Judith ducked behind a vending machine. Heart fluttering, she watched Sandra make her way towards the paying toilets and disappear inside. Jesus, she had to get a grip or she would end up following the girl she had come to meet all the way back to the AOC.

In the kiosk sat a tanned young woman with electric-blue eyeshadow and when she put her magazine aside to take a customer's money Judith glimpsed its cover with a shock of recognition. While the Archive's collection of so-called photo-stories was patchy, the three *Alexis & Star* volumes were certainly in it. So if her reading matter was anything to go by, the attendant was not only into spanking but into the variety known to aficionados as 'ff'. It was a fair bet she was one of the sisterhood and, it seemed, not concerned about concealing the fact. Cheered, Judith was struck with a sudden madcap idea and she went up to the window feeling in her pocket for change.

'Nice pics. That first one is the best of the series too, I reckon.' She pushed a coin forward under the glass. While there was a hint of curiosity the eyes watching hers were giving nothing away so Judith nodded in the direction of the entrance. In for a penny, in for a pound. 'Friend of mine just went in, the one with the ponytail. Thing is, she's been bad. And we know what that means, yeah? Needs her bum warming, like right now. OK, I've got a nerve asking, but d'you think, maybe . . .' Judith let the sentence hang, looking meaningfully at the door that opened off the back of the cubicle. There was a short pause then the girl's features broke into a grin.

'Jeez, mate. They told me to expect some queer requests in this job but that takes the bloody biscuit.' The down-to-earth response came dressed in Strine and Judith grinned back.

'Five minutes. Ten tops. OK?'

'Go fetch her. But you sure she's up for this?'

'She *will* be, promise. I mean, she might kick up a bit, but that's part of the game, right?'

'Yeah, I guess.'

The space fitted out with central washbasins was unoccupied save for Sandra frowning at her reflection with a lipstick in her hand. Before she had a chance to register her appearance, Judith was behind her covering her eyes.

'Guess who.'

'J-Jude.'

'Now you listen to me. I know a certain secretary who didn't tell her lover when she was arriving so that she could meet her. In fact the little minx didn't even send a message during the week. Not even so much as a text.'

'Jude, I didn't know – I wasn't sure –' Judith moved the hand down over her mouth and their eyes met in the mirror.

'Ssh. The point is, we have a treatment for bad girls, don't we? Do I need to remind you? Bad girls get –'

'Spanked. Bad girls get spanked. But –'

'Right, young lady. Then *you* are coming with *me*.' Judith took a firm hold of the arm and marched its owner to the exit. The attendant was waiting to usher them into the small back room.

'Be my guests. I'll keep the crowds back.'

'Jude, you can't. Not here. Oh please.' Despite the words she made no attempt to impede the trousers and pants being rolled carefully down to crotch level. Judith sat on the edge of the desk with one leg spread and pushed the body forward till the bare belly pressed against her thigh.

'Now you stay put and no arguments.' She ran her hand over the creamy skin of the buttocks that swelled out above the material bunched into the tantalisingly dark cleft. Judith began to smack, falling into a steady rhythm that was punctuated by the little gasps and cries of her plainly not-unwilling victim. She glanced over to see what looked very like a camera lens through the gap in the door and gave it the thumbs-up behind Sandra's back.

'You need to understand, sweetheart –' *smack! smack!* '– a spanking has to be given –' *smack! smack!* '– on the spot. Caning, now –' *smack! smack!* '– as you may find out one day –' *smack! smack!* '– is improved with a bit –' *smack! smack!* '– of anticipation. But when a girl's simply been asking for it –' *smack! smack! smack!* '– then it's got to be pants down –' *smack! smack! smack!* '– over the knee –' *smack! smack! smack!* '– just as soon as –' *smack! smack! smack!* '– her lover –' *smack! smack! smack!* '– gets the chance.' Six further slaps were hard enough to force some real cries of pain, then Judith was on her knees peeling down the damp gusset of the knickers. She parted the sparsely haired labia and pushed her tongue as deep as she could into the tangy folds.

'Oh God, Jude. *Jude.*'

On the way out Judith found in her pocket the printed characters she had once been given as a password. She scribbled directions on the back and pressed the paper into the Australian's hand.

'Cheers, I owe you. Take this, it'll get you into all sorts of fun and games. Hope the photos come out.'

'They're digital – for a new website.'

'Well, good luck.'

Seriously in need of release herself Judith steered the compliant Sandra into the nearest taxi. In the AOC building no one was about and they took the stairs to the upper floor two at a time. As she jammed a chair up under the door handle of their room Judith felt Sandra's hands round her waist undoing the hook of her trousers. Good, they were of one mind. At some stage there would have to be talk, but for the present, words could be left safely unsaid.

19

Theory and Practice

Constance's bid to take the lead in agenda-setting for the AOC was not going well. With the aim of highlighting its teaching mission, she had hand-picked some dozen individuals from a group of beginners in the disciplinary arts. With the aid of the newly acquired apparatus, the plan was to show that parallel genital stimulation could turn the discomfort of moderate corporal punishment into a fully sexual experience. Thus would the nervous novice become set on the path of greater severity and – so the theory went – greater fulfilment. One to one, with a partner in private, it could have worked, but what Constance had overlooked was the group setting of her attempted demonstration. While some of the women involved might have been persuaded to take up position onstage for a dose of paddle or strap, and even to bare their bottoms to a degree in the process, to take a dildo between the legs proved for each and every one to be unacceptable. Public penetration was, it seemed, an act too far.

So Helga and Niamh, fetchingly clad in contrasting black and white catsuits, stood idle by the frame while the organiser tried to cajole even one of the shrinking neophytes into coming forward from the dimly lit benches into the spotlight. But no assurances of the joys in store seemed able to banish the attack of modesty that had overcome them all and Constance was obliged to admit defeat. In the end she found only one way out: to have recourse to the young skinhead from an earlier session whose eagerness to do anything at all had her bared and impaled on the swivelling dildo in a trice. It was a properly inexperienced and satisfyingly plump arse that she presented to Constance's wicked paddle strap but, unfortunately for the point of the exercise, she was already so much into the whole thing that phallic encouragement was quite surplus to requirements.

The ecstatic cries of 'Oh yes!', 'Yes, yes, yes!' and 'Does that mother sting!' that rang round the room were enough to make Judith squirm in her seat. She herself was not dressed in her usual manner, having been kitted out in an uncharacteristic 'little black number' in order to play some as yet unspecified part in the later proceedings. It was rare to see Constance anything other than completely in charge of a situation and she had agreed readily; but now the prospect of being involved in the present fiasco was less than appealing. Judith gave Sandra's hip a squeeze and they exchanged deprecating looks as the ultra-orgasmic vocalising from the platform eventually died away.

'Any more like that and I'm away for the earplugs.' The aside from front row centre brought a laugh but also a good-natured spattering of applause as the object of it clomped back to her place tugging the denim skirt back over a scarlet backside. On instruction, the apparatus was modified to accommodate a change of gender, after which the assistants installed themselves, flanking Judith and Sandra on the bench along the side wall.

'She has the makings of a real enthusiast, I think we have to own. Not, however, quite what I had it in mind to show you tonight. That will have to wait for another time. Instead, I propose we move straight on to the exhibition that I had scheduled for a little later. It will not, I should say, be one for the faint-hearted.' While

Constance worked at recovering her poise, Judith was busy removing the hand that had crept up under the hem of her short dress.

'Stop it, Helga,' she ordered out of the corner of her mouth and shifted her weight towards Sandra.

However, the secretary was not in a responsive mood. 'I don't like the sound of that,' she said quietly but firmly, and it was a moment before Judith realised with relief that she was referring to what had been said from the front.

'Me neither,' chipped in an Irish voice from the other side. 'You're a spanker like me, girl, right? So why don't we just leave the hardcore merchants to it? I got a web stash of juicy stuff – y'know, pics and clips – and we can get online next door. If you fancy a look.'

'OK?' Sandra was glancing sideways at Judith and she nodded.

'OK.' With her track record she could hardly come the jealous mate. 'But don't do anything I wouldn't.' The moment the two had slipped away she felt Helga's touch again on bare flesh and this time it seemed churlish to object. Judith sighed. On reflection her parting remark had not been well chosen.

'I do not like this girlfriend system.' Helga pouted and stared at her trainers. 'My *offizier* is the same. When her special lady arrives she sees only her. I am –' But Judith was spared the full complaint for at that point Constance clapped her hands to bring the variously chattering members of the audience to order. As if on cue the door that led to the bar below opened and a head poked in.

'Ah, Ilya. Send our guests up as soon as you like, and you may tell them that we shall be ready for the full display.' The instruction produced an expectant hush that the speaker was quick to build on. 'Friends, I had hoped to illustrate how pain and pleasure may intermingle even in those who do not regard themselves as

184

unduly perverse. Now, perforce, we leap ahead to a further point in the process, one where we shall encounter a young male for whom pain will be shown to lead directly to pleasure. Pleasure, that is – and let us be clear about it – of the most obvious kind shown by his sex.'

There was a stir and a giggle hastily stifled from one of the formerly reluctant subjects but Judith scarcely noticed. For Constance's words had brought an image to mind and with it an idea of whom she might be talking about. Could he just be – unlikely as it might seem – the one whose blatant 'pleasure' she had witnessed before at *very* close quarters? The thought of being involved again, and for the benefit of spectators, gave Judith a twinge of pure lust and she sat up straight as the door opened once more.

But the man who entered could have been almost anyone for he was encased from head to foot in black. Male he surely was from the unmistakable package that bulged from the groin area, but beyond that who could say? Judith clicked her tongue in frustration. From the benches, though, came a different kind of stir and she realised what was causing it. Anyone who had dipped into the fetish scene would expect the pleasure of leather wrapped tight over thighs or pectorals and may even find it a little hackneyed. But the head was a different matter. The construction of the present mask – and it fitted like a second skin – made few concessions to anatomy, so that eyes, ears, nose and mouth were served by the same circular holes in the stretched material. Now she studied it, even Judith found the effect a little sinister; for the beginners who made up most of the gathering it was evidently quite disturbing.

The unnamed figure had come bearing an instrument that reinforced the impression. A yard or so the thickness of a finger that was bonded into an ivory grip, it smacked weightily into the palm of Constance's glove as she toyed with it. Neither whip nor cane exactly, but something that might very well combine the more painful properties of each. Tucking the weapon under her arm, she guided the subject into place on the apparatus and secured him at hand and foot.

'His mistress has asked me to prepare the boy for her arrival –' stroking the leather implement against the leather-clad buttocks, she smiled with evident anticipation '– and, given the protective covering he enjoys, I shall not hold back.' Turning from the audience Constance raised her arm and delivered the first stroke. In the total silence that had fallen there was a split-second whoosh of air and a meaty *thwack* that set off a collective wince. Rising on to her toes, the chastiser slammed down a second and then a third, fourth and fifth in quick succession. Even then there was no let-up, for not until Judith had counted to a breathless twenty did the blows come to a stop. Helga caught her eye, mouthing an 'ouch' with a hand to her own bottom and Judith grinned. A provisional recognition of the dimpled behind was confirmed by the stoicism of its owner and she was feeling decidedly hot. Who but Max would suffer such a vigorous attack in complete silence? However, Constance was not done. She leaned forward, put out a hand and dug thumb and forefinger into her recent target. There was a muted grunt that became a cry as the tormentor squeezed and rolled the assaulted area on each side in turn.

'Ha! Our subject has found his voice and I shall help him use it. The flesh is scarcely yet hard under its skin and the raising of real welts is going to take work. Not, of course, that we begrudge him it.' Judith's mind circled warily around the question of what would count as real in this context: as the blows recommenced and rained down she was beginning half to dread what they would see when the thrashed arse was eventually stripped bare. But only half. Constance's words showed that she knew – as only one in thrall to a flagellant enthusiasm *could* know – that the ritual inflicting of pain was an intoxicant that set the pulse racing and the head spinning.

'Setting him up good and proper, eh girl? Reckon it's time we had a look at the results.' The soft voice from behind speaking her innermost thoughts made Judith jump as if she had been caught with her eye to a keyhole. There was a hint of astringent scent mingled with garlic.

'Gwen, where the fuck did you spring from?' She kept it to an excited undertone. 'So it *is* Max – poor bastard.'

'Don't be like that, you know he loves it. Well, once the effect wears off a tad, natch. Um, guess we'll go and take over, yeah?' The brisk if muttered interchange had coincided with the last of the swingeing stripes and the black girl came round the bench to raise her by the elbow. Averting her eyes from Helga's questioning stare, Judith let herself be steered out into the light.

'Ah, Mistress Gwendoline, welcome. I have tried to prepare the boy to be handed over to an esteemed colleague such as yourself. If his vocalising was any guide then I may hope to have succeeded. Judith will, as arranged, help you in any way you require. So I'll, er, leave you to it.' Constance dabbed with a handkerchief at the beads of perspiration on her forehead and withdrew. Why the awkward deference to one who – at Judith's last reckoning – had still been barred from entry to the AOC? It was a mystery, but for the present there was a job to do and Gwen was motioning her towards the fastenings at the waistband of Max's trousers.

'OK, guys, you got the picture, yeah? My assistant –' she flashed a wink in Judith's direction '– is gonna unveil this peachy bum that's just been given the treatment. Tough, eh? I could see a few winces. But I'd put money on it there's not one of you ain't dying to give it the once over. So come on kids, gather round, and we'll all inspect the damage together.' Judith watched as the initially diffident young women were won round by Gwen's performance. It was an unlikely role, but then the immaculate white trousers were equally unexpected. What else did the lady have up her sleeve – or perhaps that should be leg? She grinned to herself and unzipped the panel that covered the part of the anatomy under discussion.

'We got some ace colours here girls, right enough.' Gwen traced a particularly deep weal with a fingertip. 'But you don't need to feel too sorry for the boy, and we are going to show you exactly why right now.' Judith anticipated what was coming and reached down to the codpiece that bulged beneath. Another zip was easily dealt with and she whipped the cover away with a flourish to reveal the sizeable erection that was Max's trademark. The girls clustered round, craning their necks for a view of the distended cock which oozed a drop of fluid from the urethra.

'Good boy.' The speaker ran a hand over the back of the tethered figure's neck. 'Now you'll do one more thing for us.' She touched the instrument of punishment to the swollen buttocks on display. 'It's gonna be six strokes and six spurts. No more, no less. Right?'

'Yes, mistress.' The words were muffled by the still-secured headpiece but perfectly audible. 'Then, if my helper will assume the position and give our subject just a little priming ...' Judith squatted as required under the frame and took the purple seeping head between her lips. The thing jacked and quivered as she moved up and down the shaft. This was not going to take long.

'OK, here we go.' Right. Now she was going to give them a display to remember. Judith pulled back, tongue out and tasted the salt flow that splashed into her mouth with each cut. Then at the count of six it all happened rather quickly. Gwen took her by the arm, hissing,

'Don't you *dare* swallow', while she tossed a tube to a goggle-eyed blonde. 'His bum could use some of this and there's plenty of the other cream left, if you get me. Help yourselves, kids. Oh, and you can remove the hood. We gonna take ten.'

In the dressing room she pushed Judith on to the table, ripped aside the thong and rammed the stock of the rod into her sopping cunt. Then they were glued mouth to mouth, tongues twisting in the wash of Max's sperm until Judith's spasms wrenched them apart and she fell back gasping.

'Jesus fuck, Gwen. Now you get those trousers off or I'm going to lay this across *your* arse.' There was – for once – no argument from the truculent domina. In seconds flat Judith's face was buried in the cunt that was satisfyingly ripe from the recent exercise, and in seconds more the black lady was in the throes of her own orgasm.

Nonetheless, it was more like twenty minutes than the promised ten before they were composed enough to make a return to the scene of the demonstration. Not that either need have worried, for the once-bashful young ladies were plainly having a whale of a time. While two were attending to the punished bottom, Max's uncovered head was busy between the spread legs of a third and two more were vying to suck the still-rampant organ. And judging by the spattered chins of each, its reserves seemed still not to be fully spent. There was just one discordant note in the form of a petulant Helga serving to support the one receiving the benefit of an expert tongue. But before she could step in Gwen had the sticky member in her hand and was pushing Judith down on to her knees.

'You started it, sister, so you better drain the last drop. And you got my say-so to drink it down this time.' To the sound of the filthiest chuckle she had ever heard, Judith did her duty and in less than a minute her tongue was again coated in the salty spurts. It was the cue for the demonstration to come to a close and the young women headed, chattering, for the bathroom at the top of the stairs. Once Max was released, Gwen shepherded him in the same direction and Judith sank down on a bench to collect herself. It had been quite a session. Then the other door opened and a head poked in.

'You're all done, then.' Sandra shuffled in awkwardly. 'Look, Jude, I don't know what you were thinking, but . . . What I mean is, well, Niamh is very persuasive and she took some pictures of me. You know, of – er – and then she, well she . . .' Red faced, the secretary looked at Judith with a silent appeal.

'Muff diving, that's the term she uses. You're going to end up on one of her T-shirts, kid. Not that the woman in the street is going to recognise you. But don't feel bad on my account, San. Five minutes ago you'd have caught me sucking on the boy's big lollipop. These things happen – especially in a place like this.' She took Sandra's arm and gave her a hug, touched and more than a little guilty. Mutual confession was good but on her side it had to be strictly limited. No way was she about to own up to unexpected and drastic sex with Gwen the moment Sandra's back was turned. Jesus, it had to stop. She had to get a grip.

20

Librarian

On the Saturday morning Judith woke at eight-thirty
with the threesome of the night before fresh in her
memory. Faced with a moody Helga, the young Irish
woman had relocated to their room and Sandra had
been surprisingly willing, even keen, to explore the
possibilities. Maybe she was branching out or maybe
she was just trying to keep her end up in a rather
intimidating environment. Whatever the psychology of
it, Judith was feeling drained by the violence of earlier
passion and had after a while left them to it. Through
fitful sleep she had remained aware of continuing
activity until sinking eventually into oblivion. Now,
stretching languorously in the top bunk she had re-
treated to, Judith peered cautiously over the side of it.
The back of a well-known body, motionless save for its
steady breathing, showed that Niamh must have returned to the fold next door. And Sandra looked out for
the count, which was providential. For she had been
asked by Miss James to make a delivery that morning
which had until that moment slipped her mind entirely.

At ten past nine, making her way up Gower Street
towards the British Library, Judith felt a strange
tingling at the prospect of the meeting to come. She
knew nothing of the new Keeper of the euphemistically
termed Rare Books except that for the first time in the

collection's history the position was held by a woman. Surprising was too weak a word for it in the light of her own encounters with the institution. Doing research into Edwardian memoirs a few years back, Judith had been left in no doubt what was thought of the access she had been granted to its graphically sexual materials, but then the reading-room staff who had looked icily down their middle-aged male noses would not have been responsible for the decision to appoint. Perhaps senior management had thought it politically expedient to have a female figurehead at the department they would rather did not exist at all: any scandal that might be stirred up might more easily be deflected by a feminine presence at the helm. But that, of course, would depend on what the lady was like and *that* was what Judith, in a very few moment, was going to find out.

Judith crossed into the tree-lined street of stone-built houses at the side of the Library complex and made her way along to the end terrace of a small crescent that was home to its disreputable contents. She stood in front of a short flight of steps looking up at the discreet sign bearing the letters BL where none had been before. As a formal messenger from one director to another, the side entrance she was accustomed to was not really on, so she took a deep breath and mounted to press the wall button.

'Yes? Oh – ah – Judith. Yes. Judith, of course, come in. Straight on through.' The voice rasped in the small speaker, loud enough to make her flinch. But she took another lungful of air and turned the handle with a firm grip. At the end of a passage the door stood half open and she had already pushed it wide at the point that the noises emerging from within could only allow for one interpretation. Across the desk between a monitor and a stack of books a bare midriff mashed into an untidy heap of papers while a veined shaft pumped deep into the distended anus. Rooted to the spot, wordless, Judith saw with a hallucinatory clarity how the stretched

192

membrane of flesh gripped the organ and followed the rhythm of the penetration: push in, draw out; in, out; in, out.

'Yes – uh – oh, yes! – nngg – don't – uuhh – stop – nnnggg – darling – uuhhuuhh – boy.' The spell was broken by the gasped words and the head turned enough for an eye to deliver a wink as blatantly lewd as any she had seen. Far from stopping, the bare-legged young man brought matters quickly to a conclusion, apparently quite undisturbed by Judith's presence. Her own loins responded in sympathy as the thrusts became deep and fast and, as he cried out, telltale double-edged marks came into view under the hem of the shirt. She turned away as the couple separated, all at once queasily embarrassed, and heard the lad being dismissed to dress in another room.

'Judith, I hope I didn't offend you by finishing off despite your arrival. You do have a certain *reputation*, you know.' The woman wriggled into the worn denims bunched around her thighs and closed the tight zip carefully over the pubic bush. She stood revealed as tall and slim with a long face, around which fine fair hair fell to the shoulders. Thirty-five, maybe, and while not pretty nor exactly handsome there was a force of personality that made those things of no account. Judith watched her push her feet into a pair of leather flip-flops and pull up the frayed sleeves of a sweatshirt as if ready for business.

'Dress down unless an absolute no-no, that's my motto. Weekdays there's a sharp young miss to fend off the suits across the road. But I am forgetting myself. How rude. Jane Barrett-Greene. With an *e*.' For a blank second it wasn't clear which of the three she was referring to, then the fog cleared. As in Graham, of course. Who knows, she might be related.

'Judith Wilson. But then you know that.' They shook hands, Judith wishing she could get more of a grip on the situation.

'I should hate you to get the wrong impression. I incline rather to our own sex, as I gather do you, dear girl. But there is nothing quite like a good arse-fucking to set one up for the day, I find. The boy's a lovely secretary and with a cane to the bum he sprouts a veritable *pole* of a cock. Such a shame to waste it.' The blue-grey eyes were unashamed and the lips curved in a wry amusement that befitted the wrapping of low sexual talk in the received pronunciation of the Home Counties. Judith thought of another young man with the propensity referred to: her mouth had milked that organ whereas the librarian opted for the anus. Whichever one chose, those stuck in the missionary position were going to see an act beyond the pale. As the notion struck her the last traces of awkwardness fell away and she smiled the smile of complicity with a fellow pervert. And then remembered that she had come on an errand.

Twenty minutes later they were ensconced in a book-lined den abutting the main office armed with steaming mugs of mocha that had been dosed with a good slug of Laphraoig. 'Try it. We need a bracer and I make a point of ignoring the purist mission to take all the fun out of life.' When Judith had expressed the view that the combination was startling but drinkable her host seemed satisfied and took a letter knife to the package she had been given. Out came a folding wallet that contained a set of six recordable CDs, each marked with a single letter of the alphabet scrawled on the face. Jane leaned forward and booted up the computer on the table in front of them.

'I think it would be a good idea if you were to forget you ever saw these, Judith. But I can't resist showing you a short extract. Now what I'm looking for is on 'B', I believe.' They waited while she loaded the disc into the tray, located the drive and brought its contents on-screen. Again there was scant information in the display: no more than a list of initials and dates. 'Okey-dokey, here we are. Look closely and I think you'll find you've seen this fellow somewhere before. But not attired quite as he is here.' Judith peered at the grainy image of a portly man in suspender belt and stockings, horsed at the disposal of a mannish woman with a rod. Then he turned his head and the picture came suddenly into sharper focus.

'Oh God. That's thingumajig at the Home Office, convener of the Libraries Committee. I actually met him when Harry . . .' Shit. Judith broke off, biting her lip. It was the last name she had wanted to bring up in the present meeting.

'My predecessor, Mr Jameson. Yes, he was on friendly terms with our man in the brothel. Shame he turned out to be such a bad lot.' Judith felt the gaze on her as she tried, eyes down, to quell a rising flush. 'Don't berate yourself, dear girl, he had a lot of us fooled. And he's gone. New era now. And that is the point of it all, Judith.' She stopped the file playing and tapped the wallet. 'While we have these, with other key players featuring therein, and are *known* to have them, the continuing existence of our little domain is assured.' Jane stood and contemplated her audience with the air of an orator about to deliver the keys to the kingdom. 'Now I don't approve of blackmail and I'd make a guess that you're with me there. But quite apart from our own security, the irony of the situation is irresistible, don't you know? Here we have one of the great and the good who would like nothing better than to close us down for documenting exactly those things he does in secret himself. Cross-dressing and caning: splendid sport! We think so and he plainly thinks so; yet we are able to survive only because, if it came to the point, we could *show* that he does. Ha!'

'That's brilliant.' Warmed by the speaker's zest, Judith drained her coffee. The department, it seemed, was in capable hands.

'So you may tell Samantha these will be as secure as if sealed in the proverbial vault. And now, if I can interest you in a refill –' the librarian took the pot from its hotplate and reached for the bottle of malt whisky '– I should adore the latest gossip from the outfit in Soho. I understand there has been something of a power struggle at the top.'

While the mugs were recharged, Judith acknowledged her own Director's dissatisfactions but stressed that as far as she knew the problems had been ironed out. She left it vague – questions about Miss James's activities always made her uneasy – but then Jane surprised her.

'I'm not expecting you to tell tales out of school, Judith, so I'll just say what I heard. It was that Samantha had made a special trip to the AOC to do a kind of penance. Not a surprising act in itself – it's no secret she goes on retreat to Brittany for that purpose – but to choose Constance, well. At first it seemed the strangest thing, but then I thought again. To submit to the whip of her rival might look like foolhardiness – to say the least – but once she has survived . . .' She let the sentence hang in the air and Judith began to nod.

'You mean, after the ordeal is over, Constance has done her worst –'

'And who, then, is the taller figure?'

'Yes, of course. And what sets the seal on it is that the whipping was sought to redress other wrongs. Nothing to do with the fights over the AOC.'

'Got it in one. So the flagellator loses out all ways except the obvious one. Easy-peasy: all you need is the courage to put yourself at the mercy of one of the cruellest women I know. Ha! That's the difference between me and Samantha James, I'm afraid.'

'And me. I actually saw her – and that was *her* idea – near the start of the night.' Judith shuddered. 'No way, and I mean *no way*.'

'Oh, I think if it came to it you might surprise yourself, dear girl. But tell me, what do *you* reckon to the new place? Are you having fun?' She pulled the stool closer in and looked expectantly at her visitor.

'Fun? Er, well, I suppose . . . Yes, of course, it's a lot of fun, but . . .' For the second time Judith tailed off and then grimaced. This was ridiculous, tying herself in knots. 'What I mean is, it's been an ace romp through the discarded knickers – in and out of the AOC – but I've been thinking it's time to call a halt. With all wearers but one, that is.'

'Ah, issues. Do I detect unresolved issues, and of a sexual nature?' The expression was keenly curious and Judith felt a confessional urge stirring. Her host glanced over at two easy chairs by the ornate fireplace of the original interior. 'Let's get comfortable then you can tell all. I'll be the good Dr Freud, not one of the latter-day pushy talkers we're plagued with, so no interruptions to impede the flow. But may I recommend – just to get the ball rolling – that you start by casting your mind back to the most explosive fuck of the past week.'

The request was forthright, even a little startling, coming as it did from such a recent acquaintance and in an accent whose reign at the BBC was long over. But the whisky had loosened her tongue and she began, haltingly at first, to talk about the surprise encounter with Gwen and its climax in the dressing room. The librarian was, as promised, a good listener and it was not long before Judith found herself working around to a statement of what was bothering her.

'Thing is, I know I have a problem saying no, but I can deal with that. I mean, I did before, but the chosen one was so fucking jealous –'

'That she thought you were up to something even when you were as pure white as the driven snow. Sorry to cut in, dear girl, but I've been there myself, and it's no joke. One's doing one's damnedest to keep the eyes averted from the delectable minxes on every side only to be rewarded by suspicion and mistrust.'

'Exactly. But that won't happen this time, though I shouldn't tempt fate by saying that. She's a sweetie – a bit odd – but a real sweetie. And thinking about that makes me feel even worse. I mean, why did I pick on violent stuff with Gwen to talk about when I had a session with Sandra that was off the end of the wet scale altogether? That girl can be every bit as horny and she's a lot easier on the nerves.'

'Well, danger is a powerful stimulant, but it has a habit of escalating. A very nasty habit.' The emphatic words made Judith look sharply at the face that had gone deadly earnest and rather pale. 'Ha. How very *un*therapeutic of me. Loading one's own stuff on to the other. Let's say no more except that I went far down that road a few years ago. Far *too* far. But leaving that aside, I get the feeling you are ready to make some decision.'

'I think so. I just can't quite seem to take the step.' Suddenly helpless, she longed for someone else to take the reins. When she allowed them, thoughts and counter-thoughts had made their procession through her mind without any resolution; the time had come for action. 'How can I get out of this, Jane? Please, can you tell me?'

'No, I can't do that; and if I *were* able, I wouldn't.' The Keeper of the disreputable books shook her head solemnly. 'But I have a modest proposal to make. When I was in my late teenage years, and with not dissimilar problems to those you're presented with, I received some help. You see, dear girl, weighing up and choosing can become endless: it is always possible to put off implementing a decision. Well I had a wicked step-mother who was only too keen to draw mental anguish out into pain of the body. In fact she rather used me as a testing ground for the development of her philosophy.' Judith sat forward, ears pricked. It was a relief to get a break from self-examination.

'I won't burden you with a lot of details, Judith. In essence I was prone to wild episodes – sex and drugs and rock 'n' roll wasn't the half of it – in which people got hurt. Fucked with, to put it bluntly. I was a beast, albeit one who suffered periods of remorse and determination to behave better. I meant it then, but the pattern repeated, seemingly without end. Until Madame Mariselle – for that is how I addressed her – cut into my self-reproaches by placing a cane on the table. No ordinary instrument, it was constructed of a bonded resin more dense than the usual rattan yet fully flexible. She assured me that applied to a girl's derrière it would hurt like the very devil; and in the process, she said, emphasising every word, bring an end to recrimination and signal a new start. My eyes must have been out on stalks at the outlandishness of the notion – my upbringing had had no recourse to physical punishment – but after a full forty-eight hours I went to Madame and asked her to use the thing as she saw fit.' She paused as if to register the effect of her words.

'And what happened? Did she do it – and did it work?'

'Well, it depends upon what you mean by "work". Though I suppose one could say it did, after a fashion.' She gave a little laugh at Judith's impatient click of the tongue. 'The point, dear girl, is not what it did to me, but what it might do for *you*. I'm not so much sharing a remedy with you as offering you the idea to consider.' She opened a wall cupboard beside the fireplace, removed a length of black rod and handed it over for inspection. There was a disconcerting weight to it and the outer sheath had a cool, greasy feel. Judith looked up at the figure standing tall in front of her for a long moment and realised that her palms were damp with sweat. It was not as if there had been a conscious choice, rather that she had become aware of being about to act, and that hadn't taken even 48 *seconds*. She struggled to her feet out of the low chair and returned the instrument to its owner.

'So the phrase is: as you see fit.' She bowed her head briefly; a bridge had been crossed. 'Is this the, er –'

'The original? Yes, indeed. I was made a present of it when I left home. They don't, of course, require maintenance or deteriorate like the natural variety.' The librarian took Judith's hand in hers and drew her to her feet, looking into her eyes. 'It shall be twelve strokes: twelve lines drawn under the recent past, and the fire of each in atonement for it. No more words are needed. Place that upright chair here, in the centre of the room, then you may bend over it to present to me the seat of your trousers. I should advise taking a firm hold of its legs.'

'Jesus H Christ. These beauts are going to knock 'em for six.' Half an hour later Judith was bending over once more in the presence of an excited lavatory attendant aiming and re-aiming her high-resolution lens. The skill and force of the beating had left her struggling for the composure necessary to shake the disciplinary hand and conclude their business. But there was a kind of chasteness to the pain that made her curiously elated: for once an initial rush of blood to the head in place of the genitals. While Judith wanted to prolong that state until her return, she thought of one *en route* under no such constraint. So she had picked her way around the main site of the British Library to the place where, just the day before, Sandra had been summarily spanked and was pleased to find the young Australian witness of the event about to end her shift. It was the work of a moment for her older replacement to stand guard over the back room while Judith bared the throbbing mounds of punished flesh.

'Your site's going to get so many hits, girl, if I say so who shouldn't. I know that wet lips framed by stripes 'always does it for me.' She let the gentle fingers explore the welts with only a token mutter but when they wandered into the moistness in between she uttered a sharp 'No!'

'Sorry. I should have known from last time you were pretty committed, yeah?'

'Trying to be. No, make that determined to be.' Judith eased up her tight trousers over swollen flesh with an unashamed display of wincing. 'Jesus. I've known sore and sore, but this is fucking *sore*. No way am I going to do any more walking: in a cab I can at least kneel on the floor. Now I think of it my email address was on that paper I gave you, so give me a shout when you're up and running, OK?'

Reaching the AOC a little after noon, Judith found the object of her affections stirring sleepily in her bed. She nuzzled into the warm neck then found a nipple to tease with her teeth.

'Hi, Jude.' The open mouth closed on hers with an active tongue, then the young woman sank back with an odd expression on her face. 'Oh God, it's all coming back. Did we, well, er, I really do all that?'

Judith laughed. 'Sure did, honey bunch. Though it was all too much for yours truly, I'm sorry to say. Now next time . . .' Shirt unbuttoned while speaking, Judith stripped her lower half and tossed aside the quilt that was covering her lover's body. 'Now let me have a proper look. Mmm, tasty. And I bet it's really scrumptious down in here.'

'Jude, you're making me blush. Jude. Oh, Jude, that's so good . . .'

Afterwards, as Judith stood up to get dressed, she felt Sandra's hand touch her flank beside the fresh weals. She turned to see the smallest of frowns clouding the open face.

'I went to meet the new lady of the Rare Books. You know, at the BL.' Judith sat carefully down on the bed. 'San, sweetie, it was an old-fashioned seat-of-the-pants caning. No sex involved. Kind of to set the seal on a resolution I've made.' She pulled Sandra up and hugged her tight. 'When we get back I'll explain it all. Promise.'

21

Emulation

'Jude, are you sure you want to go along with this? You really think it's a good idea to bring Gregor back here after the pub?'

'San, I've given up deciding what's a good idea. What I do know is that the three of us together a tad, er, loosened up, is an appealing suggestion. The question is: are *you* sure you wouldn't rather keep the boyfriend all to yourself, on the side.'

'*Jude.* Of course not. The only thing is I haven't seen him since, since – oh God I can't think exactly, but he kind of belongs to the past. And I'm still plucking up courage to come clean about that.'

'A-ha. Are we talking skeletons, even a more recent mouldy corpse or two in the cupboard?'

'Sounds like you'd be pleased. No, it's nothing like that, but then maybe it is. I went through a phase of talking to my therapist about what happened. Only he wasn't there: I talked into the tape machine pretending to myself I was going to send it off.' Judith scanned the set but anxious face and made herself ignore the impulse to fold the girl in her arms and drag her off into an endless night of hot sex with some spanking on the side. It looked as though she ought to try and hear this out.

'OK, you made some tapes. I give the empty stacks the benefit of a lecture when something's got up my nose. Creep in quietly below and you could easily catch the sound of distant ranting. Maybe you already have.'

'Pig. You've just got to make a joke out of everything.' Then the look of irritation vanished as Sandra's eyes turned to the watch on her wrist. 'God, I'm going to be late back if I don't shift. I know it doesn't happen to you any more but I get the feeling Miss J has been waiting for an excuse to exercise her strap.'

'With a bum as delectable as yours, lover-girl, who could blame her? After all, it was Marjorie did the honours before, so our boss hasn't had so much as a peek at the unclothed moons in all their glory.'

Sandra turned a little pink and let out a giggle. 'No she has *not*. And she's not going to start today if I have anything to do with it.' She gave Judith a hug and kissed her neck. 'So Gregor and me – we'll be there nineish, OK? Don't be late.' With that she was out of the flat door and clomping down the stairs as if she did it every day. Judith shook her head, wonderingly. It was barely more than a week since she had made the first precipitous move and all of a sudden it seemed to be the secretary who was at the wheel. Well, what was wrong with that? Why not just sit back and enjoy the ride? Why not indeed. And yet, and yet . . . The internal dialogue might have a simple resolution, but Judith was left with the feeling that there was something she was missing. What she needed was a second opinion, and more than that, she needed it before the evening's rendezvous.

'Well honey, if you ask me – and of course that is exactly what you *are* doing – you are way off beam. Think about it for a minute.' Judith settled in her seat with the bottle of Pils and waited for the manager of The Phoenix to develop her point. Agony Aunt was a role Marsha warmed to and while her conclusions could be succinct there was no shortcut to them. 'Here you are, a lady of some experience in the disciplinary stakes, mature beyond her years I could say if I didn't think the ego already well inflated. And there she is, the object of your desire, in recent memory quite naive and very possibly more than a little odd. And you, dear Jude, expect me to swallow the idea that she has taken charge of your relationship?'

'When you put it like that, I admit it doesn't sound very plausible. But you should have seen the way she welcomed Niamh with open legs and now she's hauling a shadowy boyfriend into the limelight.'

'Actually quite a hunk behind the specs, Clark Kent style, so I'd hold the complaints.'

'Marsha, did I turn the offer down? I'm just trying to get you to see what I'm on about for God's sake.'

The older woman slipped through the connecting door and returned with two opened bottles. She pushed one towards Judith with a pacifying gesture. 'OK, OK. Get stuck into another and chill out, yeah?' Judith looked at her friend and confidante of several years and grinned. There were undisguised crows' feet around the eyes, but with the short wiry frame and mobile features the lady mingled easily with the gaggle of young women – town and gown – that gravitated to her. But the experience was there and, on important matters, Judith had not once known her to be mistaken. After all, that was why she'd come. She took a slug from the neck and considered.

'So you think it's a kind of act she's putting on?'

'Not consciously. It's more like a style of coping. If you were out of your depth, Jude, you'd tag along and do your best to keep up until you learned how to stay afloat. Am I right?'

'Well, I suppose.'

'Now I don't know this girlie at all well, but my guess is she's doing the opposite. She's trying to prove she can swim by jumping in where it's even deeper. Risky to say the least.'

'Wait a minute now, wise one, while I try to get my feeble mind into gear. Do you mean that I should pull her back before we, er, both end up drowning?'

'Ha!' The American gave a snort. 'Aside from the fact that we've wrung that metaphor dry – sorry – then yes. To put it another way, she could be simply trying to provoke you, if not into saying no, at least into being an active guide. To which I guess there would be no objection, taken as you are with a passion for the child.'

'Marsha, she's not *that* young. But you're right. It's all so obvious really once you've pointed it out. I must be addle-brained from too much frenetic sex.'

'That'll be the sessions with the sizzling black temptress. Which you are going to renounce once you've tied the knot. As it were.'

'Stop the maternal clucking. I'm working round to it. Honest. But to return to the subject under discussion, I've had an idea about tonight. With a smidgeon of help from a certain bartender I could pull something out of the hat. And maybe give things a push in the approved direction.'

Judith made herself wait until after ten before keeping her date and even then it was a long hour until the interruption Marsha had agreed to stage. She supposed at first it was her presence that was causing the hetero pair to be as awkward as two teenagers on a first date but then again perhaps not. Gregor himself was making an effort to entertain the company with stories of breathtakingly ill-planned expeditions of geology students to remote places, but Sandra was manifestly failing to keep the ball rolling. In fact, the stiltedness of her manner seemed almost cultivated. Maybe it was, as Marsha had maintained, and the 'boyfriend' had been tossed into the ring as a gesture without the will to back it up. Well, if so, it was a bit late: there was the lady herself advancing on them.

'Hey, kids, how ya doing? Look, I don't mean to be the party-pooper but our esteemed Assistant Director is wanted on the phone. Sounds kinda urgent.'

In the small room behind the bar Judith made herself count to fifty then returned. 'Guys, I'm sorry about this but I've got to deal with a problem. It seems that we've had a double booking of a late session in the suite and the parties are in a face-off. The caretaker can't raise Marjorie and he's in a panic, so I'll have to go and sort something.' Through the effort of lying with any degree of plausibility Judith became aware of a raised secretarial eyebrow.

'I thought the suite was out of commission all week for redecorating.' Damn. She'd forgotten all about that.

'Er, well it is. But the space these people wanted has been done, and they were dead keen. Hence the reluctance to give up their claim.' She finished brightly, cringing inside at how lame it all sounded. But there was no going back. 'So, I have a suggestion. Why don't you two go on ahead and get tucked into the supplies I laid in, yeah? Then I can just go straight there when I'm done.' Catching Sandra's eye she tried out the briefest of winks and was rewarded by the suggestion of a knowing smile.

'Well, we could do, couldn't we, Gregor? I wouldn't mind a change of scenery and Jude's flat is very, er, cosy.' The boyfriend made a face that seemed to say 'whatever' and drained his glass, providing a cue for the rest to follow suit.

'Right folks, on you go. I need to pick up some stuff from Marsha. So I'll see you when I see you, and don't do anything I wouldn't do, eh?'.

It was a full hour later when she opened her front door and tiptoed quietly along the hall. The kitchen/living room had a newly acquired sofa-bed with a drop-down arm and on this were splayed out a pair of legs, trousers

207

rumpled round the ankles. That was all she could see of their owner for, crouched over, head busy at the crotch, was his partner, all bare bum and glistening vulva. Judith moved forward to deliver a ringing slap to the irresistible target and Sandra sprang up with a yell.

'J-Jude. Oh, we were waiting, and waiting, and you didn't come, and then, well . . .' She stopped, watching as Judith tossed a brief pair of nylon shorts at her and at the startled Gregor.

'Strip and get into these, while I choose the instruments. The naughty children are going to get their sex session laced with a little discipline. And less of the familiarity, girl. You'll address me as *Miss* Judith for the purpose, if you please.' She assumed a haughty stare that befitted the high-necked blouse she wore, if not the ultra-short skirt that Marsha had insisted upon: 'Severe *and* sexy; a total knockout.' However, in the silence, the situation teetered uncomfortably on the edge of farce before Sandra put her hands on her naked hips and stuck out her tongue. It was exactly the response she needed.

'Right, young madam. It is plain you need taking in hand. We see where sparing the rod has got us, and we have the means to remedy it. Now STRIP!' Turning to go out she took in Sandra's deliciously overdone pout as she bent to obey and the fact that Gregor's wilting erection had stiffened up a treat.

When Judith returned things were looking even better. There was a neat pile of clothes on the floor and the young pair sat side by side on the sofa, naked save for the skimpy items she had handed out. Keeping hold of the trimmed sole of an old gym shoe, she laid down the cane and sat on the table with one leg stretched out along its edge.

'We'll take you first, girl. Out here and bend over.' Judith indicated the expanse of bare thigh then pushed Sandra face down across it. She felt the body heat through the thin shorts and ran a hand over the buttocks. 'Hmm, quite warm already. Soon you're going to be a whole lot warmer.'

'Yes, Miss Judith. But please don't spank me too hard.'

'Whatever it takes, my child.' The crisp smacks made the bottom cheeks bounce deliciously, and Judith wriggled the free hand between her leg and the front of the skimpy garment. She rubbed her fingers against the vulval lips and felt their seeping juice as Sandra squealed and wriggled. When she was done with the rubber sole, the secretary jumped up and rubbed in furious abandon, but the 'Mistress' had taken up the other implement and was swishing it through the air.

'Feels good in the hand, this one –' she eyed Gregor who was watching closely '– and I understand you have experience of how it feels from the other end, young man.'

'Yes. At school, a private one.'

'Excellent. Then you will know the drill, though I plan to make a small variation.' She took an upright chair from under the table and placed it facing him. 'Bend over and put your hands on the seat. No jumping up and no rubbing till I say so. It will be twelve of the best. Clear?'

'Yes.'

'Yes, what?'

'Er, yes, Miss Judith.'

'That's better. The count is now fifteen.' For a moment it seemed there might be a protest, but then he leaned forward and took hold of the sides of the chair. The muscled globes made an ideal target under the clinging material and Judith laid on two cuts across their exact centre. The boy stayed quite still and she reached under the bent body with an exploring hand. The cock was stiff, stretching from crotch almost to the hip under the tight covering, and grew palpably stiffer.

She continued to assault the bum and massage the organ until the fifteenth stroke had been applied. A full-force effort, it produced a very satisfying grunt of pain for the first time and she took time to inspect the results. All across the area, ridges of welted flesh were hard to the touch. Judith knew from experience exactly how they would feel and the thought of it cranked her own arousal a notch higher. Giving the solid erection a final squeeze, she slapped the seat with her hand.

'OK. Let's have a look at the two of you. In front of me – here.' They made a pretty sight, holding sore bottoms with creased shorts variously adorned with the darker patches of genital secretions.

'Does this mean Miss Judith is done for the night? Because, if so –'

'It seems the young lady has forgotten something. Did I not make a diagnosis just minutes ago, one concerning the effects of sparing the rod?' Judith affected an icy stare and the grin on Sandra's face faded as the words sank in.

'Oh no. Not the cane. You can't, you *wouldn't* . . .' She glanced over to the doorway as if to make a run for it then looked down at her near-nakedness with a sigh of resignation. Gregor gripped her arm then, on a sign, pulled down Sandra's shorts.

'Good heavens, girl, you've hardly been properly spanked. Look at this – scarcely a blush.' Judith jabbed a finger at the bared backside. 'Come now. Over the chair. Your young man will help hold you, and we'll keep it to a single six. But first, some lubrication where it doesn't, I'm afraid, occur by nature.' The secretary submitted with a squeak to the pessary inserted into her anus and then rather noisily to a decidedly moderate striping of her behind. Afterwards, as though having divined what was to come, she lay readily across the table for the hugely erect phallus to follow the oiled path, and Judith was quick to present her bare dripping

210

cunt to occupy the girl's mouth until the spasms at the
nether end brought them all to a shuddering release.

When the tableau disengaged, Sandra stood up with
an air of authority and announced that what Gregor
had omitted to say was that in his later school years he
had become quite an expert in the use of the instrument
they had before them. So, given the positively outrage-
ous stunt pulled that evening, it was only right that the
third member of the party should feel it too. Thus it was
that 'Miss Judith' was turned back into plain Jude and
turned over the chair for a prefectorial licking that
proceeded, with painful accuracy, to re-inscribe the
fading grid of lines acquired at the annexe of the British
Library.

In the morning Judith struggled out of the mists of a
half-remembered dream and, despite a pot of strong
coffee, her brain seemed stuffed with cotton wool. What
had she done – they done – the night before? Games
were one thing, but a kind of weird enthusiasm had
overtaken the activities. Making her way through the
park Judith watched a gust of wind wipe the reflections
from the surface of the water. She hardly knew this girl
who had, in a few short weeks, gone from shy and
wide-eyed at the Archive's perversities to total immer-
sion. How different from her own oh-so-tentative two
steps forward, one step back of the early days. In the
entrance she climbed the stairs right to the top and
crossed the echoing space to her station in the far
corner. Later – after some quiet rooftop contemplation
– she would face up to the office and its occupant.

But it seemed the office had come to her for beside the
keyboard was a cardboard box with a message in the
ungainly scrawl it was impossible to mistake.

It's getting deep, so no more secrets. I'm done with
these, so you do what you like with them. S xx

Lifting the lid revealed a row of small plastic cases, each spine bearing a date. Oh God. These were the tapes that had been confessed to the day before that she had then made light of. Judith picked out one from the beginning of April and heart aflutter, slotted it into the cassette player under the desk. At first nothing happened then she became aware that a faint voice was speaking and cranked up the volume control to max.

. . . in one piece. Some date to start too, but at least nobody tried to make me the Fool. It was supposed to be only for a week but they're having problems finding anyone else and I think there's a good chance I'll be there the whole three. If I want. God, it's weird. Pretty well the first thing I saw was this book lying on the desk with a drawing of a girl in stockings bending over . . .

Judith listened to the disembodied speech with a mixture of shame and embarrassment. Is this what her lover had really intended her to do? Squirming mentally, she lasted another minute to the point where her own name was mentioned and then she jabbed the eject button. No, she wanted no part of these records of past thoughts and feelings. Sandra herself had finished with them and moved on. In that case so should she. Judith lifted the tape out of the machine, returned it to its box with the others and placed the whole thing out of the way on a top shelf. Her mind was clear for the first time that day. The point was the action itself: that was what she should emulate. She felt a wave of revulsion at her own deceit and double-dealing; it was almost certainly too much for her to come clean about, but she could make a start by cutting off relations with the chief occasioner of the duplicity.

Judith turned to her computer and, fingers drumming, waited to be connected to the server. Two regular

212

newsletters made it to the inbox where she let them sit while opening a new mail file. She keyed in 'gwendom', smiling at its suggestion of an esoteric state of servitude and stared at the screen, wondering how to begin. It was important to get a message through before the weekend that was coming up at the AOC. Not that Gwen was due to appear – it was their own Director who was hosting the prime slot – but whether she did or not, the declaration would have been made and it would be up to her to follow it through.

Deciding it was owed to the partner in such intense, if sporadic, encounters , Judith launched into a detailed statement of the position as she saw it. After a few minutes and several paragraphs, she deleted the lot and started again, only to scrub the whole thing once more. It was impossibly long-winded and the more she wrote now the more scope she would give for later attempts to make her change her mind. Keep it simple, and un-equivocal. No loopholes for argument. Suddenly it came to her and she entered the phrase 'hitched' into the Subject box then followed it with a short piece of text in the panel below.

> Hey, girl, it's been a wild ride. But I've got my self all tied up (& not with Japanese ropes!) and I'm ducking out to go seriously steady. You can call me a chicken if you like, cos I think you'd be right.
> Jude

When the message was gone she sat back suddenly enervated. That was it then. She had started the affair up again by email and had just served notice of its demise by the same means. Now all she had to do was stick to her guns.

22

Four-footer

At four p.m. on the Friday afternoon the Director of the Nemesis Archive led her small group of workers to the back of the building where a large saloon with dark-tinted windows was waiting. Judith remembered it as the made-to-order Citroën Diplomatique she had once seen whisk Miss James away to a spell of flagellant rigour in Brittany. As they rounded the corner, the door opened and a dark-suited woman climbed out. With a flourish she removed her peaked hat.

'Samantha, *ma chère*. How well you are looking.'

'*Toi aussi*, Nadine. *Il y a longtemps*.' The driver squeezed the offered hand between the two of hers, then cast her eyes over the rest of the party.

'Ah, we have the secretary and the pet. *Très charmantes*, *les deux*. But the third one, now, she is something rather more. A penetrating case study to her credit, and much yet to contribute, *je crois*.'

'Well, thank you. I, er, hope so.' While flattered, Judith was awkwardly aware of the slight that had been delivered to the left and right of her. Whatever Penny thought of it, she could *feel* Sandra's affront. It was not the best start to the journey.

The three of them occupied the rear seat while on the other side of the glass divide the conversation appeared deep, befitting a reunion of *les amies intimes*. Next to her the dismissed pair were keeping up a low and bitter-sounding interchange so Judith sank into the corner of well-upholstered leather and stared gloomily at the landscape bordering the motorway. There had been no opportunity to talk about her reaction to the tapes and in their present situation she could hardly lean across Penny to broach such a topic. So it was a relief when, at last, the sleek black machine eased itself through the archway and drew up at the door of the AOC under its distinctive correctional rebus. As they climbed the stairs with their things Judith resolved to break through the pointed silence but, no sooner were they in the room, than she was summoned – alone – to dine with a select group of invitees to the forthcoming lecture and demonstration. She could scarcely refuse, but the look on Sandra's face as she muttered 'On you go, then,' indicated there was some serious sweet-talking required before the night was out.

The meal, at a neighbouring Japanese establishment, was an exotic one of many courses through which they were guided by Constance's expert advice. Wine was poured and after a while anecdotes of past occasions flowed with it, but with an eye to duty Judith followed the abstemious example of the Director she was to serve as assistant for the forthcoming event. It was a disappointment to find that the new Keeper of Rare Books had been invited but was unable to attend, and of those present she knew only one slightly. So it was a less than ideal occasion and Judith took only a desultory part in the exchanges while devoting herself to the – excellent – food, a little irked that she had spent most of that day wishing for it to pass into its next stage.

When they returned to the AOC building, a short briefing was all that time allowed before the main action of the evening. There was no sign of Sandra, and Helga said with an 'oh, didn't you know?' kind of look that Niamh had dragged the secretary off somewhere.

Judith, though, decided to regard it as being for the best; if anything the rapport between the two should have the effect of improving the girl's state of mind. But there was no opportunity to dwell on the matter: she had been equipped with a remote control panel and the audience was assembled, so the moment had come to dim down the room and focus attention on to the raised platform.

In the sudden hush of expectation, a figure came out into the beam of light. Raven-haired, with the dazzling white of her shirt offset by the black breeches and boots, it was Samantha James at her most imposing. By her side there appeared a young woman in a pageboy haircut wearing only the briefest of red lycra hotpants with matching bra top. Beside the formal gravity of the presence she joined, the blatant undress of the young PA was a shock and when the Director cracked the riding crop she carried smartly against her booted calf a ripple ran round the benches. With the tip of it she turned Penny about and pushed up the tiny garment to reveal even more of the chubby bottom cheeks.

'A pretty sight, colleagues, I'm sure you agree. However, this is not to be the instrument to set them jumping tonight. In fact, I shall begin without the benefit of any instrument, however much this young lady may have merited one.' She smiled a patrician smile at the twenty or so devotees gathered before her who were hanging on her every word. 'My purpose is to set before you an observation about the nature of our common interest. Both simple and profound it is, I feel, one that is all too often overlooked. I shall illustrate my point with the execution of a – how shall I put it? – *full-blooded* castigation designed to stick in the minds of all those in attendance. Not for the faint-hearted, I have to say, but then I believe the present company has no need of such a warning. First, a *divertissement*, though I do not mean to imply by that term something trivial. Penelope, the chaise-longue, if you please!'

Sumptuously upholstered in a heavy green brocade, the item of furniture was positioned towards the front of the dais. Miss James sat on the end, half facing the expectant gathering, drew the girl down across her lap and without more ado began to slap her exposed behind. In a very few minutes, to the accompaniment of the victim's high-pitched squeals, the flesh glowed pink but the chastiser kept up the attack until it was suffused with a deeper red. Then she stood the PA on her feet, drew the pants right down and put a hand to the brown strands that curled out under the pubic mound.

'Oh, Miss James, please . . .' The girl squirmed with every indication of embarrassment.

'Come now, Penelope, don't fuss. With such clear evidence of it –' she held up two glistening fingers to the audience '– you should be proud to make known your state to us all. Judith, will you bring me the anal plug?' It was bulbous and black with a sheen of its own, and there was a lot more squirming before Judith had pushed it fully home. Then the Director took the hand towel that was being offered and draped it over her knee, eyeing the spectators with something close to a grin.

'If it is not already, it will soon become clear why *this* is needed. Now back over, young lady, and we will manage without quite such a raucous response. Unless, of course, you are bent on a bedtime taste of the three-tailed Lochgelly.' Plainly there was no answer to that, and the silent Penny was settled in place for the spanking to resume. In the absence of the skimpy shorts her thighs were spread and, as the slaps fell thick and fast, the lubricating vulva gaped and even the black head above blinked at them from time to time. And then, all at once, the crisis was upon them and the girl cried out again and again, the threat of leathering seemingly quite forgotten. As the spasms died, Samantha James caressed the flaming globes with undisguised relish until the figure lay quiet and still.

'Up now, dear. Don't worry: a touch of climactic excitement may I think be forgiven.' She passed over the towel which Penny clutched to herself, looking suddenly at a loss. 'Off with you and clean up. I know you don't want to miss what is to come.' There was a brief hiatus in which Judith removed the couch and wheeled into place a compact whipping horse with splayed legs that she proceeded to bolt to the floor. Not for Miss James the cumbersome apparatus that Constance had used in her session; there was only one kind of stimulation called for in the episode to follow. Neither did she allow herself to become entangled in the complexities of the desire for punishment, for once the frame was ready and Judith standing by she cut straight to the nub of the matter.

'In the frank sexual display we have witnessed there was, of course, pain. Spanking *hurts*, but the pain it creates can be placed, as we saw, almost wholly at the service of pleasure. With practice and dedication, the bodily distress that can be so transformed may be brought to a level that the novice would find unthinkable. But the question here is not simply one of severity. For at the dark heart of these preoccupations lies a scene of stark simplicity, a primal ritual of atonement in which wrongdoing reaps the consequence of retribution. What we find here is not pleasure but something profound, even transcendent: a purgation that taken to its end leaves the one who suffers it chastened utterly, yet fired with a strange exaltation. It is this, the very essence of the passion for correction, to which our institution is dedicated.' In the silence that met the eloquent words a door closed quietly at the back and the speaker raised her head. 'I bid our guest welcome. And, if she is ready, I call on her to come forward.'

Heads turned as in a swirl of rich material a figure emerged out of the gloom and mounted the platform.

The light showed her to be a young woman with ash-blonde hair falling over the shoulders of a midnight-blue cloak. Almost the height of the Director beside her she stood waiting, hands folded in front, with the attitude of one who has consigned herself to her fate.

'Ms D – for that is all the name we shall need of you tonight – I ask you only one question. In the knowledge of what is entailed, do you come here of your own will to undergo due correction?'

'I do.' The vowels were darkly un-English and there was a Slavic air about the face. It was very pale with a sheen of perspiration on the downy upper lip, but the mouth was set in a line of determination.

'That is good. Judith, please pass me the instrument.' Samantha James took the rod offered her by the leather binding at one end and bent it into an arc. 'One-point-two metres of thirteen-millimetre rattan, the modern standard; it is something very similar to the old "four-footer" whose name once struck a chill into the heart of a reformatory inmate. We have fixed your award, Ms D, at eight strokes. Are you still willing to proceed?'

'Yes.' The quiet word of assent came after a distinct pause, but it was unambiguous. It seemed there had not been doubt, more a gathering of resources to take a final hurdle.

'So be it. You will submit to preparation.' On a sign Judith went up to the young woman and reached for the diamond clasp that held the cape together at the throat. She closed it carefully and drew the garment back from the shoulders to reveal an expanse of white skin. Beneath the rich material Ms D was quite naked except for a pair of short leather boots with small spiky heels. She stood looking down, hands covering the pubic mound, and there was now a perceptible flush to the features. Judith took her by the arm and directed her gently towards the restraining apparatus. With a small

sigh she draped herself over it in position for wrists and
ankles to be buckled to its legs, and once that was
accomplished Judith fastened the transverse band tight
across the small of the back. The Director nodded
approvingly.

'It is vital, of course, that the body is tightly secured
for what is to come. When such things were commonly
used, a girl of grit could, with practice, hold herself
down for even a dozen of her headmistress's best, but
with *this* instrument –' she let the words hang in the air
and waited while Judith inserted the ball of a gag into
the open mouth then tied it at the back of the head '–
with this instrument, as few as three strokes is likely to
bring the recipient to a degree of pain she would not
have thought she could bear. So it is necessary to
preclude the withdrawal of consent. The remainder of
the punishment will not exactly increase the pain as
such, merely serve to sustain it at that impossible,
unendurable level. I speak from experience: I have been
there myself.'

There was a stir in the audience at the invoking of the
unwritten code observed by principled chastisers of the
old school. What the prone figure that had occasioned
the observations thought about it all was anybody's
guess. She would not have been consulted even were she
still capable of audible speech. The requirements of
ritual corporal punishment demanded a body for its
infliction and, bound to the horse, she had become just
that. With the tip of the rod Miss James called attention
to the feature that had been brought to prominence as
if the flesh were so much meat.

'Perfectly presented for our common purpose tonight.
These fine globes have been, in the manner recommended, massaged with a moisturising lotion thrice daily for
the past week. The measure, designed to help the skin
survive the assault of the cane without breaking, has the
added virtue of keeping the impending castigation in the

mind. Thus the offender we encounter tonight has been well prepared, mentally and physically, and to set a seal on the proceedings, the one she wronged is in the room to witness the act of penance.' The Director drew herself up and flexed the cane once again. 'Come, friends, I have talked enough. It is time to act!'

Judith moved in close to the horse and placed a hand gently on the girl's neck. She watched Miss James roll up her right sleeve and assume a position level with the waist, measuring her weapon carefully against the target. Then she raised it high above her head and, rising on to her toes, delivered the first blow. The cane was a blur, striking just below the crown of the buttocks and driving the hips hard into the frame. When it sprang back the flesh bounced and rippled and there was a choking gasp of air expelled from the lungs. Judith felt the body rigid with shock as muscles bulged and limbs strained against their bonds. A clock ticked in the silence and she found herself counting: thirty seconds was to be the interval between strokes and it seemed an eternity.

The second and third cuts forced strangled cries out past the ball jammed in the victim's mouth and the horse creaked in protest under the seizures that racked the tethered body. At four, however, the vigour of the response diminished and at five the figure stiffened once and the head slumped. Judith reached for the bottle of smelling salts kept at hand for the occasion and went down on one knee to hold it under the nostrils. There was an explosive sneeze and the eyes opened. For a moment blank, they fixed on hers, wild and desperate. A murmur was running round the benches and, keeping her back to the audience, she took advantage of it to mouth the words 'three more – just one minute', using her fingers to emphasise the numbers.

Six and seven provoked frantic writhings likely to have toppled the frame had it not been secured to the platform, and after eight the ravaged hindquarters were beset with muscular spasms that wrenched the hips to and fro. The Director stood back to indicate that her task was finished and Judith dropped down to release the wrists. Again there was a buzz and she took the chance to whisper some urgent words into the girl's ear.

'You *can* walk. Focus on your legs. *Make* them work.' She gave one of the arms a quick squeeze then unbuckled the centre strap followed by the bands at the ankles. Heart in mouth she watched the young woman attempt to rise and fall forward before pushing herself upright with her hands. A knee wobbled then straightened and Ms D took a step away from the locus of her torment. Judith had a clear view of the swollen posterior, ferociously barred, before a woman with a mannish haircut and an elegant dark suit came out of the shadows and covered all once more with the cloak. It took a perceptible prompt for the girl to shake the hand of her chastiser after which the suited woman clasped it firmly.

'Thank you so much. I – we both – owe you a debt of gratitude. One day perhaps I am able to return the favour. Come, Saskia, I shall tend to you.' It was a relief to see the beautiful victim out of the room on her own two feet before the full shock of her ordeal would set in.

Back on the top floor there was no sign of Sandra and Judith hesitated inside the door of their room. There was a quiet footfall behind her and a hand covered her eyes. A warm body pressed into her back and she recognised the slightly aromatic scent at once.

'Helga.'

'They went to where Nevie worked once. It will be late. You liked what we saw, yes?'

'Don't know about *liked*. But it was powerful stuff.' Fingers opened a button on her shirt and slipped in to caress a breast. Judith gave a little gasp, aware all at once how aroused she was.

'Look, Helga –'

'It is OK, I know she is the one. That is what you say, yes? But while we are alone, we can play a game. We pretend it is you for the beating and I tie you up. Come, Yoodit, we go to a safe place for it.'

Judith opened her mouth to demur then shut it again. Suddenly the effort that had gone into the negotiation of commitment was all too much. She was randy as fuck, the lover in question had gone AWOL and her arm was being twisted into having sex with the luscious Helga.

'OK, OK. You win. Lead the way, gorgeous.' She kissed the German girl, pushing her tongue into the welcoming mouth. Then she turned her round, slapped her bottom and followed its curvaceous progress along the corridor and down the stairs.

23

Block

At the foot of the creaking steps the basement passage had the slightly musty smell of infrequent use. The last time Judith had been through it – more than a month before – she had been incited to masturbate on camera while watching her employer under the lash, and the memory gave her a distinct frisson. Helga pushed her ahead into the main room, past the whipping bench featured in the earlier occasion to a wooden contraption that stood waist high from the floor. The top end had two hinged pieces with three semicircular holes that were recognisably part of a set of stocks but they were attached to a domed block perhaps a metre long that fell away to a padded ledge.

'Come, I show you. Over goes the naughty miss, like so –' the giggling blonde guided Judith into place '– and then we snap it shut, like so, and she is ready for the spanking.' The head and wrists were indeed securely held and the body was bent at the waist, knees on the cushioned step. Helga came behind her and fondled her bottom through the seat of the trousers, making the wet crotch of the thong even wetter. 'This is the good placing for the birch. But we must be bare, *ja*? Imagine the town square, all the people in a crowd to see.' While continuing to elaborate on the fantasy she unlaced Judith's boots then pulled her trousers down and off with them.

'The girl is going to catch it – that is what you say, yes? – and she is desperate to keep her legs together. But once they get to the second rod that soaks in the brine bucket there is no chance.' Helga paused expressively. 'Think of it: soon the sting makes her wriggle and wriggle, showing everything. The men are getting hard looking at her pussy and her bum and some women too, they are becoming wet at what they see. Just like you!' Judith pushed back onto the exploring fingers with a sharp stab of desire.

'Jee-sus, Helga. You know how to get a girl going.'

'Wait. You are not quite ready.' Ready? Ready for what? Judith tried to look round but the rough wood held her neck in a stiff embrace. Then, without warning a blindfold was drawn down over her head. 'The girl must not see who stares at her, right? And she has been plugged to heighten the sensations of the birch.' Judith squealed at the feel of something hard and smooth pumping in and out her oozing vagina, then it was pressed against the anal ring. 'Open wide like a good girl, and then we are finished.' Made slick with her juices, the head of the object was in with a single thrust and the muscle closed to pull the outer rim hard in between the buttocks. Judith gasped, her state of arousal close to excruciating. Then she heard behind her a door opening and what Helga said came from further away.

'*Es tut mir leid*, Judith. Constance says it is your need. What you want really inside, so I do it.' Then the door closed again and she strained to detect any sound above the pulse beating in her ears. Suddenly there was a whooshing through the air and a swarm of biting insects attacked her left bottom cheek. And then the right. She kicked out and yelled in pain and surprise, her upper limbs gripped tight. When the voice spoke it was one that she knew only too well.

'So it's goodbye, is it sister? Then I'd better leave you with something to remember me by.'

'Gwen.' The cold shock of realisation twisted Judith's innards. Once she had fired off the mail its recipient had been put out of mind as completely as its contents. And now here she was, large as life and twice as mean, with an audience that was quite literally captive. What a piece of folly had been the jokey little message with which she had sought to break off the affair. Judith ground her teeth: however much she repented of the flippant words already, she was likely to be regretting them still more before the night was out.

'Look Gwen, I'm sorry –'

'Save your breath, girl. You co-operate with me is your best chance. Got it?'

'Got it.'

'Then spread wide open and stick that peachy arse right out like you begging for it. We are gonna have some fun.' When the whipping started Judith breathed again: there was a degree of respite, even a glimmer of hope. It wasn't a cat with hard, unforgiving tails she was using but what Americans called a 'flogger'. Full force across the centre of the behind, the thin strips of leather left quite a sting, but Gwen was combining those strokes with wrapping the thing round under the cheeks. She had thought her arousal was at a peak but now the juices welled up afresh, demanding release. Judith became aware of the guttural noises in her throat as she strained to open to the swishing tongues and bring on the climax. Fuck, how she craved that climax! Then it all stopped dead and she writhed in an agony of frustration: the mare in heat desperate for the hard thrust of penetration.

'God damn it, Gwen. You can't leave me like this. Shit –'

'Oh sister, I ain't going to *leave* you. You see, I brought with me a nice long cane. They told me you had a girlie upstairs for cor-rec-tion.' She drew the word out almost lasciviously. 'Only eight she got, though. It can't have been that terrible what she done. Now you, on the other hand, you aimed to finish what we had going with a silly message on the computer. In my book that's a fucking insult. So I wanna know, how many is it gonna take for that kick in the teeth to be cor-rec-ted?'

Plainly lots, but it was not an observation Judith was going to make from her position in the stocks. There was no sensible answer and back-talk was unlikely to improve the situation. Then she heard the stomach-tightening swish of a flexible rod.

'We'll start with the eight, yeah? It'll get my eye in.'

No way was twice eight going to suffice, nor a third dose of the new unit of measurement. Judith clamped her mouth shut and took all twenty-four with no more than a few grunts. It was a small mercy that the instrument was not the equal of the one that had nearly done for Miss D's legs, but the cuts to the top of her thighs had come close to making her own control unravel. More of their like and she was going to plead and beg and very likely give her tormentor the satisfaction of a fit of weeping.

However, it was not yet to be for there came a change of tactic. The cane clattered to the floor and hands held an ankle. Hard metal clicked shut round it then the other as the red mists of pain began to disperse and Judith lay panting in the unexpected relief. The left leg was pulled hard over and there was the sound of a chain snapping into place, then the right was secured in the opposite direction. She was stretched tight round the sides of the block, nether regions gaping wide.

'Now lets have a good look, girl, if it's gonna be the last I get. Ah, nice.' She felt the plug in her bottom gripped and turned, sending a new wave of shivers up her back. 'And these are quite a picture. We'll have to see what we can do to liven up their colour.' Deprived of her actual sight, Judith saw in her mind's eye a vivid picture of the black girl staring close-up into the vulval folds and whorls. Then there was a sharp nipping pressure that was repeated several times.

'Oh no, Gwen, you can't. No!' There was no mistaking it: rows of small clamps were being attached to the exposed labia on both sides. She had used a couple before in a kind of rough play between the two of them, but there was nothing reciprocal about where she found herself that night. The things were uncomfortable more than painful in place, the problem came when they were removed.

'Right. These little beauties can have five, OK? While you meditate on your sins and their cor-rec-tion.' As the seconds passed Judith tried to ease the strain in her impossibly stretched muscles and marshal her resources. But it was to little avail, for when the small pincers came off in quick succession and the blood flowed again she howled and howled, the voice bouncing back at her off the rough plaster and brick of the long room. Once the sensation fell away from its excruciating peak there were fingers exploring the tender wetness and Judith writhed, trying to bring them into contact with the throbbing clitoris. The caning, the clips and now the direct manipulation had brought her to a screaming pitch of pent-up arousal that had to be released.

'Jesus fuck, bring me off. Do what the fuck you like to me after, but I can't fucking stand it a minute longer!' But the demand had, if anything, the opposite effect for there was an abrupt halt to the stimulation.

'Sorry, sister. I got something else in my bag of tricks first. You gonna have to practise some self control.' Something hard and cold pressed into the vagina and its length stroked down the backs of her thighs. It was thin with knobbly joints and Judith felt a chill at the realisation of what was to come.

'Recognise it, yeah? You should do, 'cos you're the one who told me what a malacca can do to an arse that's had a good dose already. Remember? Well now we gonna put theory into practice. But after that last earful my head's ringing, so you gonna get something to bite on, girl.'

The gag was a wodge of coarse material that stretched the jaw and made her stomach heave. Then the new instrument sang through the air and connected with raw, bruised flesh. Stroke followed stroke in a measured progression over the buttocks and down the thighs to the backs of the knees. Stifled cries wrenched at her throat that gave way in succession to heaving sobs. Before long she was all tears and snot like a child consumed by anguish and despair. The body jerked with each cut but the mind had become oddly detached from a world turned into pain, nothing but pain. Then it dawned on her, as if from a distance, that there had been a cessation. A voice – a male voice – was shouting, 'Enough, Mistress, enough!' and she was aware of a commotion behind her. But almost at once it began to fade and her consciousness slid away to join the darkness that engulfed her eyes.

When Judith came to her head ached and there was a crick in her neck. She was face down on a doctor's examination table and the starched covering was cold against her cheek. Cold too was her lower half – in fact, she was bloody freezing. She tried to roll over but hands held her in place while the icy pressure was removed.

'You're awake. That is good. I think we have done all we can with the refrigerated packs.'

'Constance.' Judith's mind, unbidden, slotted the events of the night back into place one by one. In the end she had passed out and now she was being tended by the woman who had engineered her fate. If Helga was to be believed. But she could detect in herself no swell of resentment at her treatment, only a strange reflective curiosity.

'It didn't work, you know. The ultimate fantasy, I mean. Assuming that is what you had in mind.' She

229

turned her head round to the woman who was reaching up for something on the shelf. Constance caught her eye then bent her head over the can whose top she was removing so that a screen of blonde hair hid her face.

'I believe I made a mistake.'

'I've often thought about it, well, like daydreamed, the idea of being completely in someone's power, someone who wants to hurt you. And it's not really a thing you can set up yourself. But when I was really there, God I was just terrified. Blanked out with fear, pure and simple.' Judith contemplated the awful truth for a moment then changed tack. 'But anyway, what happened? How did I get, er, rescued?'

'The young man – Max by name, I believe – appeared just at the time your secretary was becoming worried. So it seems a search party was launched, though once they had put two and two together it was not difficult to know where to look.'

'And Sandra. Did she – is she –?'

'I don't know what she saw but your party was whisked away in the big car, while you were left in my charge. Helga, too, has gone from us, summoned by her *Haupt-offizier* at the Thomas-Halle. Now, hold still, please, while I spray the worst of the damage. It promises to ease the inflammation. Then I'm going to leave you for a few minutes.'

After Constance had done her work Judith fell into a dreamlike state. The substance cooled the worst of the still burning welts and at the same time seemed to be soothing the traumatised system. She began to feel drowsy as well as oddly removed from the situation and her thoughts wandered. Then, when the manager of the AOC came back a question popped into her head.

'What did you mean, you made a mistake?'

'Well, Judith –' for the first time Constance looked straight at her, as if weighing something up '– I should dearly love to thrash one such as you myself, but I fear that I could not be sufficiently merciless.'

'But, with Miss James –'

'She is what we call an old hand. There was nothing I could do that was not a revisiting of places she knew. I thought an opportunity had presented itself to take you somewhere further, but I was wrong. That would require a detachment, not a furious spite threatening to run out of control. So when the boy burst in, it was not too soon.'

'Oh my God. You were there. Behind the window.' It struck Judith with the force of a slap in the face. Constance hadn't just brought about the event, she had been a witness in a position to intervene at any stage. And had chosen not to. 'You saw me – like that – and you just, you just *watched*?' It was monstrous – if that wasn't merciless, Judith didn't know what was – and yet the indignation in her was fighting with another reaction altogether. She had been totally on display in her extremity for the gratification of another. The fact turned her suffering into a kind of unwitting exhibitionism and the thought of it was making hot spikes of lust stab at her loins. Eyes behind the one-way mirror had savoured every detail of the 'cor-rec-tion', not as a punishment but as an exercise in sadomasochism.

'Constance, it's OK. Really.' Judith had had enough of discussion: the climax she had been denied for so long was back on the agenda, and pushing its way to the top. She wriggled down the table until her feet were able to find the floor, then stuck out her bruised behind. Damn it, the woman who had feasted her eyes on the causing of the damage could help alleviate it in the most obvious way. 'But if you could spread a little of that creamy stuff . . .'

It did the trick. Invited thus, the woman – hallmarked by a measured distance in her usual dealings – began to apply the oily salve. Anointing first the buttocks then the thighs, deft fingers were soon delving into the wetness between and the orgasm was on her in a mighty unstoppable rush.

* * *

231

Miss James, it seemed, had decreed that Judith should not return to her work until she was clearly recuperated, for what reason exactly she was not sure. She surmised, however, that Constance had been charged with supervising the recovery precisely because she was the one who had overstepped the mark, and she was certainly throwing herself into the role. For the remainder of the weekend, massage followed massage with a variety of aids to stimulation of both nether openings. Thus the time passed in a welter of exquisite sensations that left her, at the end, back in her own bunk bed and dead to the world.

At nine o'clock on the Monday morning Judith surfaced as if from a deep well of pure water and threw back the covers. It took a wince-making jump to the floor to remind her of the bruises she would be carrying for some days yet. She stuck out her bum at the wall mirror and noted the dirty yellows and the fading purples of flesh recovering from its ill-treatment. Leaving the shower she was attacked by a ravenous hunger and dressed quickly in a sweatshirt and joggers before heading down the passage. In the small kitchen space she found Constance opening a box that gave off the smell of fresh baking while water hissed and bubbled through the grounds of a coffee machine. Without waiting for an invitation Judith eased herself into the bench seat on one side of the wall table and took the steaming mug handed to her. Then she spread some soft cheese into a still warm roll and it was not until the last crumbs had gone from her plate that she looked up to see that she was being watched.

'It is good to see an appetite in the young, especially one who has come through a trying experience. So eat well, and then we shall work. There are things for you to learn.' So saying she nibbled fastidiously at a few seedless grapes while Judith wolfed down another roll and a large flaky croissant dripping with honey. Coffee cups were replenished and drained in silence, then Constance led the way through to her own quarters. Squeezing by the desk and computer work station in the cramped office they came to an inner door that she held open for Judith to enter ahead of her. For the minimally gestured manager of the AOC it was a theatrical move but one more than justified by what lay within. Occupying the centre of the sparsely furnished room was an upright wooden chair beside which stood the figure of a young Japanese woman, completely naked. So still and unblinking was she that for a fraction of a second the gaping Judith doubted she was in the presence of real flesh and blood, then Constance broke the spell.

'Mitsuko, this is Judith. With your help I shall be able to show her some of the rudiments of the art.' The head dipped in acknowledgement and there was the hint of a smile. 'So if you would be so good as to sit, we may begin. Now you will understand, Judith, that use of the chair is not, shall we say, fully traditional. But as an initial demonstration, I believe you will find the results beguiling.' She moved to the couch and took up a length of pure white nylon rope. The subject's wrists were held crossed at her back and Constance approached them, while regarding her audience in the manner of a lecturer. 'Now, contrary to untutored expectation, quite intricate bondage can be accomplished with only two simple knots, perhaps with the addition of the French Bowline. The principal concept that needs to be mastered by a beginner is that of *layering* . . .'

24

Settlements

While she had been sitting in moderate comfort at the AOC, Judith was relieved when the train at last delivered her to her home station late on the Wednesday morning. Encumbered by the extra baggage acquired as a result of Constance's tuition, she suffered the further jolting of a taxi ride to have it carried to the flat. Once the packages had been safely installed, Judith bathed quickly in a coolish tub then eased herself into a close-fitting but comfortable pair of stretch black trousers. The last parting from Sandra had hardly been on the best of terms and her unease about the reception she was likely to get at the Archive was growing. Perhaps the girl was just sick of the whole business in the wake of Friday night's excesses. At best, it would surely raise the question of what exactly she had been doing with Gwen to have unleashed such a violent response. Whatever, it was time to face the music so, boots laced, Judith clomped down the stairs and headed out at a fair lick across the park.

At the door of the office she gathered herself then entered with a firmness she was far from feeling. But the secretary was not in residence and instead the PA emerged from the inner sanctum with a pile of papers.

'Her ladyship's off for the rest of the day. Something on later, apparently. Taking advantage of the real boss being out if you ask me.' Penny indicated her disapproval with a toss of the head. 'But, Miss Judith, how are *you*?'

'On the mend, thank you Penny.'

'I'm glad to hear it. That black girl should be locked up, if you ask me. And talking of her, I don't suppose you'll have heard the news, will you?'

'News?'

'That young man she had – the one who got to you first –'

'You mean Max.'

'Max, that's it. Well he upped stakes and he's here. Had enough of her and I don't blame him neither. Mrs Rowleigh helped him get a place at the university and he's moved into her spare room.'

Judith sat down on a desk chair, open mouthed. 'That is what I call news. Wow. But what's this Sandra's up to tonight? And when's she coming back?'

'No good asking me, I'm the last person she'd tell. I would say the only way you'll get an answer is to go and find her. And now I'd better go and file these reports or I'm going to be in trouble with her nibs again.'

It would have been easy enough to go straight round to the bedsit, but having screwed herself up once for the worst, Judith was in need of a bracer. As she hoped, The Phoenix was just disgorging its terminal straggle of lunchtime drinkers on to the pavement and she was able to slip in past them and install herself at one end of the bar while Marsha finished locking the doors. When she re-appeared and took two bottles from the cooler, Judith fixed her with a stern eye.

'Now I'm going to give the bar stool a miss this afternoon and I don't want to hear anything on the lines of "I told you so", OK? That is supposing you heard.'

'About the anger of a rejected suitor and an eventual rescue party? Nothing like living dangerously while you're young, I always say. What a fund of stories you

235

will have for the teenage lovers of your later years. If you live to tell them.' Judith looked sharply at the neat features under the iron-grey crop but there was just the hint of a smile.

'Marsha, stop laying it on. You warned me and I didn't listen. I admit it, right? Let's drop the subject and you can fill me in on Marjorie's latest coup instead.'

'Well, I was given to understand – correct me if I'm wrong – that you're the one acquainted with the boy. And rather better than the sisterhood might approve. But then, as you know, I'm not one to split hairs over a male organ or two either.'

'Marsha!' Judith tried to look fierce.

'OK, I'll behave. But there's not a lot I can tell. We both have the big picture of the hunky – but plainly intelligent – lad fleeing his cruel mistress for a new life, though how exactly he came to hook up with our esteemed Vice Principal I have no idea. What I do know is that he took one look at the lady's downstairs accommodation complete with trestle and specialist book collection and decided to stay. So the bad girls she loved to chastise will have to move over for a bad boy, it seems. Or perhaps in time there will be room for them all.' Judith chuckled at the picture the American was painting and took a good mouthful of beer. 'But are you not going to find out tonight, first-hand? I thought there was a select gathering in honour of your return.'

'First I've heard of it. Though Penny did mention Sandra having something on.'

'And how is the romance? Blossoming, I hope. Or do I detect a touch of anxiety about how the weekend may have affected its prospects?'

'Damn it, Marsha, is it that obvious? Well, you know she's not into heavy stuff, and I can't help wondering . . .' Judith stopped and sighed.

'If she's backing off at full speed, as it were. Well, honey, I have a remedy for disquiet right here.' Marsha scooped out ice into a glass and splashed the contents of an optic over it. 'Best Polish. The prescription says in order to achieve relaxation swallow slowly. Then take another.'

The second turned into a third, which was followed by a fourth after which things had taken on a rosy tinge. Marsha declared that since she was off till seven they should consolidate it by an early dinner at Molly's Curry Shop. 'The food's ace and at this time of day we can chat up the waitresses. You'll see.'

The meal went well and Judith wandered back home in a pleasant haze, anxiety about the possible state of her relationship largely dispelled. But on the mat behind the door was a note that brought her back to earth with a bump. It was written in the large, rather childish hand she recognised at once and contained just a few short words.

Mrs R's at 7 for an important announcement. BE THERE.

Oh God. Judith stared at the paper, the chill in her stomach negating the effect of all the rich food. Damn the girl, what had she cooked up now? It was already after seven, so there was no time to change. Nor was there any point in a taxi – she could cut across the edge of town and be there as quickly on foot. Better just get on and get it over with, whatever it was. With rapidly sinking spirits Judith banged the front door shut behind her and set off.

When she turned into the secluded cul-de-sac of Georgian terraces, Marjorie herself was standing at the entrance in the light of the low evening sun. 'Judith!' she cried, advancing down the half-flight of steps, 'you were quite difficult to track down. I gather that in the end you were left a somewhat melodramatic little note. Well, come in, do. The culprits are waiting for you.'

Culprits? That didn't sound as though *she* was going to be put on the spot. Pricked for the first time that evening by curiosity rather than apprehension, Judith followed her host across the spacious lobby and down the stairs. In the long semi-basement, the curtains had been drawn and the parquet-floored section was lit from an angled lamp that shone on a stout wooden chair in the centre. Facing the wall were two figures, hands on their heads in the style of classroom penitents of a bygone era. There was Sandra, fetchingly kitted out in white vest and knickers, and to her right Max, all dark stubble below the streaked top, in black singlet and nylon shorts. Marjorie herself, sheathed in a dark velvet dress, motioned Judith towards the leather couch and cleared her throat.

'I'll keep this brief, though I think a word of explanation is in order. When young Max appeared at the end of last week he had quite a story to tell. I'm pleased to say the details of his stay with us here have been worked out, but there is one matter yet to be resolved. He is insistent that he could have acted earlier and possibly prevented the assault by his ex-mistress altogether. After some discussion he persuaded me to administer – in the style of the institution involved – due correction of his fault, and to do so in front of the injured party.' She took up the black rod from the side table and tapped its end on her palm.

'Twelve strokes with my favourite instrument has been agreed upon as a suitable penalty.' Judith nodded solemnly in silence. It was not for her to point out that she owed him thanks rather than anything else, for this was to be a formal caning in whose procedures he was well versed compliantly.

'Once she came to hear of it, Sandra was keen to receive the same treatment, on the grounds that her moodiness had played a culpable part in the events of the Friday night. Naturally I vetoed the request but did in the end agree to award a sound hand-spanking for the offence. So, without more ado, I call on the young lady to come forward.'

Judith settled back in her seat in an agreeable tingle of anticipation. It was going to be rather a pleasing show that had been contrived for her return and she fixed her eyes on the lush swell of the cotton pants as the secretary went down over the Vice Principal's broad lap. The palm was broad too, and it rose and fell with repeated vigour, causing the cheeks to bounce and ripple under their thin covering. After several minutes of concentrated effort, the knickers were pulled down to reveal a glowing target and the punishment was resumed. Soon gasps turned into small cries that grew sharper as tears began to spill down the face. Abruptly the spanking stopped and Sandra hauled herself up, pulling the pants back in place with a snap. In a second she was snuggling up on the couch with an 'Ooh, that's sore!' and blowing her nose with a giggle. Judith put a hand round the bare flesh of the waist with a wry smile: this was hardly the model of contrition that had been presented. Once again, she had the feeling that the girl was much more in charge of things than she would have others believe.

Meanwhile, the chair had been turned and Max was bent over its back, legs spread. Marjorie took up position slightly ahead of the tightly stretched seat awaiting its due and flexed the cane. It was a fearsome implement and, prepared as she was, Judith still flinched at the force of the first stroke. She was aware of Sandra beside her putting a hand over her eyes. There was a clear imprint dead centre and when five others had joined it the agent of 'correction' drew the shorts down around the thighs. The purple bars revealed were as thick as a finger and Judith winced again as each of four more strokes turned the patch on the right into a solid wedge of contusion. Then came the coup de grace: with a flourish, Marjorie laid on two diagonals that intersected all the preceding cuts. There was a sharp intake of breath and the right leg twitched visibly, but the stalwart recipient stayed firmly in place while his chastiser inspected the damage she had inflicted mark by mark.

'A well-caned bottom is such a stimulating sight, I always find. Do we declare this one to have suffered enough? She looked at Judith for a response.

Judith nodded again. 'Certainly. And the punishment was well taken.'

'Very well. You may rise, dear boy.' Whether he had been erect at the height of his pain Judith doubted, but in the aftermath his cock stood out firm and proud. With no hint of embarrassment, Marjorie took it in her hand and studied it for a moment. 'You know, until our friend's arrival I rather thought I had lost the taste for one of these. But now, I am afraid you are going to have to excuse us for a few minutes. Perhaps you two will be able to find a way of passing the time before we meet over drinks upstairs.' She regarded them with a look of sly amusement, then steered the complaisant Max in front of her and out of the door. After their laughter had died down, Sandra pulled at Judith's sleeve.

'Hey, am I forgiven then? You know it would never have happened if I hadn't gone off in a strop. And are you OK?'

'Course I am. Well, more or less.' Judith was glad not to be asked how she came to be tied down in the cellar in the first place. 'But I'm going to need a close look at that spanked bottom before I let you off the hook. A *really* close look.' So saying, she turned her lover round, pushed her over the arm of the sofa and yanked off her pants. 'Lovely and pink. Now if you'll just spread good and wide . . .'

The following morning Judith drove a white van on hire for the day round to the back of the Archive and parked it carefully. After fierce, hungry sex and their host's generous glasses of wine they had strolled out slowly, basking in the mild night air. Then, at the door of her bedsit in a run-down terrace, Sandra announced that she would have to find another place before the end of the month when the houses were to be redeveloped. Inside, under cover of darkness, Judith had plucked up courage to make the offer of her second bedroom, and it had been accepted at once. In the office, she had just manoeuvred the secretary between two filing cabinets with the aim of caressing a tailored thigh when the door of the inner sanctum sprang open.

'There you are, Judith. A word, please, if you will. I shan't keep you long.' Damn. It wasn't exactly in flagrante but still pretty bloody obvious. She extricated herself from the corner and blew a kiss at the beloved behind the Director's retreating back. Inside, Miss James seated herself casually on the edge of her massive desk and gathered up a sheaf of papers.

'Now, we talked a while ago about your intention to write something personal – a kind of monograph – about your own experiences and those of people close to you.'

'I haven't done a lot, Miss James. In fact, I've barely begun.'

'I do understand that things have been a little, shall we say, hectic recently.' There was an amused glint in the eyes that watched her steadily. 'How are you, by the way? Quite recovered from the contretemps with the fiery young woman of colour?'

'Er, good as, thank you.'

'Well, what I have here should help. The AOC has come up with a dossier on initial experiences: the kinds of things that set individuals off in a "perverse" direction.' Samantha James marked the scare quotes with fingers in the air. 'There are some transcripts of interviews and many more names of subjects willing to be interviewed, if you would like to take on the task. What I have in mind – waiting for your more specific input – is that the NemArch imprint will issue two titles next year on the subject bearing your name: one as author, the other as editor. How does that appeal?'

'Very much. Indeed.' Coming out of the blue, it was all a bit much to digest and she cast around for something to say. 'I'm going to have to get busy.'

'Well, yes, my dear. But first things first. Take the rest of the day off to get your lodger installed and, of course, take her with you. Penelope can hold the fort.' Judith gaped, totally at a loss for words. The Director, too, was looking a trifle awkward. 'I recall some weeks ago laying down the law about relationships among staff in a manner that was, to say the least, hypocritical. Since then, I have resolved to keep my nose out of such matters. However, I would comment that a little stability can do wonders for one's productivity.' She stood up and handed over the clutch of documents. 'So don't let me keep you any further from setting in place the new arrangements.'

It was well into the afternoon before they had rounded up a pile of boxes, packed them, transported them and unpacked them at the other end. And it was early evening before the remaining part load had been dealt with in a similar manner. While Sandra filled the built-in cupboard of her new sleeping quarters, Judith ran a steaming tub. When they had bathed she appeared at the door of the bedroom with one of her new acquisitions. The secretary was standing turned away and Judith came up behind her to cup a hand round a firm full breast. Then taking hold of both wrists behind her back she looped round them a double turn of the nylon rope and pulled her down on the bedside chair.

'Jude, what are you doing?'

'Now, I've got you here, San, you don't think I'm going to let you get away, do you?'

'Jude, that is tight. Whew, I mean *tight*. And Jude, why are you spreading my legs like that? Oh. Oh wow. Ooh. *Ooooh* . . .'

NEXUS NEW BOOKS

To be published in August 2004:

THE PRIESTESS
Jacqueline Bellevois

Gullible young solicitor Adam finds himself attracted to Megan, his beautiful fellow employee, and dominated by worldly-wise workmate Donna. The owner of a slinky, City-based fetish club finds she is being defrauded by a mysterious regular, known as The Priestess, and the three of them must learn to serve their client well. Submitting their own sexual tensions to the rules of the club, and discovering its association with a bizarre 'sanatorium', the trio discover that their lives will never be the same again.

£6.99   ISBN 0 352 33905 5

TICKLE TORTURE
Penny Birch

Jade, confident but submissive, is struggling to come to terms with the demands of her lesbian lover, AJ, to become her lifestyle slave. Matters aren't helped when her participation at a wet, kinky cabaret goes too far, bringing its shifty management after her, intent on sexual revenge. With the added distraction of her lewd friend Jeff Bellbird, and extra toppings from Doughboy the pizza man, Jade looks less likely than ever to resolve her dilemma.

£6.99   ISBN 0 352 33904 7

EMMA'S SUBMISSION
Hilary James

This fourth volume of Emma's story finds its very pretty heroine back in the thrall of the sadistic Ursula, who is now supplying well-trained young women as slaves and pleasure creatures to wealthy overseas clients. Having been trained by Sabhu – Ursula's Haitian assistant and slave-trainer – Emma is hired out to the cruel wife of an African dictator who uses her in the most degrading ways. Emma soon discovers that the woman has acquired a painting which has been stolen from Ursula. Ursula wants it back at any cost and if Emma fails in her mission to retrieve it, she may never see her beloved mistress again.

£6.99   ISBN 0 352 33906 3

To be published in September 2004:

ALICE IN CHAINS
Adriana Arden

Fresh from the adventures chronicled in THE OBEDIENT ALICE, young Alice Brown returns home to find that she has sprouted bird feathers where her own hair should be. Only another trip to Underland can solve the problem, and her bedroom mirror is the only means of return. Used once more as a pawn by the Red Queen, this time literally, and enslaved by the greedy Tweedledum and Tweedledee, Alice must use her willingness to submit to any of the bizarre demands made of her if she is to succeed in returning to normal. And that's before she's met the Jabberwock. A delightfully perverse retelling of a classic tale.

£6.99   ISBN 0 352 33908 X

SIN'S APPRENTICE
Aishling Morgan

Poor young Ysette is an orphan. Having been raised in an especially strict and unwordly nunnery, she is sent out to have her obliging nature taken advantage of again and again. First she is to learn the bizarre sexual byways of witchcraft. Then, travelling as a Sin Eater, she is tasked to remove the sin that men contain within their seed. Finally, she is taken by an elderly and perverted priest before finding her redemption. A novel of sex, superstition and religious punishment, inspired by the classics of SM literature.

£6.99   ISBN 0 352 33909 8

EMMA'S HUMILIATION
Hilary James

In the fifth volume of Emma's story, Henry, Emma's masterful lover, suddenly re-enters her life. But Emma's Mistress, Ursula, and Sabhu the gigantic Haitian slave-trainer are supervising Emma so closely that her delightfully subservient dalliances with Henry are soon discovered. Determined to enforce her dominance, Ursula sends Emma to a rehabilitation centre. Under the stern tutelage of the Headmistress and the Major, Emma learns complete obedience to her Mistress's strange desires.

£6.99   ISBN 0 352 33910 1

If you would like more information about Nexus titles, please visit our website at www.nexus-books.co.uk, or send a stamped addressed envelope to:

Nexus, Thames Wharf Studios,
Rainville Road, London W6 9HA

NEXUS BACKLIST

This information is correct at time of printing. For up-to-date information, please visit our website at www.nexus-books.co.uk

All books are priced at £6.99 unless another price is given.

- - - - - - ✂ -

Please send me the books I have ticked above.

Name ....

Address ....

....

....

.... Post code...................

Send to: Virgin Books Cash Sales, Thames Wharf Studios, Rainville Road, London W6 9HA

US customers: for prices and details of how to order books for delivery by mail, call 1-800-343-4499.

Please enclose a cheque or postal order, made payable to **Nexus Books Ltd**, to the value of the books you have ordered plus postage and packing costs as follows:

UK and BFPO – £1.00 for the first book, 50p for each subsequent book.

Overseas (including Republic of Ireland) – £2.00 for the first book, £1.00 for each subsequent book.

If you would prefer to pay by VISA, ACCESS/MASTERCARD, AMEX, DINERS CLUB or SWITCH, please write your card number and expiry date here:

....

Please allow up to 28 days for delivery.

Signature ....

Our privacy policy

We will not disclose information you supply us to any other parties. We will not disclose any information which identifies you personally to any person without your express consent.

From time to time we may send out information about Nexus books and special offers. Please tick here if you do *not* wish to receive Nexus information. ☐

- - - - - ✂ -